His Father's Blood

Book 2 in Legends of the Family Dyer

By: David W. Thompson

Part I
The Seekers

July 25, 1793: Nelson County, Kentucky

Earnest Hartman sipped his morning tea, savoring the rare stolen moment of solitude. He allowed his mind to drift back to the beginning of his family's grand adventure. For the Hartmans, the journey from the fertile soils of St. Mary's County, Maryland, to the wilderness of Nelson County, Kentucky, proved to be more grand failure than adventure. It was a hazardous trip, befitting stout hearted men of action. Indian attacks were not uncommon, but the twenty-five families under the leadership of Basil Hayden were of solid stock.

They met a flatboat in Pittsburgh, Pennsylvania, and floated the Ohio River down to Maysville. The women and children were left behind at the fortified Goodwin's station while the men traveled overland to place their claims on the lands at Pottinger's Creek.

Now eight years later, most of the settlers flourished in the new land. Nelson County became part of the new state of Kentucky, but for Earnest, nothing was left of the optimistic man he once was. The hopes and dreams he shared with his wife of building a new and better life died at the birth of their only child, Ada.

The day of her birth, savages attacked as Amelia hung the day's wash outside to dry. Three young braves on horseback—out to prove their bravery—chased his pregnant wife in their own yard. Earnest ran to get his gun and, shaky handed and weak kneed, confronted them.

One of the Indians, with a heavily painted face, turned and shook his bow over his head in a menacing fashion. He screamed gibberish that Earnest was convinced was the language of perdition.

The painted warrior rode at Earnest who stood quaking in his boots and holding his gun in a white knuckled grip. "Stop!" he cried. "You stop right there!"

On he came, and at the last second swerved his horse, struck Earnest across the face with his bow, and raced back to the others amid their cheers.

Earnest promptly shat his pants, his gun cradled in his arms, unfired.

As the three savages rode away, Amelia went into labor. Earnest knew a woman's death at childbirth wasn't unusual, yet he blamed his faith for Amelia's death—his faith, and the godless heathens of course. But God surely turned his face away from them on that day, and so Earnest also turned away from God.

Hartman's life spiraled into darkness over the following years. The loss of his wife and his religious fervor left a void in his spirit that he filled with mindless work during the day, and devil's brew at night. His fellow pioneers did not understand. They cast Earnest as a pariah for his agnosticism. Their Jesuit priest counseled a return to the faith, as only God could heal his wounds.

Bitterness, depression, and alcohol were his poor—albeit powerful—companions. It was Ada's good fortune that Monica Hagan, their neighbor, took an interest in his child's welfare.

Earnest's lowest low found him mired in the roadside mud, covered in his own vomit, and unable to stand on his uncooperative legs. It was the coldest night of the year, and Earnest scratched away the frozen drool from his chin and made peace with the universe—if not his God.

As conscious thought deserted him, he thought of his daughter. "I hope you will find it in your heart to forgive me, Ada. I failed you."

* * * *

Light streaming through the wavy window glass woke Earnest. He was in a strange bed, washed, naked, and wrapped in warm blankets. His clothes were folded at the foot of the bed and appeared freshly laundered.

His vision swirled as he sat up and took stock of his situation. The room was spare in its furnishings. A lone stand cobbled from rough-hewn pine stood by his bed. A thick and well-worn leather-bound Bible adorned the center of the table beside which a nubbin of candle rested in a brass holder. No other decor provided any hint about his benefactor.

A sharp knock sounded at the door, and Earnest dropped his head back to the pillow and pulled the blankets up to his chin.

"Come in."

"Ah, greetings, brother. I'm pleased to see that you survived the night. When you are ready, please come join us. My wife has breakfast prepared."

"Who are you? Why did you bring me here?"

"I'm Reverend George Brewster, a humble missionary in the service of our Lord, and it appears I was sent here to bring you back to the Lord."

* * * *

Over the next months, George Brewster and Earnest Hartman became fast friends. Brewster saw the hand of God in every tree, every mountain, every human smile or act of kindness. One day as the two men strolled the wildlands together, Ada on Earnest's shoulders, he realized that somewhere along the way he'd recovered the faith he hungered for, though now served up on a different platter.

That spring found Earnest as a newly ordained minister, and he considered the future of his family. As a man of God, new opportunities opened before him. Should he remain in his adopted state, raise his child in this harsh unforgiving environment, or seek their fortunes and happiness elsewhere?

Many other pioneers shared his feeling of disenchantment. Drought, rocky soils, native attacks, and disease took a toll on a man, and worse still on a family man. The past Saturday, he observed John Spalding and Rodolphus Norris in Bardstown as they shook hands. John turned his back and bent over—whereupon Rodolphus delivered a half-dozen kicks to his backside. They reversed positions and the kicker then received his six exuberant blows.

"Men, what is the meaning of this?" Earnest asked.

"Why, to inflict punishment for the horrible sin of impertinence. We abandoned God's gift to us and left the tranquil shores of Maryland for these wild forests and savage Indians." They offered to provide the same treatment for Earnest, but he respectfully declined.

Some of the members of the original group had fared better than others. Their leader, Basil Hayden, brought with him his recipe for distilling his own brand of devil's water. His corn-based elixir—mixed with rye—had become very popular with the new settlers, and too popular as a means for Earnest to drown his sorrows.

Earnest was never much of a farmer, but perhaps a congregation somewhere needed the guidance of a young preacher. Earnest recognized and accepted his shortcomings and realized that the frontier was no place for a man of his skittish temperament.

He set down his emptied tea cup, spitting out the dregs of tea leaves, and pushed himself up from the battered oak table, the legs of the chair screeching across the wood plank floors. Walking down a short hallway, he cracked open the door at the end and looked in on his sleeping daughter. *Whatever happens, I won't fail you again, Ada.*

He flinched as a pounding knock sounded at his front door, and crossing the bedroom, peered out of the lone window. Jeremiah Wathen, one of the first settlers, stood nervously shifting his weight from one foot to the other at the Hartmans' threshold.

Earnest rushed down the hall and flung open the door.

"Jeremiah, what brings you—?"

"There's been another attack, Earnest. At Rolling Fork this time."

"Indians? Are any of our people hurt?"

"Three settlers were killed, but they took four of the savages with them. Haven't heard the names yet but thought you should know. Keep your rifle loaded and ready."

"What a God-forsaken place this is!"

"But it's as beautiful a land as a mortal man's eyes ever beheld, Earnest. I suspect if it was all milk and honey, a man would have no need of salvation."

"But will it *ever* end, Jeremiah?"

"It's the frontier, Earnest. It's root hog or die. Be careful now. I'm going to spread the news." Jeremiah nodded and turned away.

Earnest closed the door behind him, and as he threw back the bolt, he made his decision. He began loading their meager possessions on his buckboard.

It was time to go back home, or Amelia's ancestral home at least. God, he missed her! He'd feel closer to her in the land of her birth, and safer too. If not a congregation, surely someone, somewhere needed an itinerant preacher.

* * * *

March 13th, 1815: Appalachian Mountains Western Maryland

The night was dark, despite the full moon. Remnant clouds from the morning's storm still blanketed the sky, and little light passed through. The haze around the lunar disk formed a halo-like effect—not the halo of angelic beings, but of far darker things. The hazed moon appeared devoted to the creatures of the night, and if somehow angelic, then that of the fallen variety, long denied heaven's light or grace.

John Dyer embraced the gloom of the evening as it echoed his mood. Being cast as a pariah and getting run off by so called civilized men seemed to be his lot in life.

In truth, John cared little for town life, just as town folk wasted no love on John 'Running Bear' Dyer. Not that he'd fared much better in the more rustic environs populated by men.

"Lone life on the road," he said to the woods around him, and scratched the thin stubble on his chin. "I suppose you're not meant to call any place home for long, Dyer."

He grabbed a wrist-thick piece of pine branch and broke it over his knee. The scent of smoldering pine sap, and the cooking flesh of the young rabbit on the spit, drifted to his nose. He drew it in deeply, reverentially, and gently arranged the pieces of wood on his campfire. The rabbit was nearly done, and he didn't want any wood ashes tainting it.

He shook his head recalling the disruption of his last meal. Hell, he'd saved the young woman from a terrible fate, and this was his reward? Running for his life on this, the darkest of nights! But it was time, the city wore on him, and nobody there meant a hill of beans to him anyway.

John held his hands up to the fire, and felt a shiver run down his back. Winter was nearly done, but the nights were still cool. Maybe he could find some land to start a small homestead before it was too late for planting. All of his life, the world had put a boot at the throat of John's dreams. Time and again, he dusted himself off and had another go. *Maybe this time.*

A deep undulating wail echoed through the valley in warning. He scooped dirt onto his fire, and waited, listening. The ten years spent living among his kin, the Conoy, had honed his senses as sharp as a spearhead's edge.

He heard the wind caress the pines, and again savored their fragrance, but underlying the scents and sounds of the woods were the approaching crashes, thuds, and the unbathed odor of the invaders. He swore he caught a whiff of their whiskey scented breath! The white men from the city followed behind their baying hounds towards him, and they were getting close—too close!

John snatched up his few meager provisions, tucked them in his satchel with his books, and trotted toward the clear mountain stream he'd drawn water from moments before. The knee-deep water of Patterson's Creek would defeat the noses of the hounds.

He spotted the rock outcropping the locals called Clark's Castle, and scurried up its craggy trail. If the dogs were able to hold his scent, the narrow trail around the rock would prove unassailable. John hunkered down and waited.

* * * *

"Where are you, half-breed?"

The owner of the voice, Karl Bauer, pointed one thick crooked finger toward the small clearing, lifted his shotgun to his shoulder, and fired into the campsite.

"We're here for you, Injun, come on out here now and face the music."

"Put the damn gun down, Karl. You boys are getting out of hand here now," Sheriff Campbell said. "I ain't figuring on having to tell your wives how it is they came to be widders tonight."

"Sheriff, we're just out here doing our civic duty, and trying to have a bit of fun while we're at it," Karl said. He took a long pull from his jug and passed it to Campbell. The sheriff pushed the jug away and rolled his eyes.

"Any luck with those dogs of your'n, Samuel?" the sheriff asked of the lanky, dark-haired man directing the hounds.

"He's gone into the creek, Sheriff. The dogs can't follow his scent in the water, and I reckon he knows it, him being half Indian and all."

"I'll bet he follows the creek clear down to Fort Ashby! He ain't worth all that trouble, boys, and he's Virginia's problem now."

"Or maybe he's sitting up ahead on Clark's Castle waiting to see what the dogs do," Karl suggested. "His campfire ain't even cold yet. He ain't got far. Let's go have a look up there first, Sheriff."

"No, not tonight. Remember what I said about making widders? We're not risking any men trying to yank that dang Indian out of there." The sheriff turned and spit tobacco juice at the ground.

"You saying you don't wanna finish the job, Sheriff?"

"I'm saying the slave girl was caught, Simmons got her back, so I reckon our work here is done. Besides, we've been in Virginia since we crossed the river—already out of my jurisdiction. Let him freeze his arse off tonight and think about things. If he shows up back in town, we'll have a nice welcoming party for him."

"He broke the law, Sheriff. Ain't it your job to uphold the law…? Well, don't just stand and stare at me! I'm going up there. I ain't afraid of him." Karl turned up the trail to the outcropping.

"Get your fat drunken ass back here, Karl. Karl!"

"Let's just make camp, Sheriff," Samuel said. "I'm not about to go up that narrow ass trail in the dark. We can stay here and have a go at it tomorrow. You know how Karl is when he gets an idea in his head, and likker in his belly. It may be a while before he either gets lost or passes out drunk."

"You're probably right. Hell, that Injun boy could have him running in circles around that rock, and he'd never even know he was there."

* * * *

John Dyer waited at the edge of the trail near the summit of the rock. It was the exact spot where one of the earliest settlers to the area, Silas Clark, held off a war party of Susquehannocks until reinforcements arrived.

The trail narrowed here and skirted a cliff. The only way forward was single file. A man seeking to defend himself against greater odds had only to wait for his enemy's advance and knock them off the trail one by one into the cold water fifty feet below. Old Silas knew this, and so did John.

Sounds funneled here from below, and John listened intently to the chatter of the men below. Two of the men he did not know, but the third was familiar. The one they called Karl was the cause of the mess he found himself in.

* * * *

John recalled the scene from the previous night. He hadn't wanted to cause any trouble. The last thing he needed was any white man problems, but then he heard the men's laughter, and heard the girl's scream.

Cloth ripping, the sound of feet slipping on loose gravel, and the malicious laughter from the aggressors. She was a slave girl, what did it matter to him? *But it did.*

"No, mister, please. I'm a good girl."

"See that you are then. You be a good girl and be still," the man called Karl said…then the sound of a hand slapping flesh.

"Be still, I said!"

"Please Mister, no, I'm a virgin!"

"What do you think we…oh, never mind, but good to know. The slavers will pay double for you! Now settle down. Buyers don't want no bruised-up breeder for their plantations."

"Don't be so hasty now, Karl. Maybe we should try us just a little taste first."

"Well, it ain't like it would be missed, but no—she's worth too much in her present condition."

John peered around the corner, and saw the big man tying the young woman's hands while the other man held her down.

The girl's screams grew in volume when Karl cackled and pretended to loosen his belt.

John stepped out into the open, and the younger man jumped up to face him.

"Best thing for you to do is back off now, and mind your own business, Injun!"

"Yeah, well see, I'm not real good at that. You boys had your fun, now turn the girl loose."

The man drew up his hands, one forming a fist, the other holding a long skinning knife. John stood his ground, and the man charged his adversary.

John swung his walking stick in an overhead arc, clipping the man behind the ear. The man had but a moment to realize his mistake, then dropped in his tracks like a sack of potatoes. John turned his attention to the other man.

Karl sat up straddling the young woman, still holding her down. He pointed at the downed man, as his other hand finished the knot he was tying. "Now why did you have to go and do that?"

"I asked nice. Now leave the girl alone."

"That's no way to be. I wasn't going to do nothing to her. I was just funning with her. Hell, this here slave will earn us good money. I reckon she was running off on her master, and we're due a reward. We'll split it with you."

"I ain't no runaway, sir. Master sent me to—" the girl began.

Karl slapped the girl again, and her head fell to the side, unconscious.

John's oak stave swung again. Karl felt the impact on his jaw, and he fell away from the girl, dazed.

John slid his arms under the girl, swept her up, and flung her over his shoulder, as Karl tried to get to his feet.

"Come back here, boy!"

* * * *

Karl stalked away from his two companions, kicking rocks and cursing under his breath as he approached Clark's Castle.

"Chicken shits! That's what they are. Both of them, scared of their own damn shadows." He turned his jug up, and guzzled the last few ounces of liquid courage, the glass shattering when he slung it against the rocks.

Karl didn't like Indians, or anyone else who didn't look like he did for that matter. He didn't even care much for his own people, truth to be told, but half-breeds were the worst. His father taught him that, and although they'd never done anything to him, they'd never done anything to dissuade him of his opinion either.

His lips turned down in disgust, deepening the furrows in his face as his mind conjured up the image of Helen, a girl he courted years ago, a girl he thought he loved and hoped to marry.

She never told him of her mixed blood, but his father knew the truth of it. Karl Senior was the first generation off the boat from Germany, real big on bloodlines and such—like he was raising a herd of thoroughbred horses instead of two dim-witted sons and a weak-kneed mule. The old man suggested Helen was painted with the tar brush and mixed up with her German heritage she had a little something extra in her wood pile.

Karl dropped Helen like a hot potato, and when she asked him why, he simply answered, "I'd never be able to forget where you came from."

He never courted another woman after Helen. He found women when he needed release, and they didn't cost much in his backwoods town. Sometimes they didn't cost a thing.

How could he trust another with his heart after Helen? He didn't forget her though. A year later, she up and ran off with some slick, smooth talking Italian grocer. Karl hated Italians.

He wiped at his runny eyes and thought the flowers must have bloomed early this year, but he didn't have time for distractions. He needed to get even with that Indian boy. Only way he'd taken that girl away from him was a sneaky punch when he was unprepared and preoccupied. That would not happen again!

He held his shotgun at the ready, and advanced.

* * * *

John smelled the man starting up the trail before he heard the rocks clattering beneath his feet. From his elevated position, Karl looked as tiny as an ant.

Or a roach. Not much time.

He pulled an ancient leather-bound book from among his possessions and opened it to a well-worn section. His great-grandfather had kept the book hidden for many years. Great-Pa said his mother, Moll, asked that it be so, and he'd honored her wishes. She said some secrets were best left hidden and some knowledge best left unknown. *Perhaps she was right.*

John's father discovered the book, along with its secrets, and took the book for his own. As much as Great-Pa reviled the book, his father, Sebastian, revered it. He embraced the words written there, even the pages written in blood. He modeled his life around them and learned to harness the powers inscribed there by his forbears. When he learned all it had to teach, he began to teach his son.

Eventually the book cost his father's life, but tonight it might save his. The pages he referenced were not those written by his white ancestors, but by the people he considered his own—the Conoy. The words were written in the precise lettering he knew as his grandmother's, a full-blooded Conoy. Her writings were done in secret, and only he and his father knew of them.

"Beware you don't become like him, John," echoed his great-grandfather's voice in his head.

He reached into his traveling bag and pulled out a dark figure, with black hair to its knees on one side, and cut short on the other. John placed it on the rock before him, altar-like.

He squatted, calmed his thoughts, and slowly released his consciousness, drifting, seeking another's spirit in the darkness.

"Great Okeus, ruler of the underworld, punisher of those who bring harm unto your people, hear your humble kwiocosuk, protect this unworthy shaman from his foe. Okeus, come!"

* * * *

Step by stealthy step, Karl Bauer progressed toward his objective. The Indian boy wouldn't catch him unprepared again...*with his pants down.* He snickered.

He sucked at the air as the climb grew steeper, and rubble moved beneath his feet, making a silent approach difficult.

The brush shook on the left side of the trail, and Karl froze. He peered through the inky black of the night. Some small animal, perhaps? He waited, but the sound did not repeat itself.

He cocked back the hammer on his shotgun and tossed a small rock into the thicket. Again he waited, but nothing emerged. *Dang 'possum, I bet.*

Karl knew the trail narrowed just ahead, and if the Indian had an ambush planned, that's where he'd set the trap. He bent down low, peeking around each bend, when a low guttural growl reached his ears.

With a howl, the naked Indian boy leapt from his hide, his black hair long and wild on one side, and pulled back tight against his skull on the other. His face was covered with red paint, his teeth bared...but his eyes? *Something isn't right about his eyes!*

Karl pulled the trigger, but only hit the stone embankment sending a torrent of rock shrapnel back into his face. The Indian boy was gone. Karl reloaded and swung the barrel right, then left, searching for his target.

"Come on out here, boy. Let's settle this."

Silence then, only the lonely call of a whippoorwill in the distance.

"You hear me? Come out here and be a man!"

The growling came from above him, and his eyes drifted up without moving his head. The boy hovered above him, squatting on an overhang, his eyes glowing red in the darkness.

Karl glanced down to cock the hammer on his gun, just for a moment, a split second at most! But when his eyes returned to the rock shelf, a giant black bear stood where the boy was a moment before! A trick of the light?

He squeezed the trigger just as the bear's huge paw slapped him from the ledge!

Falling, grasping for anything solid, but finding only air in his grasp.

Falling ever faster, his back slamming into the rock face! Again, he reached out into space, clawing to gain a purchase, and his hand seized a tree root halting his free fall.

Karl breathed deeply. "Thank you, Lord!"

He opened his eyes and looked below. Twenty feet to the pool in the river below. How deep was it? The root slipped in his fingers. *Hold on!*

Pebbles rained down on his head, and he heard the growl of the animal above. The beast clawed at the edge of the rock, and more stones fell on him.

"Leave me alone! Get away from here!"

No sound from above. He dared to look up, and his fingers slipped further! Stones fell around him as the animal clawed at his perch. Karl felt the wet chill soak his thighs as his bladder released. A long icicle of drool oozed from the bear's jaw, stretching…stretching, and finally breaking free. It floated down and plopped on Karl's lips.

"Go on now. Get away, bear!" he spat.

Then a huffing sound…the bear deciding to pursue easier prey? Rustling sounds above, and branches breaking as the bear pushed through the underbrush, moving away.

A deep human voice growled from above. "Go back to town. If you follow me, you will die!"

The air blew through his hair as the root's grip on the bank failed, and in that moment, he recognized the smell of root bear…sassafras root? Impact took seconds, then only blackness.

* * * *

Samuel jerked awake at the sound of the gunshot. Sheriff Campbell sat feeding the fire.

"Sheriff? Did you hear that?"

"Two quick shots in a row, Samuel. I was just about to wake you up. I reckon we'd better go and see what kind of trouble Karl's done got himself into."

Samuel pulled on his boots, and the two men grabbed torches from the fire and went in search of their companion.

Knowing Karl's intended destination, they moved quickly, searching for sign as they went, but they reached the trail ascending Clark's Castle without finding any trace of him.

"Only fifteen minutes or so until daylight. Let's find a spot to sit and wait for it, Sam."

Sam nodded, and looked down at his feet.

"Something bugging you, Samuel?"

"Well, no, but…about this thing with the Indian boy? Can I ask you something?"

Campbell nodded.

"I heard there was something awful strange going on in that room, Sheriff. What's the truth of it?" Samuel asked.

"Just between us, Sam?"

"Yes sir, of course."

"I can't say for sure what happened there, mind you, or what was about to happen. Karl said he saw Dyer dragging the poor girl down the street, and he tried to help but Dyer got the drop on him and struck him with a club. So Karl got one of his boys to help him, and they went after Dyer together. When he found the girl, Dyer was gone. Karl said the young slave girl had half her clothes ripped off and was trussed up like a turkey dinner. Time I got there, the poor girl was squatting in the corner, scared out of her wits. I've heard tell of stranger things, but not lately."

"Maybe Dyer was going to turn her in to her owner? Get the reward?"

"Maybe, but there's good money in selling slaves, even if ya ain't got clear title to 'em. These are sad times, Samuel. Still, if you're asking my opinion, from the look on that girl's face…and the blood? I think we got there just in the nick of time."

Samuel Nelson stood and pointed at the edge of the precipice.

"What's that moving down there?"

The Sheriff squinted his eyes. "If I was a betting man, I'd wager it's a hungover Karl Bauer. Lord a mercy, let's get down there."

* * * *

Karl's head swam as he tried to focus on the approaching men. What to tell them? They wouldn't believe what happened to him. Hell, he didn't believe it either! It must be the whiskey, or conking his head on the rocks when he landed? God, his back hurt!

"You all right, Karl?" the sheriff yelled.

Karl shook his head and waited for the men to get closer. His head wouldn't tolerate his yelling back.

"I feel purty stupid, Sheriff. I went up half ways, and saw that young Injun hoofing it on down the creek, just like you said."

"It was darker than a crow's ass, how'd you see him?" Samuel asked.

Karl's eyes closed up into slits as he stared the younger man down. "You calling me a liar, Sam?"

"No sir. Just curious is all."

Karl nodded and drew his lips back in a tight-lipped smile. "Sorry, Samuel. Maybe I heard him then. Lord knows my head wasn't screwed on right at the time."

"How did you end up all banged up and sopping wet in the river?" Campbell asked.

"I'm embarrassed to say, Sheriff, but I come on down the hill to get after him and fell face first in the river. Knocked myself clean out. Just woke up when you fellers come along."

Campbell fingered the front of Karl's shirt, and one eyebrow lifted in confusion.

"Are those claw marks, Karl?"

* * * *

Alton Bowles was tired, his youth and energy worn down by many seasons of labor on a barren farm. His hardened hands were still up to the task. His back, although weary, remained strong. The truth was his heart wasn't in farming anymore, not since his Isabella died. There didn't seem to be any point any more.

The thin hardscrabble soil barely supported the yearly crop of weeds that choked out anything he tried to sow. The ground became a quagmire when wet, and hard as a rock when dry.

The creek provided enough water for drinking and ablutions, but not for irrigation, and it dried up at the first hint of a drought.

The old log cabin, where he was born, needed a lot of work. The roof leaked over the back door, and the winter winds whistled between the logs from the missing chinking.

His children were the smart ones. Instead of lingering here, trying to eke out a living and inheriting the farm, they both left for the city to find their own destiny, and plot their own course. They were after him for years to leave the old homestead, and come live with them, share their new lives.

So when the tall, black-haired stranger made him an offer on the place, he sucked up the loss, stowed a lifetime of memories and signed over the deed.

"Now let me fill you in on everything about the place, Mister."

"Just call me John."

"John it is then. I just wouldn't feel right if I didn't tell you all there is to know. All there is to do, I reckon I should say."

Alton filled the young man in on the oddities of the soil, the repairs to be made on the old cabin, and the need to dig a small pond to act as a cistern to hold water from the stream.

"I have my work cut out for me, Mr. Bowles."

"Indeed you do, John. Second thoughts?"

"I'm not afraid of hard work. I'm looking forward to it actually."

"Stick with some goats, a few pigs and chickens, and a garden to feed yourself. Forget about any serious planting up here. Stick with hay and critters, and you'll do fine."

Bowles stood, held out his hand, and shook his head. "Well, there's one other thing I should tell you about, at least if you believe the old folks around here."

The young man looked at him and lifted his eyebrows.

"You believe in ghosts, John Dyer? Evil spirits, witches and the like?"

"I've seen some things."

"I've seen and heard some things too, but nothing I couldn't explain away with a bit of common sense. Some folks though, superstitious folks, say this side of the mountain is haunted, that no good comes to those who settle here. They call the place Devil's Peak.

"The old folks say even the Indian tribes kept away from the place, it was tainted with blood, and cursed by some evil god that them Injuns pray to. I never paid no mind to it, but say, you look like you might have some Indian in you?"

* * * *

Sally Ann O'Shea's reputation as a loose woman in Setter's Run, Virginia, was not entirely deserved, but because of it, no man ever remained steady in her life. The night before, her latest beau Lewis announced he was done with her, saying his reputation was maligned by association with her!

Sally's father always said the best thing to do when you fall off your horse was to get back on! He also claimed her mother's favorite saying was you catch more flies with honey than with vinegar. Sally Ann wasn't sure about all that, but when she spotted the dark stranger leaning on the horse rail outside the hardware store, she smiled her brightest smile, and walked on over.

He was broad shouldered, and taller than any other man in town. He seemed unaware of his attractiveness, and she never could resist a man with dimples! She'd heard the stories about him and decided to find out for herself. She figured anyone that handsome deserved a little understanding, and a whole lot of attention too!

"Sir! Sir? Could you help me, Mister?"

The man ambled over, and he looked at her reddened eyes and moist puffy cheeks even before his attention drifted to the swell of her bosom and the flare of her hips.

"Is everything all right, ma'am? Is there something I can help you with?"

Sally's eyes took a long, slow walk from the man's full head of short black hair and deep soulful brown eyes, meandering all the way down to his work boots, lingering at times along the way. She hoped he knew exactly what it was that he could help her with!

"I need help loading my wagon. Would you lend a hand?"

"I can do that, ma'am. Where's your load?"

"Sally Ann, my name's Sally Ann O'Shea. You are…?"

"John."

She held out her hand and he took it in his. She escorted him to the rear of the store and pointed out the lumber and hardware piled up for her father.

"I don't believe we've met before, John. So are you new around here?"

"Everyone around here knows everything about everyone I think, so I'd bet you already know the answer? Not that I take note of gossip, but I've heard of you."

Sally Ann flushed. "You are so right about this town. Everyone knows everything, and they are quick to share. What they don't know, they will make up too!" Her laugh was a high-pitched chuckle.

A tall brown-haired man turned the corner and smiled when he recognized Sally Ann, his unshaven face highlighting his lopsided leer.

"Why, Sally Ann. It's so good to see you again." He held his hand out to her—far enough away she had to bend forward to take it into her own. The fabric of her blouse tightened over her breasts and he shook her hand, his eyes never meeting hers.

"Hello Bradford, how have you been?"

"Fair, but I could be a lot better. Meet me tonight for a moonlit ride? Bet I can make it a lot better for you too."

"Bradford, I believe I made myself clear last week? Please stop propositioning me. I'm not—"

"I know what you're not. And I know what you are too! Seems you're fine with spreading your legs for everyone in town but me!"

John stepped between them, his palm pushing the chest of the broader man. "Time for you to move on."

"Mister, didn't your daddy teach you to stay out of what ain't none of your business."

"No, but he wasn't the best role model. I believe you were saying your goodbyes, Bradford."

"Why you…" Bradford swung a ham size fist, but John turned, caught the man's elbow and used the momentum of the blow to hurl the man head first into a post. The man stood as if dazed and brushed the dust off his stained britches.

"You ain't heard the last of Bradford Sikes, Mister. Count on it."

The man staggered across the street, and John turned back to Sally Ann.

"I'm sorry about that."

"Sorry? Thank you, John. You were amazing," Sally Ann said. *I think I'm in love.*

"We have, you know."

"We have…what, John?"

"Met, we've met before. Not properly introduced, but I remember you. I imagine I'm less memorable than a lovely red-headed lady like yourself." John's nostrils flared as he scented the air. "That's a sweet scent you wear too, it's like crushed rose petals."

"Yes, it is, thank you. But I fear you're mistaken, I'm sure I'd remember meeting you. Nonetheless, I'm pleased to meet you now." *Oh, I remembered you. You left with that holier-than-thou bitch Carolyn Beasley before I got a chance at you!*

"Well, now that we are officially introduced, Miss Sally, maybe we could take a ride together one day? Maybe pack a lunch and ride down to the river?"

* * * *

Carolyn Beasley splashed water on her face. Why couldn't she get a normal night's sleep? She had no problem falling asleep, but her dreams were tortured things, and waking up? When her eyes finally opened to a new day, it took hours to pull her head out of the fog. It had been like that every morning since she woke in John Dyer's cabin nearly a week ago.

She remembered coming to her senses in a strange bed. The room moved in and out of focus, often swirling as if in a whirlpool, but her thought processes were clear.

She squinted to steady her surroundings. Her arm hurt, and she felt a welt there. Where was she? Whose couch was she on?

"Carolyn?" She knew the voice, but what was he doing here? Where was here?

"It's all right, Carolyn." She felt a cool wet cloth swab her cheek. "You fainted in the heat, so I brought you back to my cabin."

John, this was John's house.

"I'm sorry…" she started and rubbed her arm. *Bee sting?*

"No need to be. It's fine."

Carolyn sat up and surveyed the room. John stared down at her with a glass of water in his hand. His shirt was open, and she stared openly at his muscled chest.

She wiggled to straighten her skirt and felt cool air on her chest. She glanced down at her partially unbuttoned blouse and pulled it together. Her face flushed the color of a blazing fire.

"Did you…did we…?"

"No, nothing happened, Carolyn. I just tried to cool you off. I didn't even look," he said.

"I mean I like you, John, but…"

"Nothing happened, Carolyn. I swear it's so."

* * * *

St. Clement's Bay, Southern Maryland

Ada stepped into the small kitchen where her father, Earnest Hartman, sipped his morning tea. His lips moved as if in silent argument with himself. She hoped it was a sign of the degree of his agitation, and not of his encroaching age.

She knew he had much on his mind and hoped to be of some comfort to him. The previous night, Earnest stated his intention to again pull stakes from their Southern Maryland home.

"It's provided a good base of operations for my evangelical mission. It's true the Catholics have taken it over again, but there are some righteous people here, and at least they've driven off the godless heathens. In a day's ride from here, I could preach to congregations from the mountains to the sea, but it's no longer safe for us here."

"The British have gotten quite close, Father. I know your political friends say it will be over soon, but I've heard about the civilian homes and farms they've destroyed. One family on the Patuxent has a cannon ball lodged in their wall!"

"It's been a good home to us, but the safety and convenience of the area is now outweighed by the dangers."

"It will be fine, father, we will be fine. You know how I feel—we've been in one place too long—I miss being on the road."

Ada kissed her father's forehead and retreated to her room to pack up her belongings. The next town beckoned, and she couldn't wait to see what tomorrow might bring. Her father's mission to fill the world with the word of the gospel fit in with her own quest—to see as much of that world as possible.

She brushed her blonde hair from her eyes, fastened the buckles on her travel bag and carried it into the parlor. Her father sat on the couch, a dog-eared Bible open in his hands.

"Father? Are you ready? It's a two-day ride, and we want to get there before too late tomorrow. We must consider the comfort of our generous benefactors."

"The Jordan family is strong in the faith, daughter. Whenever we arrive, we will be greeted with open arms."

"Nonetheless, we mustn't take advantage of their hospitality, Father. They have an infant son, do they not?"

Preacher Hartman stood and touched his daughter's cheek with the back of his hand. "Your mother was the same, always thinking of others."

"Thank you, Father. That means a lot to me. I wish I'd known her."

"She would be proud of the young woman you've become. You have her hair, her sky-blue eyes, even her figure…"

Ada smiled, such compliments were rare from her father.

"Just remember, from those the Lord has given much, he expects much in return."

"I will do my best."

Reverend Earnest Hartman shook his head, his eyes watered, and he looked at the floor.

"I fear my calling has been unfair to you, Ada. If your mother had lived, I'd have my own congregation, and we'd have a place of our own to call home—not traipsing all over the country seeking to convert the godless rustics."

"This has been home, Father. Our frequent trips provide fodder for my appetite for travel. I'd not have it any other way. I love seeing new places and meeting new people. I'd soon get bored twiddling my thumbs in the same old place every day."

"It will have to end soon. You need to find a young man, a decent God-fearing man to take care of you, and give me some grandbabies before we are both too old."

"Too old? Father, I'm twenty-two years old! And do you think I need someone to take care of me? Haven't you raised me to be my own woman, independent in thought and deed?"

Earnest smiled and said a small silent prayer. *Lord, please do not make my devotion to you harm my greatest joy—my daughter. Do not test me as you once tested Abraham!*

* * * *

John's arms encircled Sally Ann's waist as he drew her into his embrace, but with a light touch she pushed him away.

"Now, you just stop, John. Let me unpack our lunch first."

Sugar cured ham, venison jerky, and smoked fish were on the menu, with fresh peaches for dessert. They washed it all down with the homemade elderberry wine thoughtfully left behind by Alton Bowles.

"Where did you come from originally, John? Does your family live near here?"

"Close enough, I guess, but I don't think about them much, not since my father died. Family is just a word, and the only two of them I cared about are gone now."

"Your father?"

"Yes, and my great-grandfather."

"I'm so sorry."

"It's been a while since they passed on, but what about you? Have you lived here your entire life?"

"Yes, since birth, but I wouldn't mind getting away from here, seeing something of the world beyond the mountains. There has to be more to life than this." She stretched out her arms to include the woods and mountains around them.

John poured her another glass of wine. "We need to drink this before it gets hot."

"Why John Dyer, are you trying to get me tipsy and take advantage of me?"

"Is that something I'd need to do, Sally Ann?"

Her lips constricted into a knot, her eyes darkened, and she pushed him away. "Who do you think you are, talking to me like that?"

John lifted her hand from his chest and kissed it lightly. "I think you are a beautiful, desirable woman. A woman who knows what she wants."

He gazed into her eyes and drew her into his embrace.

* * * *

John left the woman sleeping and stalked away from the cabin towards the creek. He'd discovered no pure blood since the young slave girl. Only the blood from a chaste woman held the power he might need, but again John's conscience ate away at his resolve.

What right did he have to take even this small thing from another human being? Was this the path that started his father's fall from grace, and led to his death? One question served him well as a moral compass over the years: Would his great-grandfather approve? He bowed his head in silent supplication, praying to hear his voice again.

You are my true heir, John. Do not become your father, nor follow his path! Do not know his shame!

John slowly nodded his understanding. Sally Ann was the last. He would not take the blood again.

"Great-Pa, this is the only peace I know, help me," he pleaded and touched the stone knife on his belt.

He sat beside his fire pit and started a small fire with his striker and a piece of flint. He took the small long-haired figure from its bag and stood it on the rock before him, then placed his great-grandfather's stone dagger beside it.

He searched for the bear, his spirit animal. It grew easier every time. His thoughts faded away, as his essence strengthened, pulled away and drifted on the sweet, pine-scented breeze.

He felt the inhuman power of his limbs, the moral certainty, and the tenacity of spirit. His life force coursed through the veins of the indomitable beast!

He was free, and where he belonged—home again.

He raced to the small peak behind the log cabin, surveyed the valley before him, and saw that it was good. He scented the air, sucked in the flavors of the mountain laurel blooms, and the musky taste of rotted leaves.

A young opossum stalked the night just below him. John could smell the dead frog it feasted on upon its breath. He heard and smelled the termites and grubs within the rotted log at his feet. He ripped the punky wood apart to savor the delicacy, when another scent tickled his nostrils.

He stood on his hind legs and stared down into the valley. A horse pulling a small wagon. An old man and a young woman arriving in the town below.

The bear stretched out on an overhanging boulder and rested its head in its paws as the night faded, satiated and at peace.

* * * *

Hours later, as the sun threatened to crest above the mountains, John returned to himself, his fire reduced to warm embers.

He sat up and reached for his clothes.

"Who are you? What are you?" Sally Ann asked, her eyes as wide as the full moon, and her face the color of the ashes in the fire pit.

John stood, holding his clothes in front of himself, and reached one hand in her direction.

"Sally Ann, I…"

She ran toward the house, mounted her horse, and raced away down the mountain.

* * * *

Setter's Run, Virginia

As Ada feared, it was full dark when their wagon arrived at the home of their host and hostess, the squeaking wheels much in need of grease. Her father was also right, in that both Mr. and Mrs. Jordan met them at their door with open arms.

Well, mostly open arms, as Mrs. Jordan held a squalling baby boy at her hip.

"Reverend Hartman? Wonderful to meet you, sir, and your beautiful daughter as well! Ada, I believe?" the man asked.

The two men shook hands, and Ada approached the mistress of the house, surprised to see that she was about her own age.

Ada put her hands in front of the young babe, and lightly tapped them together. "May I hold him, Mrs. Jordan?"

"Of course, but do call me Kate." She nodded at her husband. "My husband William, and this little monster is Billy."

She passed the lad into Ada's arms.

"Shall we go inside then? Old and foolish habit I fear, but I am still cautious of being out at night. I thank our Lord the recent unpleasantness with the English hasn't reached our mountains."

Kate escorted them inside and led them to the small repast laid out for them in the dining room. They wiled away the hours before bedtime with idle chatter designed to get to know each other better.

"Ada, how do you ever manage all the jumping around from town to town?" Kate asked. "Do you ever feel at home? You must either have a boyfriend in every town, or no time to meet any at all. Which one is it?"

"I love our life on the road, Kate. I don't think I've missed out on anything—although it is my father's constant concern. Men? I've not met any who are more interesting than the next town over the horizon."

"That may change one day. I hope it's in time for you to have your own family."

"Now you sound just like the Reverend," Ada said, nodding at her father.

Kate left to put the sleeping baby to bed, and said she'd turn in for the night after.

"Shall I show you to your room, Ada?" she asked.

Ada stood and kissed her father's cheek and bid him good night. As she left the room, she overheard Mr. Jordan ask him about their trip.

"It went fine, until we were almost in sight of town. Ada swore something watched us from the wooded hills. She was absolutely convinced of it, and then our horse whinnied and reared up! A good stalwart mare she is, and I'll tell you, it sent shivers up my spine."

"I hope you're not a superstitious man, Earnest, but they've named that area Devil's Peak. Perhaps the spirits that dwell there heard you were coming."

* * * *

Sally Ann puzzled over what she saw, and even what she heard. Was it truly the figure of a bear she saw in the dim light of the dying flames? Was it a trick of the light? A fantasy conjured by her fugue state? The man moved like a bear, and she heard him growl like a bear! But did he really *look* like a bear, or did her imagination fuel a bizarre, and horrible hallucination?

Her imagination? Perhaps, but more likely it was that damn book putting ideas into her head! When she awoke to an empty cabin, she yelled John's name into the darkness, then lit a few more candles and toured the home.

She thought the symbols painted on the walls a bit odd, and the strange long haired Indian doll even stranger. In fact, it gave her the creeps! She took a close look but couldn't bring herself to touch the grotesque image.

When she stepped into the bedroom (there was only one), a book sat on a small table beside the bed. She wanted to know more about this man she befriended, and sat to see what he liked to read, and what captured his imagination.

Spells, incantations, and bloody stories of horror and dread danced in her head as she perused the pages. Many appeared stained with blood! Those she would not touch, and flipped through them so fast, she cut her finger. She sucked at the blood and turned another page. When her bloodied fingertip touched the paper, a thin tendril of smoke curled upwards.

That did not just happen! Am I still tipsy from the wine?

No, there was a thin line of brown ash at the edge of the dog-eared page—just where she had touched it! That's when the book slipped from her hands, and she ran from the house, only to find that...thing outside.

Despite everything, or because of it, here she was at his cabin again. She cast a glance behind her at the fire pit, took a deep breath, and knocked on John's door. She heard his footfalls inside as he approached. The door creaked open, and John poked his head out.

"Sally Ann, I'm so glad to see you. Come in, and let me explain about..."

"I'm not here for that, John."

"That's fine, I understand, but if I could explain..."

"No, John, you can't explain that away."

"Then what? Why are you here?"

"Teach me. Teach me everything you know, and your secret will be safe with me."

* * * *

John knew it wasn't a good idea. He knew the dangers associated with sorcery, even the Native American version, shamanism.

How could he teach her what he'd learned over a lifetime? How could he share the secrets and spells earned by the blood of six generations of his ancestors? Lore extracted and gathered from three continents?

He couldn't, but what recourse did he have? He feared her thinly veiled threat to expose all she'd seen last night. The rustic xenophobes in town considered anything they didn't understand to be evil. The spiritual plane was foreign to them, and he'd be run out of the county just as surely as had his ancestor, Moll Dyer. She was abused and turned away to her death. *You'll never find a home, John!*

"I cannot do all that you ask, Sally Ann, but I'll tell you what I will do. Come back tomorrow, and I will give you some training. I will show you the herbs that heal, and if you are a quick study, I will teach you the most beautiful thing I know. It gives a person the freedom you seek and hurts no one."

"What I saw in the book, John, I want freedom, yes, but also power. The power to amend wrongs. I wasn't always known as the town whore, you know."

John's lips tightened in a straight line, and his eyelids clinched so close to his eyes, his pupils barely showed.

"You looked in the book? What gave you the right?" John asked darkly. Sally Ann winced as if struck and recoiled from his voice.

"I'm sorry, John. I shouldn't have. Please don't be mad at me. You're my only friend." She watched as the tension in his face slowly dissolved, and waited.

"Never again, Sally Ann. So much as touch that book again, and you'll have one less friend. Understood?"

"I understand, and I am sorry. I shouldn't have. I just wanted to know more about you, John."

His head bobbed in a short nod, and he turned back to the cabin. As he pulled open the door, he glanced back at the sound of her voice.

"Will you still show me, John."

"See you in the morning. Bring lunch, and enough clothing to last the week."

* * * *

The arrogant ass, Jimmy Haas, along with Mister High and Mighty Frankie Johnson, and of course the first—Momma's boy Lewis Boyle, be warned—justice will be served!

A smile split Sally Ann's face, and escalated into a full-blown laugh as she rode down the mountain trail toward home.

John didn't want to show her the means to do that, but she'd get it out of him. She had her ways. The reputation the boys branded her with might keep her from holding a man, but short term? Sally Ann could get them to do whatever she wanted. And this was something she wanted, and she wanted it bad!

John Dyer, what a man he turned out to be, if he even was a man? Or was he something else entirely? He was like her, with no one's love to warm him at night, and no family to speak of. *A week he said.* Maybe a week alone with him was just what she needed to win his heart.

She felt for the necklace she always wore, her only remembrance of her mother. She drew it out and examined the tiny emerald encased in a gold heart, kissed the stone and smiled. *Wish me luck, Momma!*

She'd tell her father she was visiting with her old school friend, Beatrice, in the next town over. Hell, she could tell him she was flying up to visit with the man on the moon! He'd be fine with it, if he ever sobered up enough to even notice she'd left.

She knew raising a daughter alone was hard for him, and he tried. When her mother ran off with a farm implement salesman days before Sally Ann's tenth birthday, she drew closer to her father, their father-daughter bond enhanced by the shared grief.

Life was good with them until Sally Ann began to fill out. Then a distance developed, a wedge driven between them, and Sally Ann questioned what she'd done to drive her father away. In the years that followed, they were unable to recapture the closeness they'd known. At a time a girl needs her father, he drifted away from her, and sought comfort in the bottom of a bottle.

His wasn't the biggest male disappointment in her life, only the first, nor was it the first betrayal in her life. But it was the worst, the one that plagued her on sleepless nights.

Perhaps Sally Ann's life would be different if her mother stayed, or if her father was a stronger man, or hell, if she didn't slip at the fair and the whole county saw she wasn't wearing any knickers! None of that mattered now. With John's help, and with or without his love, she would make it all right!

* * * *

Kate and little Billy accompanied Ada to town to purchase some necessities at the dry grocer's. The two women had become fast friends, and their excursion was as much an excuse to spend time together as it was born of need.

The Reverend remained at the Jordan residence to prepare his homily and promised them a real old-fashioned fire and brimstone sermon!

They placed their order with the proprietors, a middle aged Italian man with a dark moustache (too dark for a man of his age and likely supplemented with stove black), a receding hairline, and his much younger blonde-haired wife.

As the pair bustled about gathering their goods, the bell over the entry door rang.

A tall dark-haired man, perhaps twenty-five, Kate thought, strode in, and set about picking items from the shelves.

"Can we help you, sir?" the owner asked.

"I just need a few things, and can help myself, if that's all right?"

He nodded his agreement, and the younger man soon gathered his requirements, his arms laden with candles, beeswax, paraffin oil, salt, and sugar.

"I don't believe I've had the pleasure, sir?" Kate asked. "Are you a new settler in the county?"

"No ma'am, well I guess you'd say I'm rather new. I bought the Bowles homestead up the mountain a couple months back. I sure hope to make this my home."

"I can't say as I've seen you in church?"

"No ma'am, I'm afraid I'm not much of a church goer. I mostly keep to myself. I find it's better that way."

"Nonsense, well you simply have to come to town this Sunday for services. My young friend's father will be preaching, and we'd sure like to have a good turnout. We might even convince them to stay in our little town."

"Your young friend?" he asked, smiled at little Billy, and touched the tiny hand with his finger. The lad grabbed on.

"That's quite a grip your young friend has."

"No, this is Billy, my son. Where did...I didn't see her leave..." She looked around flustered, and then noticed Ada returning.

"Ada, say hello to our new neighbor, our 'rather' new neighbor, that is," she laughed.

"Hello." Ada offered her hand to the stranger. His gaze moved from little Billy's brown eyes to Ada's azure blue ones, and his mouth dropped open.

"I'm...ah. I don't...I do beg your pardon, but what was your name again, Miss?"

"Ada Hartman, and I'm pleased to meet you, Mister...?"

"John, ma'am. I'm John Dyer. If you don't mind my asking, is it Miss or Misses Dyer."

"It's Ada, John, and I'm happily *unmarried*."

"I see...will you attend Sunday services, Ada?"

"I'd not be a proper daughter and miss my father's first sermon here, would I?"

The store owner yelled from the back of the store. "Helen? Would you tally up the young man's order?"

John opened the shop door to leave as the grocer returned with the women's goods. He turned at the jingling of the bell, smiled at Ada, and bowed his head as the door closed behind him.

Kate lightly slapped Ada's arm. "What a thing to say! Happily unmarried, really? That man is clearly smitten with you!"

* * * *

On the ride back to his cabin, John replayed the conversation at the grocer's. In all his life, he'd never beheld a woman of such beauty!

No, Ada wasn't beautiful. Sally Ann was beautiful. Ada Hartman was angelic, a tall, blonde-haired vision surely conjured by the gods! Her eyes held a natural lushness, reflecting all of nature, deep pools of sky blue that a man could easily lose himself in. *She cannot be for you. What are you thinking? Remember your calling.*

His horse sensed his mood and moved forward in a slow trot. John kicked in his heels, and they sped uphill, soon reaching his cabin.

A horse stood tied to the hitching rail by his front porch, Sally Ann's horse. Hurrying inside, it seemed as if time turned backwards, the scene was one he remembered well.

Sally Ann reclined on his couch, seemingly asleep. He noticed her unbuttoned blouse—just like before. As he entered, she stretched out her arms over her head pulling the thin cloth tighter over her ample chest.

"John, you said early, but am I too early?"

"Not at all, I had errands to run to prepare for you." She sat up, and he took a seat beside her. "Are you ready to learn about the healing herbs? That's the best place to start."

"I am, just give me a chance to wake up." She stretched again and draped one arm over John's shoulders.

"Thank you for this, John. It means a lot to me." She placed one hand on the front of his shirt, and slipped it inside, playing with the hairs on his chest.

"This isn't a good idea, Sally Ann."

"Of course, it is! You're a man, I'm a woman, and I like you a lot, John." She leaned over to kiss him, but before their lips met, John placed a palm on her shoulder to hold her back.

"Stop, Sally Ann, I won't do this. I am the teacher and you, the student. This is how it must be between us. I am a kwiocosuk, a shaman."

"I don't understand. Don't you like me? Don't you find me attractive?"

"Any man would be a fool not to, Sally Ann. It's not that."

"The men in town…they've poisoned you against me? Made you hate me?"

"I do not know the men in town, Sally Ann, and we are friends, but I am a kwiocosuk."

"I don't understand…"

"You will."

* * * *

"Ada? Ada, where is your mind?" Kate asked.

"What? I'm sorry, Kate. I was daydreaming I'm afraid. Did you ask me something?"

"Which strong, darkly handsome young man might you be dreaming about, I wonder?"

"Kate, I'm a Christian woman, and the daughter of a preacher!"

"Ada, how naïve do you think I am? A Christian woman is still a woman. The good Lord blessed you with great beauty—no don't shake your head! Do you think He did so just to torment men? To lead them into temptation?"

"I'd truly hate to think of myself as a temptation to damn men's souls!"

Kate's laugh was pure and self-confident. "Then be honest with me before we get home, while we can still openly discourse without the men."

"Between us? You won't ring like a church bell?"

"Of course not, and who would I tell? Your father? I suspect he would welcome a suitor for you."

"No, not this one he wouldn't. I've heard it said that his ancestors were witches. I'd think we were above such superstitious foolishness in this modern age but…Father also believes the natives are the descendants of Cain. So what do you think the Reverend would say about John Running Bear Dyer?"

"I think it matters what *you* think, Ada."

"I'll admit he is pleasant enough to look upon: muscular, and with strong hands that are no strangers to hard work, and deep soulful eyes…"

"Not that you noticed, of course."

"But he's not for me, Kate. He's a lone wolf, and either an agnostic, or worse yet, an atheist!"

"A beautiful woman can turn a man's head, Ada. A strong *and* beautiful woman can make his head spin like a whirligig!"

"Kate, you are determined to cast me as a temptress!"

Kate felt the smile crease her cheeks and pulled it back into a straight line. She was only a few years older than Ada, but the girl knew so little of men, and perhaps less of love.

Kate's knees went weak when she'd seen the look that passed between John and Ada! If her friend was right about her father's reaction to John, the fireworks were just beginning.

"He'll be at services Sunday, Ada. I'll bet you a fresh baked apple pie!"

* * * *

Sally Ann was tired of traipsing through the woods. John led her on a not so merry chase through the swamps to show her the dreaded poison sumac, and then how to harvest cattail roots. The meadows yielded purslane, lamb's quarters, jewel weed, and further warnings about nightshade.

Whenever Sally Ann touched his hand or brushed against him, he pulled back as if repulsed. Was something wrong with her, or with him?

John said they'd barely touched the surface of nature's apothecary, and there were many more plants she'd need to know. He promised a full week of this! Now they were back on the mountain digging ramp roots—these not for medicinal purposes, but for dinner.

"Tomorrow we'll start on the fungi. We won't have time for me to teach you all the edible and medicinal mushrooms, but hopefully enough so that you'll not poison yourself or anyone else."

"And what you promised? The secret to the freedom you spoke of?"

"After, but the plants first."

Back at the cabin, John gave Sally Ann the bedroom, and took the couch for himself. When she carried her bag to the room, she immediately noticed the thick leather-bound book no longer graced the bedside table. *He doesn't trust me.*

They ate their meal facing each other across the small kitchen table.

"John, can I ask you a question?"

He nodded around a mouthful of venison stew.

"Is there another woman in your life? Is that why you won't let me get close to you?"

"No, Sally Ann, there is no other, and cannot be. You want more than I am able to give, and I don't want to hurt you. We are friends."

"I'd not ask more than you wish to give, John. I never asked you for forever."

"I cannot be with a woman, Sally Ann. I am kwiocosuk."

"So you've said, but what does that mean?"

"Most of the men who've chosen the same path as I have, remain celibate. It is believed this brings the spirit world closer, and grounds a man to the earth."

"John, you're a strong, virile young man. Are you saying that you've never, that you *will* never, be with a woman? I've heard the stories in town about you."

"People tell stories. You of all people know that, and I'm not strong enough to say never, but to find a woman I love? Love stronger than my calling, stronger than the freedom of my soul? I doubt it."

"What about Carolyn Beasley? You remember her, the tramp you scurried off with? She said after lunch with you, she woke up on your couch, just like me! How about that John? You're lying, trying to sell me a dog! You're drugging women to steal their affections!"

"I'm not, Sally Ann."

"Then why?"

"I needed their blood!"

* * * *

Ada brushed her hair and wondered again about what Kate said. Would John Dyer show up for the church service today?

She sat the brush down on her bedside table and considered it. Why did she even care? Despite what Kate said, she doubted the man's interest in her.

Too skinny, too dark, and too opinionated were the descriptors Ada thought about herself. She wasn't good wife material for the backcountry. Wife? Lord, did she just think that—even to herself? What a fool she was! Her life plans did not include being tied down in some tiny backwoods town in the middle of nowhere!

A vigorous knock sounded at her door. "Ada? I'd like you to listen to a part of my sermon. See if you understand what I'm trying to get across. Are you there?"

Ada opened the door to greet her father.

"Are you feeling all right? You're all flushed, child," the Reverend said. He pressed the back of his hand to her forehead. "You don't appear to be hot."

"I'm fine, I was just primping for church, trying to make a good first impression for our hosts."

"Now that's something new. Didn't you postulate to me, as recently as last week, that vanity is man's greatest sin?"

"The root of them all, yes, but that was also when you asked me to fancy myself up for that dull Simpson man."

"I just want you to be happy, Ada, and Simpson was a good man. You could do worse."

When Ada rolled her eyes, Reverend Hartman laughed. "All right, I confess, he is a bit slow."

Ada listened to her father's sermon, stopping him several times to suggest the addition of a biblical reference, or clarity on an idea he put forward.

When the sermon was polished to his satisfaction, the Reverend placed his hand on her shoulder.

"So, tell me, who is it that you've really gussied yourself up for?"

"Father, can't a woman attempt to look her best?"

He only stared at her and she knew he waited for her honest response. She dropped her eyes to the wooden floorboards.

"It's no one, Father, just a man Kate and I met at the grocer's, but I doubt we will see him today."

"Please do not misunderstand, Ada. I want you to be happy, but you mustn't rush, or give your heart to an unworthy man! Blessed is the man who will have you as his life partner."

* * * *

The church wasn't a proper church at all, but rather a cabin left vacant when Deborah Henning met her maker two years before. Her husband preceded her in death, and the elderly couple left no heirs to their humble estate. The town accepted the building as their own, and repairs long overdue were quickly undertaken. The outside was painted, and most interior partitions removed. After a thorough cleaning, a large wooden cross was affixed to the roof, and a church was born.

John paused outside the door, still indecisive about entering. No one knew him here and, churchgoers or not, most would see the coppery shade of his skin, and dismiss the integrity of his heart. Why was he subjecting himself to this torture? And for a woman he didn't even know?

He was different from them, physically yes, but spiritually also. He did not share their beliefs, but surely righteousness crossed all lines of faith? He remembered the Conoy saying, 'there are many paths to the top of the mountain.'

You were a fool to come, you are an outcast here.

A dizzy-aged lady, white haired and bent over by the years, hesitated at the base of the church steps, and John offered his arm to her.

"Thank you so much, young man. Would you do an old lady a favor and join me?" she asked, as he opened the door for her.

John smiled, nodded and peered inside. The room was dark, and he squinted his eyes to adapt to the light. Reverend Hartman stood at the front of the gathering, greeting parishioners, and shaking their hands. Rough-hewn benches stood end to end in rows, and several simple wooden crosses adorned the walls.

John's eyes swept the congregation, searching...and then met Ada's gaze! She quickly looked away, as the old lady tugged at his elbow.

"Come along now, young man."

"Yes, ma'am."

John retained little of the day's homily, distracted as he was. His stare rarely left the visage of Ada, sole occupant of the bench in the front row. Did she feel the weight of his eyes on her? As this thought formed, Ada turned her head, and caught him watching. She smiled!

Ten years had passed since he last entered a white man's place of worship, but he soon recalled the prayers and responses. Tradition and religion were familiar bedfellows.

Reverend Hartman painted a vivid view of the horrors waiting for unbelievers in the fiery pit. He detailed how Satan and his demons lavished their hellish punishments on sinners and spoke as if from personal experience. John wondered if the man's understanding of heaven was as intricate, and as passionate?

At the end of the service, John faced the moment he both anticipated and dreaded. Would she be pleased to see him, or even remember him?

The Reverend Hartman and his daughter, along with Mr. and Mrs. Jordan, led the congregation's exodus, and stood just outside the door to interact with everyone as they left to begin the rest of their day.

When it was John's turn, Jordan clasped his hand. "I don't think we've met before? I'm William Jordan."

"William, this is the nice man I told you about from the grocer's. John Dyer, this is my husband, William. He's a lawyer, but don't hold that against him. Reverend, this is John. John, meet Reverend Hartman," Kate said.

Everyone exchanged handshakes, and John moved forward as the line pressed in on him from behind. As the crowd thinned, he mustered his courage, and approached them again.

The Reverend's eyes narrowed as he drew near. "Mr. Dyer, is it? What can we do for you today?"

"I was hoping to have a word with…"

Ada shook hands with the last couple in line and turned to him.

"John, I hoped you hadn't left. Kate and I wondered if you would join us for lunch."

* * * *

Sally Ann dug the roots from the last plant on John's list—a test he said—designed to measure what she'd learned. She suspected it was his way of keeping her busy and out of the way for a few hours. She wiped the sweat from her brow and returned to the cabin.

As she entered the clearing around the house, no horse grazed in the small fenced-in meadow, and none stood tied to the hitching rail. John was still in town, supposedly to purchase poultry!

Why he really went was a mystery to her. No stores opened their doors on a Sunday. John was up to something, and whatever it was, it required him to wear his finest clothes!

She entered the cabin, and made her way to the dry sink, poured in water, and scrubbed the dirt from her face and hands, aggressively attacking the black soil embedded under her fingernails.

She rubbed repeatedly at the pine sap she'd gathered for making pitch, but it proved particularly difficult to remove. The lye soap didn't help, but she scrubbed until her skin hurt. *All this, and John still won't share his secrets with me.*

She dried off, and stepped out on the porch, and glared down across the valley. John's horse was nowhere to be seen. The man selling him the chickens must be a real talker. *You know he's lying.*

Sally Ann went back inside, poured a glass of water, and retrieved a biscuit from last night's dinner. She plopped herself down on the couch.

"Ouch!" Her butt smacked something hard beneath the cushions. She stood and yanked the cushion to the floor. There it was—the book!

She rubbed her thumb over her mother's emerald necklace and smiled. Let John lie and keep his secrets, she held the key to everything in the palms of her hands. She opened the cover.

She flipped through the writings on healing plants and continued on. It was the last section on plants she searched for—plants to enact revenge.

Part II
The Path Chosen

Reverend Hartman couldn't keep his eyes off the stranger, nor could he keep his dislike for him out of his voice. He had the wild-eyed look of a savage Indian about him. Earnest had met a few of his kind in his life. The man was a godless heathen, unless he missed his guess, and Earnest Hartman was seldom wrong about such things.

William Jordan pulled him into his study to discuss the day's sermon, and unless he missed his guess again, to also get him away from the young man, John Dyer.

Earnest wasn't confident in Kate Jordan's ability as a chaperone, being nearly as young as Ada, but his daughter was a strong, independent, and Christian woman.

In most things, he trusted her absolutely, but she knew nothing of men. Her beauty intimidated most of them, but he wasn't without fault for her ignorance either. When on the road, they never stayed in a town long enough for Ada to meet potential suitors. And a hundred years after the Glorious Revolution that nearly wiped Catholicism from the New World's shores, their former home became infested with papists again. There was no potential there.

He noticed the way John Dyer looked at his daughter, but that wasn't unusual, few men could turn away from her. What concerned the good Earnest Hartman was the way his daughter looked back!

"Come in," William said, in response to the knock at the door. Kate entered with a tray full of sandwiches.

"I thought you men might like your meal where you'll not be disturbed."

"Excellent, Kate, thank you, my dear!" Kate sat the sandwiches between them on his desk and excused herself.

"Tell me, Earnest, why is it that you never took another wife? I understand you've been a bachelor for a very long time," William said.

The Reverend's head jerked up. "I'm sorry, William, did you ask me something? Do you think the young people should be left alone? We don't even know this young man."

"Dear sir, no disrespect, but your daughter is a grown woman, and they are certainly safe under my roof."

"I don't trust him, William, there's something strangely primal about his soul. Yes, Ada is a grown woman, but as you will discover when your own son matures, they never stop being your little ones."

William Jordan nodded, and an awkward silence filled the room. Reverend Hartman wolfed down his sandwich and grabbed a second one. His eyes focused on the closed door.

"So, getting married is not in your immediate plans?" William asked.

"What?"

"Did you never consider getting married again?"

"No, my calling to preach His word, and properly raising my daughter, consumes my time, and I am grateful for both. They are my salvation."

William nodded, and the dead, uneasy silence returned. Hartman was not in a conversational mood.

"If you're done with lunch, perhaps we should join the others?" William asked as he hastily swallowed his last bite of sandwich.

Hartman stood abruptly and led the way to the dining room. At the table, Kate took a nibble from her sandwich, then dabbed the corners of her mouth with a napkin.

"The sandwiches were sublime, Kate. Thank you," Reverend Hartman said.

"I'm glad you liked—"

"Where did Ada get off to?"

"She and John took their sandwiches down to the river, Reverend. That's not a problem, is it?"

* * * *

The long slow walk to the river exhibited nature at her most beautiful. Ancient oaks and maples shaded the path, while squirrels danced through their branches. The clean scent of the woods filled Ada's senses and cleared her mind. At the river's edge, they surprised two otters. As joyfully as children they played, tumbling over one another in a sliding race to the river, unconcerned with the worries of men.

These things she might have spotted on her own but seeing them through John's eyes added a whole new dimension. His awe and exuberance at all the natural world brought her long-forgotten delight. Her heart embraced the feeling of innocent contentment, as a grandfather might feel when seeing his grandchild's smile, only to recall the times his own child's face beamed in recognition of him.

They sat together on a blanket Kate thoughtfully provided, and despite the continual flow of conversation, managed to finish their sandwiches.

"Where are you from originally, Ada?" John asked.

"My mother's people come from Southern Maryland. By the way, there's a legend there of a famous witch named Dyer. Are you any relation?" Ada laughed.

"Actually, I am. Are you superstitious, Ada? Moll is my great-great-grandmother."

"Is? Not was?"

"Is. Do you not believe in eternal life of the spirit or soul?"

"Who are you, John Dyer?" Ada asked, and John laughed.

"Who am I? I'm John Dyer. I live in a cabin on a small homestead on the top of the mountain up there." He pointed toward his home.

"You can do better than that, John. You have a different perspective on everything and I'd like to know more."

"I fear you'll be disappointed, as I'm a simple man. But what do you want to know?"

"Well, where is your family from? What brings you joy—besides nature obviously. What do you want from life? Do you believe in God?"

"Whoa! Very well, I'll try, if you promise to reciprocate?"

Ada nodded.

"I am John 'Running Bear' Dyer, so that should tell you a little bit about my roots. My father was a violent alcoholic, and a bum. When I was a young boy, he beat my mother after a fight, and she left him.

"I didn't see him for a year, when he showed up at our house one morning while my mother was at work. He packed me a bag, and we rode for days. We finally found the Conoy, the tribe of my ancestors, and the people my great-grandfather still lived with.

"I never saw my mother again, though I'm told she died of a broken heart soon after. We lived with the Conoy for ten years, until my father died. I stayed with my great grandfather for a while. Great-Pa I called him. Anyway, after a few years I set out to find my own path."

Ada sat open mouthed as she followed his story. "You've been through a lot for someone so young."

"I'm sorry, too much?"

"No, not at all. You still owe me what makes you happy, what you want from life, and your beliefs..." Ada clicked the three things off on her fingers.

"I don't know. This makes me happy, being here with you. Sharing actual thoughts with someone genuine, and not just idle chit-chat that passes for conversation with most people. Even better when that person is as beautiful as you are."

"I may not agree with your assessment, but I appreciate the thought. I know I'm too skinny, almost boyish, and my skin is too tanned, but I love being outside, so I'll suffer the consequences. Still, beauty is a gift from God, not something anyone earns of their own accord. But based on the beautiful women I've known, I suspect physical beauty is more of a curse than a blessing."

"If given your choice then, what divine blessing would you choose for yourself?"

"I'm abundantly blessed, John. But if I was so covetous as to pray for another? Then I would be a healer—like in the Bible. To be able to heal the pain and suffering in a world full of both. How blessed would that be?"

"Well, whether blessing or curse, your beauty is undeniable, but I confess that time with you is as healing as any potion or salve." Ada felt the color rise to her cheeks as he spoke.

"Forgive me if I've been too bold. Did I embarrass you?" he asked.

"No, no…not at all. Please continue."

"Oh…well then, your eyes are the intense blue of an indigo bunting, my favorite bird, but the depths of your eyes, such as I've heard about the ocean. Your smile…"

"No, John, stop!" Ada laughed. "I mean thank you, but tell me the rest about you, silly man."

"Oh. Where was I? What I want? I don't know. What I want can change depending on where I am, or a new experience, and even the people I've met. I guess just to be happy, free, and to be as good a man as I can. I'd like to be the kind of man who would make my great-grandfather proud."

Ada nodded, and smiled. "What about your faith? Do you believe in God? I am a preacher's daughter, you know!"

"I believe God is in everything and everyone. Doubting the existence of God, by whatever name you call him, is the same as doubting the existence of yourself. Look around you, Ada. Seeing all of creation spread out before us like this? Who could doubt Him, or more likely, Her?"

"I suppose you're right, although if you called God by a different name in front of my father, or used the feminine pronoun, you'd better prepare yourself for a long theological discussion, better known as a tongue lashing, at the end of which he will have converted you or pronounced you irredeemable." John's face showed concern, but Ada's laugh was clear and contagious. He had no recourse but to join in.

"Wait now. It's your turn, Ada." John smiled.

"I am Ada Hartman, and I live everywhere, or at least whatever town my father gets invited to preach at next. I've travelled up and down these mountains and even to the cities on the coast a few times while father was based in the southern part of Maryland. I've seen the humbling magnificence of the ocean that you so extravagantly liken me to. I love seeing new places, and faces, and I'm a little nervous because, besides my father, you are the first man I've been alone with in over a year. I'll bet my father is close to having a fit." She laughed, and then the expression on her face turned somber, and her voice lowered.

"I'm sorry about your mother, and I miss mine too, although I never knew her. She died during my birth." A tear slipped from the pool gathering in the well of Ada's eyes and slid down her cheek. John reached out and wiped it away with his thumb.

"I don't know where that came from!" She dabbed at her eyes. "I'm sorry, I'm being silly. It was so long ago."

"Never be sorry for feeling, but a safer subject then? Tell me what you want from life?"

"At the risk of spouting cliché, I want to make the world better. I know everyone says that, and it's a grand aspiration, but not like saving the world. I'd be content to make a few lives better for my being born. And my thoughts about the divine? Well, you were at services, so you already know my feelings about God."

"Well, I know what Reverend Hartman's thoughts are anyway. Pretty dark I thought, but I'll give you a pass on that one." John laughed. "So, what makes you happy?"

"Traveling, family, the outdoors, and puppies, and oh, did I mention traveling?" She laughed.

"There's nothing out there that you can't find right here." He touched his index finger lightly against the center of her forehead.

"There's a whole world out there to see and explore, John. Have you seen it all? I want to!"

He shook his head. "No, but I've seen enough. People are the same anywhere you go, so it's a matter of who you are. Change who *you* are, and you change *where* you are."

"That's an interesting point of view, John. Still, there is so much beauty in the world…"

"Look around again! Can you imagine any place more beautiful? Or anywhere that could make you feel closer to the Creator?"

"My father would say you are making a serious theological error. One he felt his mentor was guilty of. He says you must not make the mistake of worshiping the creation instead of the Creator."

"I mean no disrespect to your father, but anyone who would say that has never created anything. How can you separate the two? Whatever we make, we put a piece of ourselves in it, our spirits, or our souls if you prefer."

"And you believe God did the same?"

"Yes, there's a piece of the Creator in each of us, and in everything, perhaps especially so in you."

"I'm not sure if you're trying to seduce me, or if you're the least superficial man I've met, John Running Bear Dyer. If it's the first thing, I should be honest with you. I know coming here with you seems forward, so perhaps you've misjudged me, but..."

"Your honor is safe with me, Ada Hartman. *You* are safe with me."

* * * *

Sally Ann discovered a patch of interesting mushrooms that she recognized from drawings in the book and gathered them to dry. *You never know what a girl might need.*

She returned to the cabin with her muslin bag full of plants, ones not requested by John, but helpful for her own purposes. She entered the shed behind the cabin and hung the plants in the darkest corner to dry and draped a worn tarp in front of them.

She looked at the darkening sky. The sun flickered its last rays before disappearing over the mountain, and the silver sliver of moon promised scant light.

Inside the cabin, she lit the lone lantern and a pair of candles and opened the book on the floor before her. She sat reading, the glow of the lantern flickering on the pages as she waited for the sounds of John's return.

The dark, slithery, and powerful things described in the book filled her with dread, and yet consumed her with desire. They fed on her need and infused her with their false hopes. She practiced invoking the names, pleading for their intervention.

A series of shivers ran down her spine, over and over, with each new name she called upon. Her body shook as if each of her nerve endings were tweaked, electrified.

Unseen hands caressed her, gently at first, but then roughly twisting her about, manipulating her body to meet their desires. Needle like teeth nibbled at her ears and moved over her body.

One by one, and two by two, the spiritual assault continued, ravaging her until she reached an unknown peak, and cried, "Stop! Please stop, I can't take any more! Please..."

The spirits washed over her in a wave, and a searing heat filled her loins, and her hips flailed with them. Stars flashed before her eyes, finding a release she'd never known, and her mouth opened in a silent scream. Finally, she curled up in a ball, limp with terror and a sordid, satisfied exhaustion.

Minutes or hours might have passed when the sound of galloping hooves yanked her back from this other world, yet the ancient voices still whispered her name.

"Hide the book, Sally Ann. He approaches. We are with you, and we are one."

She stood, weak kneed, and replaced the book beneath the cushion, then sat at the kitchen table, waiting.

John entered the cabin, and Sally noticed the broad smile on his face and the swagger in his step.

"Welcome home, John. Did you have a good time with the chicken farmer?"

"No, I didn't get to his place. I went to church to hear the new preacher though."

"Church? New preacher? You? That's not how I'd guess you'd choose to spend your Sunday."

"How did you do today? Any problem finding everything?"

Sally Ann reached under the table for her bag and separated the plants on the table.

"You found everything I asked for, even the ginseng root! You certainly had a productive day, Sally Ann. Wonderful job!"

"Thank you, John, that means a lot to me," *and you have no idea how productive…*

* * * *

Kate bustled around her kitchen, preparing breakfast and wishing the walls weren't so thin. She placed a pot of sausages—what her husband called "bags o' mystery"—on the wood stove and began to mix up the pancake batter.

Her curiosity battled with her sense of decency, but the former won out as she listened in on the battle of wills.

"Father, he is a good man. We only ate our lunches and chatted. Nothing else happened. I cannot believe your trust in me is so fragile," Ada said.

"Ada, you are a warm, intelligent, and trusting soul, but I fear what you see in this man is subterfuge, a façade he is using to take advantage of your caring and innocent nature."

"This isn't something I intend to argue with you about, Father. I love you, and I respect your opinion, but I am a grown woman. I barely know this man, but I do find him interesting, and if I choose to see him again, I will do so."

"Ada, he's an Indian, a half-breed heathen with no religious upbringing, no background in the faith. He is everything we stand against."

"Really, Father? I thought we were bringing Jesus' love to everyone. I believe your very words were, 'no man is beyond salvation.'"

"Yes, and the words so often spoken by young maidens: 'I can tame the savage in him!' Why do naïve young women feel this ludicrous attraction to such unsavory men?" The Reverend stomped his foot to punctuate his words.

"Father, I've only just met him, and we've made no plans to marry this week. Didn't mother's family rail against your own marriage?"

"If your mother was here, she'd be ashamed of your behavior, she would tell you…" but the rest fell on deaf ears, as Ada slammed the door behind her.

"Ada! Ada, I'm sorry, I didn't mean…"

Kate heard the door, and her heart wept when Ada dashed through the house, tears raining down her face.

* * * *

Flames licked at the oak slabs in the fire pit, and sparks danced when John tossed in another sizeable piece.

"This should last until we return. Are you ready?"

Sally Ann smiled. "I am, finally!"

"I will try to explain, and I have tools to help. You must relax, and find yourself, your true self. I want you to calm your mind, and identify all that is you, not who others say you are, but the undisguised you, your being with none of the trappings. Only then will you see another. A spirit animal who is you, only another you."

"I'll try, John, but I'm confused."

John placed a dark, hideous figure on the large flat rock in front of her.

"This is Okeus. He is a god of my people, the Conoy. He is often seen as a god of war, but when appeased, he also aids our journey into the world of the spirit. Never call upon him, or any of the others to seek revenge! Avoid black magic at all costs or you will be consumed. You cannot use the spirits for gain, except spiritual gain, and you can never use them to harm another. Understood?"

Sally Ann's head nodded up and down.

"Are you sure you want to continue?"

"Yes."

John opened the vial, and placed a smear on the rock, and touched each of Sally Ann's cheeks.

"This will help you to find your way, at least until you become more proficient."

"What is it?"

John lowered his gaze and stared into the dancing flames, then stared at Sally Ann as if in challenge. "Blood from an unsullied woman. It is the most powerful."

"It's virgin's blood? John, what have you done?"

"Not what you think, although I suppose it is bad enough. Until I learned to skin-walk on my own, I put women to sleep with a mixture of valerian root and chamomile, plants I learned from my European ancestors."

"You drugged women and drained their blood?"

"Drained? No, I added the extracts to their wine, and they fell into a deep and peaceful sleep—just as you experienced. I took a very small amount of blood, not much more than the swamp mosquitos took from us our first evening here. The worst side effect for the woman is being sleepy for a few days."

"John, my blood...I am not a..."

"Innocent? I know, still all blood has power, but I just needed you to sleep, so I could...change."

"You stopped doing it? You said you don't need it anymore?"

"I've discovered I don't, but I retained some as a teacher, in case it's ever needed—as it is now. After you, I swore to my great-grandfather I'd never do so again. You are a friend, and I crossed the line. I'll not become my father!"

"Yes, you did! That's disgusting, John, an invasion of the worst kind...so what does the blood do anyway?"

"It's used as an offering to Okeus, a payment for him serving as your guide. It appeases him and prevents him from taking his payment in more distasteful ways. This was the last of it." John tossed the empty vial into the flames.

Sally Ann glared into the fire, her mouth opened to speak, but no words came out.

"Do you still wish to continue?"

"I've come this far, but why are you avoiding my eyes with that faraway look of yours? What are you holding back?"

"It's just that..."

"Spit it out already, John."

"Well, some initiates say it is easier if the seeker is open to the natural world, their hair loose, and clothes..."

"Well now, John, why didn't you just say so." Sally Ann smiled, and John stared at the fire as her clothing fell at his feet.

"Then let's begin," he said. "Okeus..."

* * * *

Ada slipped through the woods, no destination in mind and replaying her father's words over and over in her head. Her vision was too blurred to enjoy the wonders spread out before her.

How could he speak to her so? Was it so important to him to be right, to drive home his point that he needed to wound her so grievously? She loved her father, but for the first time in her life, she questioned his love for her!

Deeper and deeper she strode into the woods, questioning, hurting. A raised maple root snatched at her ankle and threw her to the ground, and she found the woodland carpet of leaves to be a good spot for her sorrows to overtake her.

The solitude of the forest did not reflect her sobs, but rather absorbed them. There was no condemnation in the gentle wood, and her anguish spent itself in its tender embrace.

She wiped her eyes (*stop being a fool*) and looked around to get her bearings. She didn't know how far she'd travelled, or how long, but she could still hear the flow of the river below her.

What now, Ada? Go running back to your father? She knew how worried he'd be, but she needed more time to think, and perhaps he did as well.

"John, I'll go see John. He will at least be glad to see me," she said out loud, but only the lonely pines heard.

She knew he lived on the mountain's summit, somewhere, so how hard could it be to find? From his description, he was in an isolated location, and he didn't say he was one of the homesteads at the mountain's top, he said it was *the* homestead at the top.

Ada picked herself up and continued onward and upward. The sound of the river faded, as did the light from the sun.

"The mountain is blocking it," she thought, "but it should be light for hours yet."

Her steps slowed as she feasted her eyes on the glory of creation, spread out across the mountainside for her enjoyment.

"John is right about this. You cannot separate the Creator from the creation!"

On Ada walked, and she knew it couldn't be much farther when she spotted the silhouette of a cabin ahead. Darkness closed in, and she hurried toward it. Father will be so worried, she thought, and she wouldn't be able to get back tonight in the dark! Perhaps John would hitch up his wagon and take her back to town? What if John isn't home?

She reached the small clearing that housed the cabin and broke into tears. The cabin was obviously an old coal miner's cabin, abandoned and unoccupied. The holes in the roof were large enough for a man to crawl through, and the chinking on the logs was cracked or missing. Glass from the broken windows glittered in the feeble moonlight.

"John!" she yelled, expecting no reply.

I cannot find my way in the darkness. She decided the best course of action at this time was none at all. She would wait for the morning light and pray the night didn't get too cold.

She curled up on the decrepit front porch to await the dawn. Distressing sounds reached out for her as the stillness of the day-lit woods gave way to the intrusions of the wandering creatures of the night.

She backed up to the cabin wall and drew her knees up to her chin. The sound of a screaming woman echoed through the night! Close to her! *Sweet Jesus, too close!*

"Who's there? Stay away!"

Soft padded footfalls were the only answer, moving closer, stalking her? The scream rocked her back on her heels. There! At the edge of the porch! Silvery moonlight peeked through the trees revealing the tawny fur, and the lash of the long tail.

Mountain lion!

Ada folded her hands in prayer, remembering her father's sermon about Daniel and the lions.

"Help me, Lord," she prayed.

The beast leapt, eyes glowing green. She felt the weight of the beast slamming into her, then only blackness.

* * * *

Earnest Hartman led the search party. His hosts implored patience for hours, their town was safe—nothing bad happened here, but eventually, even they admitted their concern, and gathered the community.

The Jordans said Ada was too grounded and smart to stay out at night alone. What they didn't say was that meant she was either lost in unfamiliar woods, or abducted. They would not entertain the second possibility.

Preacher Hartman didn't mind sharing his ideas. He knew the half-breed Indian boy took her, and it was his fault. The pain he inflicted on his daughter was inexcusable, but didn't she know it was his love for her that drove his hateful comments?

With one breath, he berated himself for his behavior, and then excused his actions with the next. If she'd listened to his common-sense concerns, the heathen bastard couldn't have captured her!

Earnest directed the men and women to split up, to cover as much ground as possible. One group followed the river, while the Reverend's group moved steadily uphill, circling the mountain. Some were on horseback, but most walked to preserve every sound that might reach their ears.

The lights of two dozen torches moving in opposite directions flickered through the night, and yells of "Ada" filled the air.

Reverend Hartman prayed to his God for deliverance, and the words written in Titus popped into his mind: "To the pure, all things are pure, but to the defiled and unbelieving, nothing is pure."

The words provided clarity for him. He knew Ada's purity prevented her from seeing the true nature of the defiler. He must save her from the evil of the man, and he quickly made his decision. He turned toward the Jordans.

"William, take me by the fastest route to the top. You know where I want to go."

He saw a stout branch at the side of the path, and picked it up, felt its weight and tested its strength. It took all his weight against its center to break it into a maneuverable club length.

"Reverend Hartman?"

"One must be prepared, William. We are told in 2Timothy 3:17, 'so that the servant of God may be thoroughly equipped for every good work.'"

* * * *

Sally Ann felt the animal's presence before she saw it in her mind's eye. There was another there also—a bear. It appeared to be waiting for her as it sat on its haunches observing.

A tannish figure stood before her. It stepped forward until its face was inches away from hers, and scented her breath, which now came in gasps.

The jaws of the mountain lion spread open, as if in a yawn, but ever wider it stretched becoming an unnatural gaping hole. Sally Ann felt herself sucked forward, her breath resonating with the breath of the beast. Her eyes looked through the eyes of the giant cat.

She felt the cat's unbelievable strength. The powerful scents and sounds of the woods created a sensory overload, disorienting. The feeling of the cat's fangs was an adjustment, but contributed to her sense of invincibility, and dominance.

A soft huffing sound, and the bear moved away from her. She turned to follow, feeling the flex of her bundled muscles, and then sensed another presence. The cat in her shied away from this dark spirit, and growled, but her human curiosity held her there.

The entity remained unfocused to her eyes, as if hovering between two worlds. Sally Ann could only make out its dark wavy hair, and...red eyes?

"Enjoy your adventure, my lady. I am Laris, remember the name, for we will meet again." She slashed at the figure with her cat's claws, and the apparition faded away.

Another huff, and Sally Ann fell in line behind the bear. John set a fast pace, but she kept up easily. Who was this Laris, she wondered, but the cat forced her concentration back to their surroundings, ignoring all else. She was the queen of the forest! Nothing could challenge her here, perhaps not even the bear racing in front of her.

She didn't know John's destination, nor did she care, the freshness of her experience overwhelmed her, and set her free. Oddly, she knew every smell she encountered! A fat opossum crossed their trail here, and she sniffed the raccoon above her, trembling as it hid in the fork of a tree. She sensed where a rabbit's resting spot was disturbed by their passing, and then...?

The spore was human, but not of anyone she recognized. Her cat's intuition screamed "Danger! Enemy!" She glanced at the bear as it continued toward a herd of deer, and then turned to follow this new trail.

It was a human dwelling ahead, and the cat was repulsed by the old aromas of the place. It screamed its anguish, but Sally Ann grew stronger and forced the cat on. She tasted the air around the porch. *Enemy!*

The hated creature sat just before her, quivering in fear. The odor of its enemy's terror fueled the cat's anger, and it crouched, gathering its muscles to spring.

The woman spotted her in the dim light, and the cat pounced before she could scream. Sally Ann felt the fragility of the creature beneath her. She extended her claws and felt them slide effortlessly into the flesh of the woman's shoulder. She licked the human's neck and felt the warmth of her jugular vein under her tongue.

Her jaws spread to rip open the woman's neck, when a tremendous weight smashed into her side, flattening her against the cabin walls.

The bear!

Sally Ann screamed her cat's indignation, and then stood, and shook her head. She felt the cracked ribs, and the bruises, and growled.

The bear stood on its hind legs and roared its challenge. Bruised and battered, the cat turned and raced away.

Another day, Sally Ann thought.

* * * *

John came back to himself in the hazy moments just before dawn. He was curled up beside Sally Ann near the fire-pit, and instantly recalled the night's events…*Ada!*

His head still filled with cobwebs, he mounted his horse bareback and galloped toward the old coal miner's cabin. Once there, he hurried to her side, anxious about her wounds.

Her injuries weren't severe. The bump to her head probably knocked her unconscious, but the deep gashes on her shoulder concerned him. A cat's claws often created a difficult to heal wound and could lead to putrefaction. He picked her up in his arms, mounted the horse, and raced back toward his cabin.

As his horse trotted across the meadow in front of his cabin, he noticed Sally Ann still sleeping beside the fire pit. *What have you done, Sally Ann!*

The cabin yielded fresh clothes, clean water, and the bandages he needed. After having treated many injuries, John observed that a good cleaning helped wounds to heal, but as soon as he touched her injuries, Ada's eyes popped open and she screamed.

"Get away from me!"

"It's all right, Ada, you're safe. It's me, it's John…I found you in the woods. What happened to you?"

"John? Oh John, it was terrible." She wrapped her arms around his neck. "I was looking for your place, and I got lost. I decided to wait for morning, and this huge cat…it was a mountain lion, John! It attacked me!"

John held her, and promised her she was safe, and began to clean her shoulder wounds. He applied a honey-based poultice and covered them with a clean cloth bandage. The gashes were not wide, but they were deep.

"I'm so sorry, Ada," John said.

"Why are you sorry? You saved me."

He nodded. "I should have been there to protect you. If anything worse happened to you, I don't know what I'd…"

"Now you are being silly. You didn't even know I was coming to visit."

John dropped his eyes to the floor, but Ada cupped his chin in her hands, lifted his face, and looked into his eyes.

"My hero!" she said. When her lips softly touched his, the warmth filled John's heart, and became a yearning ache migrating to his loins. His arms reached out for her—

Crash! The door flew open, and the Reverend Hartman stormed in with the Jordans filing in behind him.

"Let go of her, you filthy beast!" Hartman yelled, striding across the room.

Ada jumped up from John's table. "Father, it's all right, John saved me…"

Hartman swung the improvised club sideways and hit John solidly in the neck, knocking him from his chair.

"Stop it, dammit! Stop it, now!" Ada yelled, and snatched the weapon from her father's hands.

John stood, rubbing his neck, and approached the older man. "I believe there's been a misunderstanding, sir."

The Reverend grabbed his daughter's arm, and half dragged her toward the door. Ada winced.

"Reverend, she's injured, her shoulder..."

"You stay away from my daughter, Dyer, stay away or you will be sorry! Come along, Ada, we will discuss this on the way home."

As they all cleared out of John's home, Kate stepped up to him before leaving, shaking her head.

"What were you thinking? You messed up, John."

He shrugged his shoulders. "I didn't do anything wrong, Kate."

"Right." She winked at him, though her eyes burned with hatred and pointed her thumb outside. "By the way, Earnest was focused on your cabin, so I don't believe he noticed, but there's a very attractive, and very naked woman sleeping in your front yard."

* * * *

The search party caught up with the Hartmans and Jordans on their way down the mountain. One of the men brought his wagon, which sped up the trip downhill.

After thanking everyone for their help and concern, Ada rode in silence. She knew Kate was trying to pull her out of her shell, perhaps concerned with her drifting into shock, but she felt shaken and hollow, and disinclined to share the particulars of her attack, when Kate tried another tack.

"So, tell me all about this handsome fellow, John? What's he like?"

"He certainly deserved better than he got from my father."

"You know how worried the Reverend was. I'm not excusing it, but he was a man protecting his family..."

"I didn't need protecting, not from John, anyway. My father owes him an apology."

"You know your father better than I do, but my impression is he's not a man readily given to apologies, nor am I convinced one is deserved."

"What do you mean, Kate?"

"Forget it. Guess I was just worried about you."

The wagon bounced over a rock, and Ada grabbed at her bandaged shoulder.

"Slow down up there, Ada is hurt," Kate yelled to the driver. "What happened last night, Ada? What did that to you?"

Ada let her mind travel back in time to the attack. She remembered the moment just before the big cat pounced. Even now, she could see its eyes clearly, and the almost human intelligence reflected there. *My imagination going wild.*

"Do mountain lions hunt people? I mean, are they smart enough to go looking for people?"

"What? I don't know…a few years ago, the men hunted down a cat that killed a young boy. It was old, and nothing but skin and bones. Its teeth were so worn it probably couldn't find any other prey."

"There was nothing wrong with this one's teeth, or claws," Ada said.

"When did John enter the picture? How did he find you? Was anyone else there?"

Ada rubbed the back of her head. "I don't know much that happened after the cat jumped on me. I guess it knocked me out. John found me somehow, and he carried me back to the cabin and bandaged me up. I don't know much else. We just arrived at his homestead when my father broke in like some Old Testament avenging angel."

"It's truly amazing you survived, Ada," Kate said. "What a horrible experience."

Lucky, yes, she was that, but was it all luck, or was there something else? After the cat leapt, her vision blurred, darkened, and her mind floated away, but did something happen to the big cat. Or was the bear just a dream?

* * * *

There was no reason for John to treat her this way. He took her on a journey beyond her experience, and beyond her wildest dreams. Then he expected her to somehow know what was expected of her, and to know the inherent dangers lurking in the dark? How could she know that *she* was the danger!

She had found her way back to herself, back to her human self at the homestead, with no thanks to John. She was battered and sore and that *was* entirely thanks to John!

The woman, why was she there? Sally Ann sensed the threat from her, and that is why the cat attacked. Who was she? Why did John protect her?

The questions raced through her head as she rode down the mountain toward home.

John is lying to me! That woman is the one he wants. He thinks I am not good enough for him. It's been her all along. He is just like all the rest of them!

Sally Ann was a novitiate to an unknown world, he should help her, show her the way, not curse her and order her out of his sight! Whatever happened henceforth was on him.

Her thoughts fell again on the woman, the trembling fearful lump of humanity impaled on her claws, writhing in terror and pain. She had watched as the light left her eyes, unconsciousness—a small death, and she thought to end her permanently. Her cat craved the coppery taste of the woman's blood.

That's when John swooped in, and she remembered little else other than her red rage, and the consuming need for revenge.

Sally Ann remembered waking at the sound of the others breaking into John's cabin, amazed that she retained some of the cat's hearing, and its sense of smell.

She slid behind a rock to hide and observe, but she knew one of them spotted her. Kate, one of the holier-than-thou women from town. She knew Kate was there for the other woman—her enemy, and probably John's lover. She drew in her scent, the marker special to her, a scent she'd remember.

She waited for them all to leave, and then dressed and walked up to the cabin.

John sat at the kitchen table rubbing his swollen neck.

"What happened to you? Did your girlfriend's daddy take exception to your overnight visitation?"

John continued staring at the floor.

"What did you think you were doing, Sally Ann?" he asked. "You were not in control. You could have killed her! You would have!"

"My cat felt threatened."

"You allowed the cat free reign, Sally Ann. I made a mistake. It wasn't your fault. You weren't ready, and anger consumes you. I cannot teach self-discipline. I never should have shown you."

"I will do better next time, John. You'll see, but I don't like that woman."

"She's a good woman, Sally Ann, but there will be no next time, not with me."

"What do you mean, John? It was my first time. It was amazing. You cannot take this from me!"

John didn't answer but shook his head.

"Is she the reason why, John? That woman? Why did you lie to me about her?"

"I never lied to you, Sally Ann, but I owe you no explanation. We were friends, you and I—that's all we were."

"Were, John? We *were* friends?"

John shook his head and raised his eyes to meet hers.

"Were, Sally Ann, I think it best if we don't see any more of each other."

* * * *

John wondered how everything went so disastrously wrong. He never expected Sally Ann to be so totally absorbed by her spirit animal that she forgot her humanity! It was a terrible mistake, a wanton lack of judgement on his part to introduce her to her spirit animal, and it nearly cost Ada's life!

Over and over, he replayed the night in his mind. Why didn't he end it before she met up with Ada? Something wasn't right from the moment Sally Ann's spirit animal embraced her. A dark spirit waited, his image no more than a shadow. Was it another guide? Not Okeus—he would recognize that dark god, but another presence, a dark and foreboding entity, John could feel it there…

No, he couldn't blame Sally Ann, the fault was his alone, but he'd learned his lesson. He would show her no more, and she'd never find her way back without his help. He knew he hurt her, dismissing her from his life and withholding his friendship, after all she'd been through with other men, but he saw no way around it! She was a dangerous and angry shifter, and he was a terrible friend, a source of pain to everyone close to him.

He touched the hooved up bruise on his neck and smiled. "Guess I had it coming," he said, but the four walls of his cabin did not respond. How could he make this right?

Kate wouldn't trust him now. Earnest Hartman considered him some sort of fiend, and Ada? He didn't know what she thought, but he knew the best thing for her. If he cared for her at all, he needed to stay out of her life.

A week ago, he didn't know her name, and this morning, he couldn't get her out of his head! Her smile could light up the whole of the outdoors, her sparkling eyes rivalled the stars, but with such depth! The sweet smell of lilac on her skin…

Stop it! She isn't part of the life you chose; your path is different from other men. The old man did you a favor by forcing her away!

Yes, his path forward was clear.

* * * *

Ada knocked on the carved wooden door leading to William Jordan's study, and waited a moment for her father to respond. She knew he made her wait to unnerve her, as he often did with a parishioner he intended to shame back to the path of righteousness.

Ada was not in the mood for games, or lectures, so she knocked once again, lightly, and went inside uninvited.

"I am here. Did you want to see me, Father?"

"How are you healing, Ada? You've hardly left your room since your terrible experience. Is your shoulder better? What did the doctor say?"

"I'm fine, Father, thank you. The doctor thought the wound was healing nicely, and seemed surprised. He requested that I ask John about the ingredients in his poultice when I next see him."

"Do you intend to?"

"Ask him about it?"

"No, see him again, Ada. Is that your intent?"

"I do, Father, and I know you do not approve, but…"

"But you are twenty-two years old, and a grown woman."

Ada smiled, and nodded. "I love you, Father, but yes. As a child I followed your every word, as is the way of a parent and child. But I *am* a woman now and if I follow anyone, it is because they lead where I would go."

"Have you been practicing that little speech?"

Ada smiled. "I have, but that doesn't diminish its truth."

"What happened in that cabin after the attack? Please be honest with me. Did he try to take advantage of you, Ada?"

"Of course not, Father! Do you think I'd entertain his company again, if that was the case?"

"Do not chase that man, Ada. I know you are a grown woman, but I also know people in small towns like to talk. A young single woman seeking a man's company, unchaperoned and staying out all night?"

Ada's lips drew taut in a straight line on her face. "It may look bad, Father, but nothing happened between us, and what is the quote you love so? 'To the defiled and unbelieving, nothing is pure?' But you know what? He saved my life! Anything he wanted, I would have gladly given!"

"Ada! If we're quoting the good book, it also says, 'Do not make your daughter common by letting her become a loose woman.' I would not be a good father and let that become your reputation."

"I think my reputation and my honor are intact, Father, but I will wait for John to call upon me. We can't have it said that the righteous Reverend Hartman's daughter is a fallen woman of ill repute now, can we?"

"It's not my reputation I am trying to protect. I just want…" The rest of his thought fell on deaf ears, and for the second time in a week, Ada stormed away from her father. This time, there were no tears, only anger.

* * * *

Sally Ann fell into a fitful sleep, after a full day helping her father nurse a hangover. She looked forward to a long restful slumber, but it was not to be. Strange and darkly vivid dreams haunted her slumbers, jerking her awake in a cold sweat, trembling in fear.

The scene she recognized, a small island in the middle of the river. It was a spot where Jimmy Haas took her frequently, peaceful and secluded, a beautiful setting for young lovers to spend time together.

She later realized Jimmy liked it there so much because he could be with her, and take advantage of her affections, without sullying his precious reputation. It just wouldn't do for the educated son of the oldest local family to be seen with the lowly daughter of the town drunkard!

Sally Ann climbed out of bed to throw some water on her face, trying to shake the feeling of dread left behind by the nightmare, but still the images crept into her waking mind.

She and Jimmy skinny-dipping in the river, and then cuddling by a small campfire to dry off. In the warmth of the flames, Sally fell asleep, and woke up alone.

She called out repeatedly for Jimmy, but he did not respond. She walked through the brush to the water's edge, and the chill of the night sent a shiver down her spine. She returned to the campfire to warm up and retrieve her clothes, but they were gone. *That damn Jimmy, pulling one of his childish pranks!*

"Jimmy! Damn you, bring my clothes back! What are you, ten years old?"

She waited for his answer, but the only sound was the crackling embers of the campfire. She stomped her foot, and again yelled for her inattentive boyfriend.

"You're gonna be sorry, James Haas!"

Her face burned in anger, and she stalked away from the river, hoping he might hear her better from the center of the island. She followed a well-worn path, and wondered if it was worn by the hooves of deer, or the heels of men?

The night was black, even the stars hid behind the clouds, and she measured each step, not wanting to stub her toe on a rock, or worse. As she ducked under some fox grape vines, and side-stepped a clump of poison ivy, the moon slid out of its veil, and she beheld a small clearing ahead!

She made use of the available light and raced into the center of the glade.

"Jimmy! Jimmy, can you hear me? Where are you?"

She heard a rustling in the brush, and…what animal made a noise like a child's laugh? She took a tentative step toward the sound, the meadow brightened, and suddenly the woods filled with the sound of children's laughter—snickers really.

A dozen scruffy ten-year-old children surrounded her, standing just outside the full light of the moon, pointing at her, laughing.

It couldn't be? She knew them all, but they were still young! As young as when they laughed at her bare ass at the county fair! They were the children of her childhood, unchanged.

She used her arms to cover herself and fell to the ground.

"No, no, no! Leave me alone! You can't be real!"

Sobbing, she wiped repeatedly at her face, but even now, awake in her bedroom, the tears wouldn't stop.

* * * *

For the next three days, Kate watched Ada with increasing concern. She watched as she paced the front porch; she noticed when she began sleeping later in the mornings. A woman with a healthy appetite, who never missed a meal, now picked absently at her dinner. Kate felt her friend's pain.

Where are you, John Dyer?

When Kate stepped into the kitchen garden to cut some asparagus for dinner, Ada squatted by a row of beans, pulling weeds.

"The beans are going to be late this year. The ground stayed soggy all spring, and William couldn't get them in any sooner," Kate said.

"I'll bet you're looking forward to the first fresh ones cooked up with a piece of fat back? Thinking about it makes my mouth water. The first ones of the year are so good after a long winter chewing leather breeches beans."

"Wonderful, you're getting your appetite back then? I've been worried about you."

"I know I've been mopey, but I'm fine, Kate, thank you. It is hard to admit it, even to myself, but it appears my father was right about him. John isn't interested in me, and that's fine. I'm forgetting about him, moving on. He owes me nothing, and we made no promises to each other, but…"

"But you felt there was something special there?"

"Yes, I guess so, and it has me questioning my feelings, and my ability to read people. I thought it was real, and I hate that it matters to me…stupid. I never wanted to settle down in one place anyway, but sending out roots, and creating a home is very important to John."

"He's a man, Ada, maybe he's been distracted. Something may have come up," Kate said, and nibbled on her lower lip.

"Kate, even if I misread him, misread us, you'd think he'd find the time to stop by and check on my injuries? Make sure I'm all right? A half-dozen men from the search party have done so."

"Yes, I believe all of the young single men? Oh, and the one wishing he still was." Kate laughed. "There will be no shortage of suitors for you in this town. John Dyer will soon be forgotten."

"It's just that there's something different about him. I like the way he makes me feel, and I like how I am with him."

* * * *

John Dyer, or the bear that was John Dyer on this night, hunted the game trails near his cabin. Guiding his spirit animal required constant attention. The bear's essence filled his soul, but his mind controlled the bear. It must be so, or the wild creature within him would act solely as its nature directed. Such raw power, coupled with the mental ability of a man, could only spell doom for anyone caught in its path, as Sally Ann discovered.

He followed the scent of a shoat pig, likely escaped from a farmer's pen in the valley, and his mouth watered in anticipation, his pace quickened.

A grey fox ran across the trail, but John's bear was focused. The other small predator scurried off in peace to pursue his own meal.

The aroma of pork grew stronger, the pig closer, and then the shoat dashed from the bushes on his right, squealing in fear, dashing down the trail.

John's bear pounced, slapping the pig with one giant paw, snapping its back. He held down the squirming animal, grasped its head in his jaws, and crushed its skull.

The warm blood and raw meat fed his body and his savage soul! The bear feasted until he had his fill, then John lifted his shaggy head. Seeking the place where he'd been fed and protected, the pig's life had ended behind a house near the town, a house John knew. It was the house where Ada slept.

His paws pulled leaves and small branches over the pig's carcass and circled the house. Ada's scent lingered everywhere, lilacs and honeysuckle! He paused in the garden, and his nose trailed where her steps fell earlier in the day.

John had seen Ada often since the attack—only through his bear's eyes. Her recovery was swift, but her soul seemed troubled, and unhappy.

He picked at the raspberries along the fence line, and licked his lips, exposing his teeth.

The man inside knew he must stay away, for Ada's sake, but the bear understood none of the man's concerns, only the man's yearning. He grunted and stepped up to the front door of the human dwelling and stood to his full height. His paw ripped across the wood leaving claw marks embedded in the old oak.

The man pushed him away from this place, and the bear swung his massive head side to side in agitation. He slapped the ground, tossing chunks of sod into the air, and slowly disappeared into the woods.

* * * *

Sally Ann crawled back in bed, praying for the torment of her dreams to abate. She tossed and turned, trying to locate a comfortable position, and a dry spot in the bed not drenched by her own sweat.

When sheer exhaustion snatched away her consciousness, it deposited her back in the same clearing on the island. She raised her swollen, sodden eyes, and surveyed the perimeter. No tiny figures pointed at her. No cackling laughter filled the night. She was still dressed for skinny dipping, and well snacked on by the hordes of mosquitoes, but she was alone!

Alone also meant no Jimmy, but the island was small, no more than five acres, and she knew their campsite was close.

Needle sharp thorns pierced her flesh, and vines reached out, snatching at her to impede her progress, but she pressed on. Why couldn't she see the campfire?

Jimmy picked the campsite because of the ancient maple tree growing on the riverbank. He liked to dive off the lower branches, and display his tree climbing skills, thinking his prowess put her in an amorous mood.

The tree was there. It had to be the same one. She examined the bark at waist height, where Jimmy carved their initials last year. There they were! S.A.O. + J.H., except someone had scratched through the J.H!

The fire pit was cold, damp, and looked as if it was unused for some time. There must be another tree, another camp site! Sally Ann ran into the woods looking for the other camp.

The trees seemed to mock her, branches slapping at her face as she passed them by. She tripped over a rock in the twisting trail and skinned her knee. Forced to slow down, she faced her fears. She was lost and couldn't find her way in the dark!

"Jimmy! I can't find you, where are you?"

Small shrubs shook in front of her.

"Jimmy? If that's you, you better answer me!"

"Hello, Sally Ann," said a voice in the gloom.

"Who...who's there?" The voice did not belong to Jimmy, not unless he disguised his voice, and if so, she'd kill him!

"Have you forgotten me so soon?"

Sally Ann folded her arms over her chest. Whoever, or whatever, it was, it wasn't Jimmy!

The large leaved sycamore saplings shook in front of her and parted to reveal a dark wavy-haired man. He looked to be in his mid-twenties, but something about him suggested that his was a more ancient vintage, a very old soul.

"Who are you? What do you want?"

"You may call me Laris, and I'd ask nothing you wouldn't readily give in exchange for what I can give you."

"What is it you offer that you consider so priceless?"

He stepped toward her and smiled. She relaxed, fears melting away. *No, be afraid! This is not a good man!*

Where did she know this man from? Laris reached out his hand and touched her lightly on the cheek. Desire engulfed her loins, and her arms dropped to her side of their own volition. She reached for him.

"Not now, Sally Ann, but soon. There's time for that, but first see what else I offer."

He leaned forward and touched his forehead to hers. The image of her mountain lion flooded her consciousness, and for a moment she felt the cat's strength, its freedom. She saw the woman caught in her claws, and ripped at her throat, tasting her life's force.

"No, not that one, not yet," the man said, and pulled away, breaking their link.

"No! Take me back! I could taste her," Sally Ann growled.

"She must not be harmed. The three of you must be friends. You will be the cornerstone of my triumvirate, a perfect trinity of devastation."

"I hate them. We will never be friends."

"Three young people, motherless due to death, abduction, and lust. Raised by fathers made absent by their addictions: alcohol, power, and self-righteousness. It's quite perfect, your experiences groomed you for what is to come.

"Please Laris, take me back to my cat!"

"Do as I say, and I will show you the way."

* * * *

The bell on the grocer's door tinkled its warning as Kate entered.

"Mr. Rossi? Helen?" she called.

"I'll be right with you, Mrs. Jordan," came the answer from the back room, just a moment before the little man bustled up to the counter.

"I believe I have everything here for you." He lifted a bundle onto the counter. "Nice fabric it is too, ma'am. It will make a lovely dress. Your husband will be proud to have you on his arm at the town dance."

"Thank you, although this dress will not be for me. It is for a friend. You remember Ada?"

"Indeed I do, she's a lovely young woman. The single men will be tripping all over themselves for a chance to escort her on the dance floor!"

"That is my hope. The dance will be good for her, and all of Setter's Run can use a joyful diversion."

"Ah yes, that unpleasantness at the top of the mountain. I've heard rumors…"

Kate knew rumors had spread and had no doubt Mr. Rossi was the origin of many. Men belittled female gossips, but many of them rivalled the loosest tongued of women, and Rossi was their champion!

"Thank you for the material, Mr. Rossi, and please tell Helen I asked about her."

She heard the bell tinkle again as she left. Rossi was right about one thing; the men would definitely notice Ada in the dress she planned to make for her. One way or another, she'd make Ada forget the seducer, John Dyer.

"Hello, miss? Are you Kate Jordan?"

Kate turned to face a familiar young red-headed woman. "I am, but I don't believe we've met?"

"I am Sally Ann O'Shea." She held out her hand.

Kate took her hand and shook it firmly. "We haven't actually met, but I think we almost did? At John Dyer's cabin I believe? I'm pleased to see you didn't catch your death of cold."

"I know what you must think of me, Mrs. Jordan, and I don't blame you for that. It's a long story, and one I'd prefer not to repeat, but the blame is mine alone. John Dyer was innocent, or as innocent as any man can be anyway."

"Tell me what it is that I can do for you, Sally Ann?"

"John and Ada are our friends, and we both know they belong together."

* * * *

John sat at his kitchen table with his face in his hands. He sought relief from his heart's pain through communion with his spirit animal, but for the first time it failed to provide him with release from his human tribulations.

He picked at a splinter raised in the table's wood grain.

Was Ada all right? Did the deep gashes inflicted by the cat heal, or fester? Did she hate him? Perhaps it was best if she did.

The sound of a horse galloping toward the cabin stirred him from his reverie. He peered through his lone window as Sally Ann tied her horse and small carriage to the hitching rail.

What does she want?

A knock sounded, and John pulled open his door.

"Sally Ann, what are you doing here?" he asked, blocking the entrance.

"May I come in? I'd like to talk to you…just talk."

"I think we said everything that needed saying, Sally Ann."

"It's about Ada."

John paused, took a long look at her, and stood aside beckoning her inside.

"What of her?"

"I thought you should know, she's healing nicely, almost as good as new."

"Thank you, Sally Ann, I'm glad to hear it, but how do you know? Have you seen her?"

"I have seen her, but it was her friend, Kate. She told me. She also said that Ada pines for you, all the while trying to wipe you from her heart."

"That is as it should be, and you shouldn't be here either, Sally Ann. I cause suffering to everyone close to me. We were friends, and I nearly made you into a murderer. The path that I am walking can only be walked alone."

"You are right, John. The path of the skin-walker draws me in, but you were right to deny me, I can see that now. I am not as strong as you are, and it puts me at the mercy of my inner demons. Still, I would like to be your friend."

Sally Ann stuck out her hand, and John reached for it, then stopped.

"Friends, Sally Ann? Only friends?"

"I will be whatever you'll have me be, John, but we both know she captured your heart the first time you saw her—even if you try to deny the inevitable. I can't compete with that, and I have too much pride to try." Again she stuck out her hand, and John shook it.

"Friends we are then, Sally Ann, but you are wrong. There can be nothing between Ada and me."

"Think on it between now and the weekend."

"The weekend?"

"Didn't I mention it? There is a dance this coming weekend, nothing fancy like back east, but old man Haas has this big old empty barn this time of year…anyway, I told Kate you'd be there, and Ada will be expecting you."

* * * *

The woods grew darker as Sally Ann pushed her horse toward home. She'd tarried too long at John Dyer's cabin, but she accomplished all that was required of her. The dark man kept his promises, and once home and in her dreams, she'd get her reward.

Beware of him, and his promises! He is not a good man!

After seeing to her horse, she scurried inside, and found her father sitting in the dark in their tiny parlor.

When she was a teenager, her visiting so-called friends called the room a broom closet with a high opinion of itself. Sally Ann would laugh along. After all, the joke was on her father, and by then she'd lost any sense of loyalty toward him.

She walked in, stepping lightly so as not to disturb his slumber, and removed the large earthenware jug from the claw foot side table. Sally Ann retrieved a cloth from the kitchen and wiped up the alcohol he'd spilled on the aged walnut. Her father told her that the table was the first thing he and her mother bought together.

Sean O'Shea opened one eye and smiled when he saw his daughter standing over him. The smile was an expression Sally Ann hadn't seen on his face in many years.

"Sally Ann, Daddy's little girl. Bless you, sweet child." For a moment, the years fell from his face, and he was the father she loved as a little girl, bouncing her on his knee, telling her everything would be all right. Tending her scrapes and putting an extra helping of food on her plate when there was never quite enough to go around.

He was the father she knew and loved before her mother left, and the bottle took her place. *Daddy, I was always here! I never left!* Then his one eye closed, and his smile gave way to an alcohol fueled belch.

A tear streaked down her cheek in memory of what once was, and what might have been. *If only.*

She placed a pillow behind his head, wrapped a hand stitched blanket around his shoulders, and went upstairs to her own bed.

Sleep came as soon as her head sank into her feather pillow, and just as quickly, the dark man found her. Again, she found herself on the small island, but there was no Jimmy here now. No trees shook, no children laughed, no bright lights or explosions, just one second, she was alone, and then she wasn't. Laris was there.

"Ah, dear Sally Ann, I was worried about you. I am so pleased to see you are safe."

"Take me there, Laris. I've done all that you asked, and you promised."

The dark man squatted in front of her and extended his hand. "Sit," he said, and held her hand as she squatted on a flat rock.

"Close your eyes and open your mind to me."

Sally did as instructed and looked into the darkness around her. She heard her cat purring and felt its warm breath on her neck. When the cat's whiskers tickled her lips, she let go of herself and floated toward the feline.

A sharp pain pierced her forehead, and her joints twisted in pain. Bone and muscle elongated as she poured her being into the cat. *Or became the cat?* She looked through its eyes and grinned a toothsome smile. At last, freedom!

She ran through the trees, down the trail, and across a narrow spot in the river. Her feet got wet, and she stopped to lick them dry. Then she resumed her trek toward the swamp, the farthest point from human habitation.

On and on she ran. She was tireless, with no end game other than feeling alive in this glorious body! The scents and sounds of this new world swarmed over her, and the spoor of a large bear reached her quivering nostrils. A bear she knew…but what was it about this bear? Danger? The need for revenge?

She climbed into the branches of a large hickory and surveyed her world. The traces of the bear were clearer here, but she sensed they were at least a day old. She dropped her guard and stretched out on the limb.

Something felt different this time, not at all the same as it was with John. Both the change and her total absorption into her spirit animal! Perhaps each time it became easier to control? But she didn't just control the animal…she *was* the animal!

She felt a burning sensation in the center of her forehead, just above her eyes, and heard Laris' voice within her.

"We are together, Sally Ann. I possess you as easily as you do your cat. We are one."

Part III
What the Heart Wants

Ada felt the gentle tug through her hair as Kate brushed it.

"I'm really not sure why I am doing this, Kate. Father and I will be gone in less than a month, and even if that wasn't the case, I have no interest in flirting with young men in their cups, drooling over every female old enough to sprout bosoms."

"You will enjoy yourself, Ada, and that's reason enough! It will be good for you, and yes—the young men will certainly drool! I'm going to make sure you are the belle of the ball!"

"It has been a while since I dressed in such finery, Kate. I thank you for this beautiful dress. It must have taken forever to sew!"

"It was my pleasure, and in defense of our young men, do tread lightly, remember my own William Jordan came from their ranks."

"I fear William is the exception to the rule, but I will take your recommendation under advisement." Ada laughed.

She kissed her friend's cheek, and ran her fingers over the blue cotton linen, a light sky-blue. Kate said that it complemented her eyes. The floor length gown was trimmed with a thin darker blue brocade at the bodice—a scandalous bodice—and the hem was adorned with lace. A dark blue belt sash completed the outfit.

The Jordans and the Hartmans loaded into their carriage and drove the mile to the Haas farm. A hundred lanterns glowed around the barn turned dance hall, and night turned to day. Gay flowered decorations hung from the weathered boards, and ribbons were draped along the paths.

"I'm amazed old man Haas allowed such frivolity on his property," William said, admiring the display.

Kate laughed. "I assure you, it had more to do with old woman Haas than old man Haas, and the womenfolk of town took care of the rest."

"It's beautiful, Kate, and now I know what you were doing every moment you weren't slaving away on this dress," Ada said.

Earnest Hartman held open the door, and waved the women inside, but a flash of scarlet red womanhood surged through.

"Reverend, so nice to see you," the woman said. The Reverend took her proffered hand and kissed it.

"The pleasure is entirely mine, Miss O'Shea."

She then turned her attention to the women.

"Kate, you are as beautiful as ever, and Ada...my, you are stunning, absolutely scrumptious!"

Both women thanked her and bestowed some compliments of their own. The foursome moved inside, finding themselves at the opposite end of the barn from where the small band set up their tables and chairs.

"I didn't know your father knew Sally Ann O'Shea," Kate said when the men left to procure drinks for them all.

"Oh yes, I suppose he thinks if he can't stop his own daughter from acting like a trollop, he might as well take an actual one under his guidance and try to convert her!"

"Ada! Sally Ann isn't so bad, she's had a hard life, but I've never heard you speak so ill of another. Are you all right?"

Ada shook her head, and her eyes welled up. "You are right, Kate. I'm ashamed of myself, especially as I hold no ill will to Sally Ann. I'm lashing out. God, I'm horrid, certainly unfit company for this dance."

"You are nothing of the kind, but who or what has you acting so out of character and ornery?"

"I don't know…well I do, but it's silly. I am perturbed with John, my father, and especially myself. I care for John, my father hates him, and John couldn't care less what either of us feels."

Kate glanced over at Sally Ann as she pulled a tall man out on the dirt dance floor.

"Perhaps that's best, Ada."

* * * *

The music started just as Sally Ann spied him slipping in from the side door. It was the only part of the barn that no light from the lanterns penetrated. Before his backside found its resting spot on the pine board bench, she latched onto his arm.

"Oh no you don't. You will favor me with the first dance of the night."

The beginning threads of the Sussex waltz floated down, and tuning adjustments were made on the instruments by the musicians. The man pulled his arm away.

"My dancing is such that it would be no favor to you, Sally Ann, I assure you."

"Nonetheless…" She caught his arm again, inside the elbow, and pulled him along. To resist would cause a scene, so he followed with his head bowed, a lamb led to slaughter.

"Put your right hand on my shoulder, and your left hand in mine. Very good, now simply keep counting to three."

The musicians found their beat, and he moved with her, trying to shadow her movements.

"One, two, three…do you have it?" she asked.

A misplaced foot answered her question, tripping her up. He faked a dip and guided her back to her feet.

"I am so glad your reflexes are better than your dancing, or I'd be on my back with my legs in the air," she whispered. "Now, there's a pleasant thought!"

"He's not for you!" the voice in her head said.

"I know, Laris, I'll do as you asked!"

The melody softened, then slowed as the dancers retreated to their seats.

"Before you return to your dark corner, join me for a glass of punch?"

He nodded, and they moved together to the side table holding the refreshments. He ladled out a cup for them both and passed one to her.

She reached out for it and tripped, her elbow colliding into his chest, and knocking him backwards into another dance patron. Landing side by side on the edge of the table, he turned to apologize.

"Ma'am, I'm so sorry, I...oh, Ada!"

"John!"

* * * *

She was as beautiful as he remembered! The past weeks, trying to convince himself otherwise, failed miserably now in her presence!

He was desperate to find a flaw, any imperfection that might dilute her desirability! *Be objective, John!* Perhaps she was too tall? *No, just the right height to reach my lips.* She said boyish. *Hardly.* Her skin too ruddy? *Not as much as my own.* Too outspoken? No, these were all part of her distinctiveness, and her charm.

Frantic to find something, he managed to focus on a small mole peeking out at the edge of her bodice, only to discover how much he wanted to place his lips there! His eyes returned to hers and found them misted over.

Sally Ann poked him with her elbow. "Well, at least say hello, John. Did the cat get your tongue?"

"John, where have you been? What happened to you?" Ada asked.

John started to speak, but the words would not come, and he stood open mouthed, like a fish out of water, gasping for air. Ada's lips turned down at the corners, as a thin trickle leaked from her eye.

He watched as Ada swung away from him, about to walk away. Sally Ann punched him between his shoulder blades.

"This is probably your last chance, Romeo, don't be an idiot!"

John moved as if in some puppet master's thrall. His hand reached for Ada, caught her arm at the elbow and drew her in. One arm wrapped around her waist, the other cradled her shoulders. Their eyes met in a silent plea as his lips tasted hers.

It didn't matter where they were, neither did they care about a room full of prying judgmental eyes. What happened before carried no weight, only this moment in time, and the comfort and pleasure they found in each other's arms.

John heard Sally Ann's voice as if from a great distance, but his lips were greedy, and his passion was not to be distracted.

Angry hands grasped John by the shoulder and whirled him around.

"Wait, Reverend..." Sally Ann started.

"What do you think you are doing?" Reverend Hartman hissed, and shoved John's shoulder. "Well, I'll tell you! You are making a laughing stock of me, not to mention ruining my daughter's reputation!"

"I didn't...I wouldn't..."

"John was just asking me for the next dance, Father. Won't you please excuse us?" She turned her back on her father and pulled John away. They stepped into the center of the barn. Tendrils of music floated down to them, teasing their ears and warming their hearts.

* * * *

After a pair of dances, another amorous couple attracted the attention of the self-righteous, and the couple used the distraction to slip outside for a moment of privacy.

"Well? Where have you been, John? I gave up on you. I thought the worst of you, and now you show up here?" Ada asked.

"I'm sorry, Ada, and I've been ripped apart about it too. Didn't Sally Ann tell you I was coming? She said you would be expecting me."

"Perhaps she said something to Kate. They've become the best of friends, but she did not mention it to me."

"I wanted to be here, but I fought against it, until I couldn't anymore."

"Do you find my company so repugnant, John?"

"No, dear God no, Ada. I couldn't disappoint you, or myself, again. I tried to reject how I felt, but the denial wouldn't stick. I am so sorry, I…"

Ada held one finger to his lips to quiet him, then replaced her finger with a kiss.

John tasted her hungrily, then pulled away.

"The two of us together, Ada? It is the exact opposite of what we want, or wanted, from our lives. What are we doing?"

"Do you have designs on replacing my father, John? Because that role is filled, and I'm a grown woman. I'll make my own decisions, good or bad, thank you very much."

John smiled and shook his head. "What is it then that you've decided?" He brushed the hair from her eyes.

"To give you one more chance, and we'll figure it out from there, one day at a time."

"One day at a time, those are words to live by."

"We better get back inside. My father and the town busy bodies will be watching for us." Ada pulled him toward the barn door.

* * * *

"You did well, Sally Ann," the dark man said, crawling into her bed, and cuddling up to her, spooning.

"Did I earn my reward? Will you show me the way, be my guide again?"

He didn't answer, but she felt him shift in the bed. His hands roamed over her body, barely touching, but raising goose bumps, and sending sparks sizzling along her nerves. Unwanted desire flared up with every touch.

He flipped Sally Ann over to face him, and she gasped at the sight of him! His eyes were black as coal, his skin red and leathery! Sally Ann blinked, and then Laris looked like himself again. A slick talking, well-groomed and refined ladies' man, a Jack-a-dandy.

He leaned over to her, and his sharp teeth nipped at her ear lobe. "Yes, you did well, Sally Ann, but soon I will need more from you."

"Ah, yes that's nice…more? More of this?"

"We will become closer."

"Ah…Laris…"

"Is that what you want?"

"Yes, please Laris…"

He leaned in closer and whispered in her ear, her eyes widening as his soothing voice revealed his plans. Laris sat up in the bed.

"You understand what you are to do, what we will do together?"

"Yes."

"Will you be my sweet girl?"

Her breath came in gasps as he continued his attentions.

"I…will be…whatever…you need…me…to be."

"There, there, my girl." He patted her thigh, and then brought his forehead down to touch hers. "Now let's find your cat."

* * * *

At least one day of each week John and Ada were together. She visited John on the mountain most often due to her father's low opinion of her suitor. She told Kate she wanted no altercation between the two men spilling over into their home.

Despite the Reverend's protests against the relationship, Ada did not bow to his demands, but she did make one concession. She took Kate along on these social calls out of respect for him.

On this day, Kate rather wished the Reverend would get past his resentment of the man and allow John and Ada to court in the open like other young couples.

Kate's young son, Billy, spent the night before in the throes of teething agony, despite the hours Kate spent massaging his gums with diluted corn alcohol. As it is with all parents, Billy's pain was her pain.

Kate had promised Ada this visit, as a week had passed since their last one. She craved a midday nap to recover, but the thought of disappointing her friend kept her silent. Then her sweet William offered to keep the toddler with him for the day. He said that working up a new deed for Silas Emory could be accomplished at home as easily as at his office. As for Billy, his pain seemed forgotten, as only the very young can, and he did his toddler's dance at the suggestion of a day spent with his father.

Kate's mind wandered as their wagon ascended the mountain. She suspected Ada's silence was due to her thoughts mirroring her own—hoping her efforts to help Ada and John weren't foolhardy and futile.

Her concerns were not unfounded. She'd noticed John's efforts to win over Ada's father. He'd made church attendance a weekly Sunday event, and interacted with the townspeople at every opportunity.

At Sunday service, a gruff faced Thomas Henry pulled John aside to inquire about a goat illness plaguing his herd. Wayne Burrows and his wife asked him to lunch after services to discuss next year's planting.

"I'm sorry, Wayne, but I have a lunch date today," John answered. He stared past the eclectic assortment of farm wagons and fancy carriages to where Ada waited by her father's side.

"Of course, the young lady is welcome also," Mrs. Burrows added with a knowing smile.

Yes, the town had warmed up to John, but despite his efforts, Kate noticed no discernible difference in Earnest Hartman's attitude. *Perhaps with time.*

Kate tried to keep her concerns about John from Ada, but they both knew there was something unsaid between them. As they crested the trail leading to John's cabin, Ada opened up about it.

"Kate, you are my best friend, so may I ask you a question?"

"Of course, Ada..."

"I've never had a friend like you before. I've never been in one place long enough, but I know something is wrong. You've been acting strangely around John, and have for some time now. I've seen how you watch him from the corner of your eye, just like you watch Little Billy when he gets too close to a fresh baked pie. What's wrong?"

"Ada, you are my best friend as well, but Sally Ann's my friend too, and...it's nothing, old news. I don't want to betray either of you."

"Please, Kate, what could possibly be so bad? I think John and I are getting serious, and I don't want questions shadowing my feelings."

"Have you asked John?"

"John doesn't have an issue with you. I'm asking you."

Kate shrugged her shoulders in defeat. "Very well...do you remember that first awful night...when we found you at John's cabin?"

Ada nodded.

"Sally Ann was there that night also."

"Really? I didn't see her, where was she?"

"She was behind a rock, Ada. She was sprawled out naked in John's yard!"

Ada's mouth flew open, and she covered it with her hand. "Kate, what...?"

"I don't think anything happened between them, and Sally Ann swore it didn't. She placed all the blame on herself, and said she threw herself at John, but he wanted no parts of her. I think I believe her, Ada, but keeping this secret from you has haunted me."

"If that's all true, and with all you've told me of Sally Ann's life—the poor girl, denied love her entire life, bullied by her peers—I'd seek out any form of human interaction I could too. I hope John let her down easy," Ada said.

"I know, and that's very...understanding of you. Not sure I could be as Christian."

Ada nodded, and nibbled at her bottom lip. "You really believe what she said, Kate? That nothing happened?"

"I do, but just in case, I'd keep my eyes open around them if I was you, Ada."

"Oh I definitely will, Kate. I trust John, but I've seen how easily men can be lured away. Sally Ann is so beautiful, and I imagine quite a temptation."

* * * *

John finished his morning chores as the sound of approaching hoof beats reached him. The chickens were fed and watered, eggs gathered, and his goats, Moll and Nema, were cared for and milked. The weeding could wait for another day!

He wiped the sweat from his brow on his shirt sleeve, and hurried back to the cabin, arriving just as Ada and Kate pulled their carriage to a stop.

"John, it is so good to see you." Kate smiled, as he helped her down.

"Thank you, Kate, and the same to you." Did Kate seem friendlier than usual, her smile more sincere?

John then took Ada's hand as she stepped to the ground. Their eyes met, and sparks still crackled between them. Would he ever get his fill of this woman? He took Ada's hand in his and turned toward the cabin.

"Please let's go inside, ladies, it is cooler out of the sun. I've begun nothing for lunch, and I fear a bachelor's cupboard leaves much to be desired."

"I'd fall asleep and drown in a bowl of soup, John. Billy and I had a rough night," Kate said, "but perhaps Ada…"

"I'm fine as well, thank you. I fixed a late breakfast for the men. That's the one meal my father will not miss."

"Is Billy doing all right? Nothing serious, I hope?" John asked.

"Teething is all, and I'm sure he's in much better shape than I am today."

John laughed. "Good then. It's been a long time, and I've missed you both. Fill me in on all the doings in town."

"Ada has some news you might find interesting," Kate said, sitting in the seat John pulled out for her.

"Indeed?"

"Well, last night Kate and William informed us that the congregation wants my father to stay on as permanent pastor. Hopefully, because they've grown enough to need someone full time, and not because of any arm twisting by our hosts."

"That's wonderful news for Reverend Hartman…but what does that mean for you, Ada? Will you stay on also?"

"For now…I'm young, and there's plenty of time to see the world if I choose. I've never had a home, or needed one, but family is important, and my father is all the family I have…and well, there's you John…"

John nodded, his smile appearing forced. An awkward silence echoed from the cabin walls, a soundless reverberation.

Kate lifted her chin high. "Well, I hoped for a bigger reaction than that, John Dyer. Are you tongue tied?"

"No, I..." The sound of approaching hoof beats halted further conversation. John stepped over to the lone cabin window and glanced out. Kate walked up behind him and peered over his shoulder. Her eyebrows raised, and her nostrils flared as she turned back toward Ada.

"It's Sally Ann."

* * * *

"Do as I say, and you will get your revenge," the dark man had said. Sally Ann planned to do just that. Nothing and no one would stay her hand. Only revenge could assuage the pain of the many indignities, and her countless spiritual wounds. Men were the scourge of creation! Only the dark man understood, and only he could fulfill her desires.

Tied to the hitching rail outside the cabin was the Jordans' carriage—just as Laris said it would be. She saw the faces peeking out at her. John's eyebrows flew up, and his jaw dropped. For some reason Kate looked pissed, what was her problem? She did nothing to Kate, nor to her namby-pamby friend, Ada...not yet anyway! Laris wouldn't allow it.

Sally Ann stepped onto the porch, smiling at the thought of wiping the grins off their insipid gigglemugs, and knocked on the door. *They actually made me knock? Did they think I couldn't see them staring out at me?*

Just as she was about to knock a second time, the door creaked open, and John poked his head out.

"Sally Ann, well this is a surprise. What brings you here?"

"I came to see you and my friends, John, and just in time too, I'd say. It looks like there's a party."

"No, just catching up with Ada and Kate."

"Are you going to ask me in, John, or are you going to leave me out here baking in the heat?"

"Yes, yes, come in Sally Ann." John swung open the door.

"Good afternoon, ladies." Sally Ann gave both women a quick hug. "Did you hurt your back, Kate? You are so stiff."

Kate shook her head and dropped her eyes to her hands folded on the table. "I'm fine, Sally Ann."

Silence again filled the cabin as John crossed the room to the table, and pulled out a chair for Sally Ann.

"We were just savoring Ada's good news. The good Reverend is staying on in town as our permanent pastor."

"That's wonderful news, Ada! It is good news, don't you think, John?" Sally Ann asked.

"Indeed, it is."

"Then we need some wine to celebrate! John, do you still keep it in the cupboard there?" Sally Ann pointed to the hand hewn wooden cabinet.

John shook his head, and she stood to retrieve the wine. John grabbed three mugs, and with his back turned toward his company, rubbed the dust off them with his shirt tail.

* * * *

Ada felt the tension build in the room as soon as Sally Ann crossed the threshold. Kate made no attempt to hide her displeasure, but Ada welcomed the redhead's arrival. What better way to measure John's reaction to her?

The wine was a nice touch, and before their third cup, but after the cork was pulled on the second bottle, tongues loosened and inhibitions dropped.

"Ada is too much of a lady to ask, John, so I will," Kate began. "What are your intentions with her? You didn't seem particularly enamored with the notion of her staying."

"Kate, I..." John turned his attention from Kate to Ada. "I don't think this is the right time or place to..." Ada dropped her eyes to the table and sniffed.

"It's all right, John. You don't have to..." Ada began.

"I think I love you, Ada, but I bring only pain to those I love, and those I've loved always deserted me. I'm not a brave man, but I would prefer a broken heart to causing you pain."

"I feel the same, John," she answered and touched his cheek. "Perhaps we can be scared together, or brave together? Until we figure out what this is that we feel?"

Sally Ann cleared her throat. "Kate, do you want to take a walk? The wild flowers are in bloom in John's pasture."

The two women stood, and Ada caught Kate's eye just as she winked at her. "You two behave while we are gone now."

"Of course," John answered, but as soon as the door shut behind them, he reached for Ada, picked her up and carried her to his back room.

"John, I don't…"

"It's all right, I only want to be close to you." His lips tasted hers as they curled up on the bed together.

"What are we doing, John?"

"For now, I only want to hold you," he said, and kissed her again. "For now, that will be enough."

John pulled her into his embrace and breathed in the fragrance of lilacs.

Ada lifted her head, and then rested it in the hollow of his shoulder. She reached over and touched his cheek.

"I love your dimple, John. My mother had one too. Her family said it meant you were kissed by an angel."

"You are the only angel that's ever been in my life, Ada."

Ada curled back into his chest and sighed.

"Is this what it feels like? Being in love, I mean?" she asked, and yawned.

The soft contented rumble from deep in John's chest served as his answer.

It must be the wine, she thought and dozed off in his arms.

* * * *

Kate hoped the time alone helped the couple define their relationship. It wasn't fair for Reverend Hartman to place so many restrictions upon them. Kate could see how much in love they were, even if they had yet to realize it themselves!

She found herself reevaluating Sally Ann yet again. First she felt sorry for her, given her rough upbringing, then tentatively accepted her as a friend until convinced she wasn't a modern day Jezebel trying to steal John from Ada. Now? Sally Ann making excuses so the young couple could spend alone time together? That was not the act of a competitor for John's affection.

Sally Ann took her hand and pulled her out of her reverie.

"The meadow is beautiful this time of year. I used to ride up here sometimes before John bought the place. Mr. Bowles always welcomed me. To tell the truth, I think the old man took a liking to me. Did you notice the flowers on your ride in?"

Kate shook her head no and followed her to the edge of the clearing. Sally Ann was right. A huge bouquet of wildflowers spread out before them. Bluebells, daisies, black-eyed susans, woodland sunflowers, Indian paintbrush, and bloodroot displayed their vibrant beauty.

Kate entered the field and picked some of the showiest blooms.

"These are for our kitchen table at home. I'll have to see if John owns a vase that I can borrow to put them in. Little Billy loves black-eyed susans!"

"I think I'll do the same, although my father won't notice. He is partial to dandelions, you can ferment those you know…" Sally Ann dipped her head.

"I'm sorry, Sally Ann. It hasn't been an easy life for you, has it?" Kate draped her arm over the younger woman's shoulders.

"It's getting better." Sally Ann sniffed. "It's amazing the new lease on life that a new friend or two will give to a person. Justice comes for everyone, and my reward is coming too."

"I'm sure it will." Kate squeezed the other woman's shoulders.

Sally Ann wiped her eyes, smiled a brave smile, and nodded back toward the cabin. "I think it may be too early to disturb them? Maybe we should sit out on the bench by the fire pit for a while? Chat some more?"

Kate smiled. "I think that's a wonderful idea!"

Sally Ann's shoulder bag made a tinkling sound as it jostled against her. She reached inside and pulled out a loosely corked bottle.

"I snuck some of John's wine to help us wile away the time."

The two women relaxed on John's bench and drank straight from the bottle until their giggles gave way to yawns.

"Oh my," Kate hiccupped, "what would William say? I'm getting very tipsy."

"A little wine won't hurt you, Kate. You look like you need a nap more than the wine though. Rest if you'd like, and I'll wake you up in plenty of time."

"Yes, I'm so tired. Little Billy, so whiny all night. Rest my eyes a bit…let them have…time. Then go home."

Kate's eyes closed, and the heavy breathing sounds of deep sleep began. Sally Ann sat cross-legged on the ground, closed her own eyes, and whispered, "It's time, Laris, come…"

* * * *

Even in her sleep, Ada recognized John's earthy aroma. Freshly scythed hay, pine, and rose water? She never noticed the rose scent before. *What a strange fragrance on a man.*

John reached for her, and drew her in, chasing the thought away. Her lips hungered for his, and his own lips answered their silent plea.

"John…"

"God help me, I love you so much, woman!" His lips followed the curve of her neck, kissing, nibbling…

"John, we shouldn't…"

He pulled his mouth away from her and brushed her hair away from her eyes. "It's all right, sweet Ada. I will never ask for more than you would give."

Overcome by the tenderness in his eyes…*his dark eyes, were they so dark before?*…she pulled him back to her. She felt the strength of his arms as he wrapped them around her, and sensed his desire, his need for her.

"John, I've never…"

She felt the cool air flow over her chest, and John's lips followed his eyes. There was a sharp sting, and then they rode the ocean waves of desire together, each wave surging them forward—higher…and higher.

Ada felt the blood rush to her face and chest, and tears swam down her face. O*h God, I never knew it would be like this!* She felt him nibble at her ear, his warm breath on her neck.

"Oh, John…" A flood washed over her, and she trembled uncontrollably.

"Oh, John…Ow, John!" she said as his needle-sharp teeth pierced her ear. Her eyes flew open to see green eyes and flaming red hair hanging over her. *Sally Ann! Oh dear God, how could it be Sally Ann!*

Did you like it? It was good for me! Sally Ann ran her tongue over her lips. A trickle of blood from her teeth fell on Ada's bare breast, and she licked it off with a grin.

The image of Sally Ann morphed into another dream image and an olive skinned, dark-haired man gyrated his hips above her, probing her! His eyes were as black as night, ogling her.

"Say hello to Laris," Sally Ann's voice purred.

"Get off me!"

* * * *

John woke from a tortured yet stimulating dream with Sally Ann's name on his lips.

Dear God, what was in the wine?

He shook his head violently, trying to chase the cobwebs from his mind. He ran his hand over the wetness on his chest, and it came away red...blood? Ada squirmed about in the bed beside him. Were her dreams as perverted as his own?

He stood, and his pants fell to his knees. They were unbuttoned and loose, as was his shirt!

"What...?"

Ada's attire was also in disarray, and he tucked and pulled at her clothes to preserve her modesty. The same reddish liquid covered the top of her chest. She stirred, tossed her head from side to side as sweat beaded up on her brow. Should he wake her?

Surely what he experienced was a nightmare...they didn't really...they couldn't have...he would remember, and not as a dream! That much he knew! Sally Ann did something, drugged the wine probably...but in a drugged and drunken stupor did they...do it? Ada tossed about on the bed, moaning.

"Ada," he whispered. "It's all right..." He touched her cheek with the back of his hand.

"Get off me!" Ada screamed, struck John in the center of his chest, and then bolted upright in the bed.

"John? It's you. What happened, did we...? Where's Sally Ann?"

"I don't know, but I'm certainly going to find out!"

John flung open the cabin door, and immediately spotted Kate and Sally Ann asleep by his fire pit. He closed the distance to them in a dead run.

"Sally Ann! What did you do?"

Ada ran behind him, adjusting her dress. Kate and Sally Ann stirred when John shouted for the second time.

"What? What are you talking about, John?" Kate asked.

"She knows! Don't you, Sally Ann?"

"No, I have no idea what you are talking about."

"The wine...what did you put in the wine?"

Sally Ann held out her hands palms up and shrugged her shoulders.

"Calm down, John," Kate said. "I think we all had a little too much of that wine of yours. It's potent stuff!"

Ada stepped around John and reached out for Kate's hand. "We should go home now, Kate. It's getting late and the men will be worried."

Kate stood, swaying on her feet, and grabbed Ada's hand.

"Whoa, oh my, like I said—potent stuff!"

* * * *

After a hurried exchange of goodbyes, Ada and Kate unhitched their carriage and headed for home.

"You are unusually quiet, Ada. What happened between you and John? John seemed so angry!"

"John was fine!" Ada replied.

"All right, my friend, we don't need to talk about it then. Let's talk about something else."

But no other subject came to mind, and the two rode on without speaking. Kate, tired and irritated with her friend, hurried her horse down the narrow dirt trail. Halfway home, Ada broke the silence.

"I'm sorry, Kate. I didn't mean to snap, not at you of all people. I just don't know what happened! I fell asleep and dreamt this horrid nightmare. I'm not sure, but I think we might have...you know, been together..."

"Been together, of course you were, we..." Kate noticed Ada's tight-lipped expression, and her hands folded in her lap. "Oh...Oh Ada, no...! But what do you mean you might have? How could you not know?"

A sob burst free from Ada's chest. "I know...I know, but I'm just not sure. I might be wicked, but I wanted him so much. I love John, but I just don't know what happened!"

Kate pulled the horse to a stop and wrapped her arms around her friend.

"It will be all right, Ada. No more crying. If you keep on, you will wash that beautiful blue right out of your eyes."

Ada smiled. "You're a good friend, Kate. What did I ever do to deserve you?"

"You're just lucky I guess!"

The women laughed, and Kate pulled away and turned Ada's head.

"What happened to your ear? God that must hurt! I saw the same marks on John's ear. Is this something you young people are doing nowadays? Marking your territory or something?" Kate laughed.

"No, not at all." Ada's face fell, and tears again threatened to flow as her eyes welled up.

"Oh no, don't start, Ada, I'm sorry. It's all right. It's just a nibble, barely anything. I doubt the Reverend will even notice."

"Kate? Did you see anyone else there? A dark man?"

Kate shook her head no.

"And Sally Ann? Were you with her the whole time?"

* * * *

Sally Ann sat twirling her red curls with a finger, as Kate and Ada boarded their carriage and began the trek down the mountain. As the wagon wheels kicked up dust, John's inquisition began.

"Tell me what you did, Sally Ann. What was in the wine? How did you get into our dreams?"

"Do you know how crazy you sound? Get into your dreams? I didn't think I was your type, but I'm glad you think of me, even if only in your dreams. What kind of dream was it? What were we doing, John?" she fired back.

John put his hands on her shoulders and gave her a shake. "I've never felt any desire to hit a woman, but you are surely testing my resolve."

"What is wrong with you, John? Your eyes look like my father's do after a Saturday night's drinking binge."

"I know you did something, Sally Ann! I don't know what, and I don't know how, but I know that you did!"

Sally Ann's mouth formed a pout, and her eyes clouded over. She lifted her hand, paused, and then touched John's arm.

"I'd never do anything to hurt you, John. You are my friend, and one of the few! I told you I'd be whatever you wanted me to be, but I know Ada has your heart!" The dam of her tears burst, and she openly wept. John looked confused, and Sally Ann saw the anger melt from his face.

"How could you even think such a thing of me, John? What have I ever done to you, other than be your friend? Is this still because I couldn't control my spirit cat? Was that my fault too? You knew I wasn't ready!"

Sally Ann twisted on the fire pit bench, and presented John with her back, her head in her hands as sobs racked her body.

John lifted his hands, dropped them, and lifted them again. He opened his mouth to speak, and finding no words sat beside Sally Ann, shook his head, and scratched his chin whiskers.

"I'm sorry, Sally Ann. I shouldn't have...I didn't mean...I know you are my friend. Forgive me?"

Sally Ann did not answer, but lifted her head, and encircled John's shoulders in a hug. She didn't move until she felt the chest of his shirt soaked by her tears, then pulled away and stood up.

"I better go now, John. Thank you for a lovely time," she said, choking on her own sarcasm. She turned toward the hitching rail. Halfway across John's yard, her tears were dried and a smile crept to the corners of her mouth.

As John waved goodbye, she dabbed at her eyes. Men are such simple creatures, she thought, and she never met one able to resist a woman's tears.

* * * *

John stalked back to his cabin, confused by the day's events. What happened in his bed? Did he and Ada consummate their relationship, as he feared? Feared because he knew Ada's upbringing, and her moral objections to wanton women.

He prayed his craving for Ada hadn't led to a callous disregard of her feelings. His guilt gave way to shame for the man he used to be, the sentiment even stronger since meeting Ada. He knew the only way to redeem himself was living the life of an honorable man. He'd not follow his father's path!

Ada's virtue had to be safe. It couldn't have happened. He recalled every detail of each brief, precious moment spent with her, and knew he'd not forget loving her! He thought back on his dream and smiled, recalling the fleeting moments of fulfillment in her arms, the moments before his dream turned ugly, dark, and nightmarish.

His love's sweet embrace changed, became violent in intensity, just as her face also changed. Changed to Sally Ann's face! How could that be? But this was a different Sally Ann, a slightly older, and if possible, an even more sensual version of her!

A necklace swung like a pendulum between her breasts, hypnotizing his dream self, and his eyes fixated on the emerald at its center. Sally Ann's necklace—no, Sally Ann's was framed in a heart—this one was set in a golden owl. Its emerald blazed with an unearthly light.

He tried to pull away, but his muscles did not respond. A dark, derisive laugh filled the space around them, a man's laugh! How could Sally Ann be the source of that? No one ever accused her of being, or sounding, masculine!

Ladonna! He remembered the name he heard over and over as the man snickered, and the woman ground into him. If only a dream, why did he still feel where her cold slimy tongue assaulted his mouth, and smell her fetid breath? It was the putrid stench of rotted meat and death.

John's father knew and practiced the darkest aspects of a tainted shamanism, and tried to teach him all there was to know about shape shifting, but did he?

Was there a way to invade another person's dreams? He thought not! His father proved the tribe would cast out such a man for trying! Likewise, white society isolated and ostracized anyone practicing the black arts. Still, John had never heard of any shaman or sorcerer with such an ability! A darker being then?

John's head hung low as he walked back to his cabin. He grabbed the bottle from the table and sniffed at the dregs of wine within. The smell of rancid peanuts and cabbage assailed his nostrils, an odor he knew well—jimsonweed, the devil's trumpet—a plant he never showed Sally Ann!

How would she know its effects? Few white men understood its hallucinogenic, and often deadly power!

Drugged wine explained his dream state, and their sudden drowsiness, but there was more to it than that! The nightmare was too real to be fantasy! He touched his ear, feeling the punctures left behind by the mocking woman's teeth! No, not a woman—John suspected he knew the dream creature for what it was.

He dug through the chest holding his meager wardrobe, and retrieved the old leather-bound and dog-eared book, handwritten by his ancestors. He prayed one of them confronted the darkness he now faced and survived to write about it!

John flipped through the brittle pages searching and stopped when he came to the writings of Moll Dyer, his ancestor. He read the entry in her precise hand, the words faded from time, and the pages crinkling under his trembling fingers.

"Oh Sally Ann, what did you let in?" he moaned. He knew the demon who stalked their town!

Part IV
Hell's Fury

"I summon you, Laris, on the strength of your task completed. Fulfill your promise, lead me to my revenge."

"Ah, sweet Sally Ann." The dark man's voice oozed over her and sent shivers up her spine. She kept her eyes closed, in a trance as Laris taught her. She felt his black cat nuzzling her neck.

"Come then," he purred. Sally Ann found her cat waiting, and leapt inside its skull.

The two large cats ran on padded feet through the streets, unseen by any, save one little boy. Sally Ann felt the young human's eyes upon her and heard Laris growl as he hastened his pace. The house they sought was in sight.

Lewis Boyle was the first on Sally Ann's list, the spineless momma's boy. Her first beau, her first lover, and the first man—besides her father—to break her heart.

She remembered her time with him well.

* * * *

"There's something I have to tell you, Sally Ann, and I'm sorry, this is so hard for me. I'm not good at this sort of thing," Lewis said, after making love to her on that long-gone day.

"What is it, my love? Tell me?"

"The truth is…well…I can't see you anymore. It has to be over between us."

"Lewis, what do you mean? You said you loved me, and even spoke of marriage! What's changed? Did I do something wrong?"

"My mother says you've been with other boys, Sally Ann, and you're the daughter of a drunkard. She says I have a future in this town, but I won't with you at my side. I'm sorry, but I know this is the best thing."

"Best? Who is it best for? You were my first, and I've never been with anyone else, Lewis!"

"Best for both of us, Sally Ann. You'll see in time. Can't you see how hard this is for me?"

Sally Ann soon did see, and the town did too. Lewis bragged about his conquest, and other boys followed suit, lying about her virtue, or lack thereof. Mrs. Boyle's deceitful tongue flapped even faster, and combined with her own father's reputation, her lot became that of the town outcast, nothing more than a whore.

Younger women giggled whenever she walked by, and the older women spoke to each other with their hands hiding their mouths when she met them on the street. Many crossed to the other side of the road to avoid her, as if she carried some disease, a leprous slut who'd infect them with her soul's perceived corruption!

The men were no better, but at least they were honest in their disdain, groping her whenever they could corner her at a party or social event. Propositioning her, enticing her with what they could ill afford, though never promising love, nor even affection.

* * * *

Sally Ann smiled, revealing her cat's fangs, as she thought about the big man Lewis became—failing at everything he tried! Fired from the mercantile, he tried his hand doing manual labor for the grocer, then worked at feeding the chickens and cleaning out the coops at the local hen yard. Seven years later, and Lewis still lived at home, doing odd jobs and shoveling out the stalls in his father's stables. Town gossip said that only Mrs. Boyle's nagging kept his own father from firing him!

Her cat's nostrils flared at the scent of the man she came for. It was true the boy suffered in life, she thought, but not enough…not yet. His suffering would match her own before this night was done.

* * * *

Little Billy's cries reverberated through the house, and Ada jumped from her bed. His cries were not those of a discomfited toddler but screams of real pain or even terror!

She ran down the short hallway barefoot, dressed in only her nightclothes. She grabbed little Billy from his crib and placed him against her chest.

"There, there, little man. What has frightened you so?"

He hugged her hungrily as tears washed over his tiny face and wet the front of her nightgown, but the screams abated, muffled against her breast.

"It is fine now, Billy. I'm just glad I got to you before you woke your poor mother again! You've been an absolute terror these past few nights. Let's have a look at you."

Ada sat in the rocker beside the crib and placed the boy on her knee. She probed his gums with her finger, but Billy showed no reaction, no sign of pain.

"What is it then? Did you just get lonely?"

"Ki-ey cat, ErrRowl…big ki-ey," he said, and Ada smiled.

"A big kitty was it? That's what has you all stirred up? I'd tell you it was nothing but a dream, little friend, but I know too well how real those can be! How about I rock you for a bit, and we both forget about bad dreams for a while?"

"ErrRowl," Billy growled, and drew his tiny hand into a claw.

Ada giggled. "Enough kitty cat noises, now go to sleep, little man." Ada rested his head back against her shoulder and began to rock. Both blond heads fell into a deep and well-earned slumber.

The slamming of the front door woke Ada, and she looked around the room to get her bearings. She yawned as the first rays of the morning sun flickered into Billy's room. *It's early even for William*, she thought.

She felt the pins and needles prickling her arm where Billy's behind had rested for so many hours and switched arms slowly as the rapid clump of hard soles across the pine floors reached her ears.

Ada smiled when she heard the hinges creak on William and Kate's bedroom door downstairs. *Did your loving husband miss you so early in the day, Kate?* William's voice then, quiet so he'd not wake the house.

Kate's response was less reserved. "Oh merciful God, William, you're kidding me! No, of course you're not, not about such a thing!"

She heard her father's door open and close beneath her feet.

"What's all the ruckus about?" he asked, but Ada couldn't make out William's answer.

She stood, with Billy in her arms, amazed the lad slept through all the noise, and rushed to the top of the stairs.

"Kate?" she called down. "What's the matter?"

"Lewis Boyle is dead, killed by some vicious wild animal!"

"Well, we don't know for sure what it was..." William began.

"I'll get dressed and be straight down!"

The excited hum of voices filled the house, but after the initial shock, their volume decreased, and Ada heard little of the conversations. She hurriedly threw on a work dress, buttoning it with one hand while getting Billy dressed for the day with the other.

Ada descended the stairs with the toddler in her arms, and Kate looked up at her from the sitting room couch.

"Dear Lord, I'm so sorry, Ada, with all the excitement, I forgot all about getting him up. Never heard a whimper out of you, Billy. I see that Aunt Ada took good care of you though." She reached out her hands, and Billy climbed into her arms.

Billy smiled at his mother and drew one hand into a claw. "ErrRowl," he said swiping at her.

Kate looked at Ada with her mouth agape. "Ada, does Billy somehow know what happened last night?"

"Well, I didn't tell him anything, Kate. Billy had a bad night at first and woke up screaming. He did that with his hands, along with the cat noise. He said something about a big kitty. You don't think he saw the thing, do you?"

"God, I hope not, he won't sleep for a week. His crib is right by the window facing the street though."

* * * *

John immersed himself in the story penned by his great-great-grandmother, Moll Dyer. Any knowledge he gained could only be an asset, but the fact of her death at the hands of the demons did not bode well!

His well-loved Great-Pa Zachary finished the tale when his mother could not, and described in gory detail the cost of fighting demons, and Moll's ultimate demise!

He touched the stone dagger at his side, only now realizing its significance! The blade, Great-Pa's most treasured possession, was a gift he passed on to John just before his father spirited him away. Knapped by the Conoy from the rock where Moll died. A rock said to be imbued with the power of her spirit.

John reflected on what he'd read. Moll had the support of her closest friends in preparation for her battle, but in the end, she faced the evil alone. Her only reward for her selfless act was society's scorn, and a tortured death. John planned a different fate for himself.

The more he read, the greater his concern grew—for Ada, Sally Ann, the town, and even himself. He chewed on a piece of venison jerky, and fresh picked blackberries, and began reading Moll's story again from the beginning.

Somehow he must warn the town, but who would believe him? Could he turn Sally Ann from her path? Did she even know what it was she was dealing with? Most of all, he must protect his true love.

Tomorrow morning he'd ride into town, and safeguard Ada—her father be damned!

* * * *

Billy's crib no longer faced the street, and its position on the interior wall prevented a window view. There was enough talk of the killing in town, and Kate took no chances on the possibility of Billy spotting another late-night mountain lion visit. For so it was, according to the men in town who knew about such things. A large mountain lion had crept into their small town in the dark of the night, murdered and partially consumed the carcass of one of their citizens.

Kate prayed that Lewis Boyle had indeed departed this world before his evisceration and the consumption of his entrails! To imagine otherwise…it was too disturbing to consider!

The men were puzzled that such an animal would enter the town—and even more surprising a home—but concluded the age of the cat must have driven it to desperate measures.

Two weeks passed since the killing, and still the town posted armed guards to walk the streets. Women feared to leave their homes, even to cross the road to the grocer's. Kate felt content to spend her day entertaining, and being entertained, by her son.

The only good, if it could be thought of as such, to come of the tragedy was that one of the families with a home adjacent to Lewis Boyle's place headed back east. The wilds of western Virginia proved too much for them.

The church purchased the house, and the Reverend and Ada Hartman intended to move in as soon as the Reverend returned from a last-minute emergency at a parish he was in much demand at. This too was a mixed blessing.

Kate knew her friend needed her own space, but unlike most extended guests, her welcome was not worn. Kate knew she and Billy would both miss the daily interaction with their new friend.

As if on cue, Ada called from the hallway. "Kate?"

"In the sitting room with Billy."

"Kate, how are you feeling this morning? I wonder if the chicken I bought from Mr. Rossi had turned. Are you feeling any ill effects?"

"Not at all, and thank you for preparing it, not to mention the adventure of going to the store!"

"I doubt we have anything to worry about in the daylight, but that's why I'm wondering. With so few shoppers, perhaps the bird sat there a while?"

"Are you all right, Ada? I know you're worried about John…"

"I'm sure he heard about what happened, and is smart enough to stay away, don't you think?"

Kate shook her head. "You are probably right, but I only know the reception my William would get if he stayed away while I was in harm's way! It wouldn't be pretty, Ada!"

"Oh, Kate, you are such…umpf…urgh…" Ada's cheeks puffed out like Billy when he held his breath, and she held her hand over her mouth as she ran from the room. Kate heard the rattle of the chamber pot in the back room, and then the sounds of gastronomical distress. A few heaves later, the back door opened, and the outside privy door slammed open and closed.

Kate folded her hands and prayed it was only the chicken that was tainted.

* * * *

"When can I go out again?" Sally Ann asked. "I can't even taste Lewis's blood in my mouth anymore, and my spirit animal is hungry for more!"

"Soon enough," the dark one purred. "Your friend John will be here shortly, and I suspect I've had dealings with his family before. He may know what we are. This town is on alert too, but things will get back to normal soon. Then we will strike again."

"But it's not soon enough! Last night wasn't soon enough! The night before that wasn't soon enough!"

"Watch your tone with me, woman child! You forget your place! Do not make the mistake of thinking we are equals! You've enlisted me in your fight for revenge, and you've shed blood at my side. I own your soul!"

"I'm sorry, Laris. I didn't mean to anger you, but I've never felt such power, and so much control! I'm hungry for more."

"I'll feed your hunger," Laris said, and threw her to the floor.

"No, Laris, please don't hurt me again."

"You'd tell me no?" he cackled.

Sally Ann wept, curled up in a ball when he next touched her. A caress on her shoulder belied the strength and dormant violence of his hands, and shivers ran up and down her spine.

"Oh, Laris…"

"Perhaps there is a way to hurry things along, my delectable young friend. Ladonna is helping us even now."

* * * *

The early morning light beamed through the window and burned through the thin skin of John's eyelids. He rubbed his eyes and shook his head, feeling the crick in his neck from sleeping at the table.

What day was this? Incantations and pages of notes taken from his ancestor's book covered the table in front of him, as well as most of the bearing surfaces in the cabin. The truth was, he'd lost all concept of time!

Was Ada safe? What must she be thinking of him? Was that why she'd not come again to visit with Kate, or did he offend her? Perhaps she remembered more of their last encounter than he did, and more than she'd let on? No, there was nothing false about Ada! If she told a lie, she'd likely break out in a rash from head to toe!

Dear God, what if she was in trouble? But wouldn't Kate get word to him? Maybe Kate was involved too? Or did his absence anger her? He needed to see her. Make sure she was well before he moved forward against the demon!

Approaching hoofbeats broke his concentration, and he hurried to the lone window, anxious to see the rider, to learn if his concerns had merit, and praying they did not.

The dry road threw dust up in front of the horseman, and the rider was at the hitching rail before John could make out the stranger's features. An older man, dressed in worn town clothes, dismounted and tied his horse.

"Hello, the cabin," the man yelled.

John stepped to the door and opened it a crack. "What can I do for you, sir?"

"I reckon I'm lost, and I'm hoping to impose on your hospitality for a swallow of water for me and my horse."

"Not much of nobody up here except me, and you can't get anywhere from here, the road dead-ends. Back the direction you came from though, the road forks. You can go right and head to Setter's Run or left to go back the way I reckon you came from."

"I'm much obliged. I heard there was a homestead in these parts that might be for sale. Is this the one, and is that still true?"

"I'm afraid you missed out, stranger. I bought the place some months back."

"Figures, my luck and all," the man said, and rubbed his grey whiskers. "Sure could use that drink of water before I head back down though. Maybe fill my canteen too?"

"Come on in out of the heat." John threw open the door.

The man followed him inside and sat at the table while John poured a tall glass of water from the pitcher.

"Thanks for that, Mister...what did you say they call you, friend?"

* * * *

Reverend Earnest Hartman greeted his daughter, and his former benefactor Kate, at the door of his home.

"Welcome my dear lovely ladies." He bowed with a flourish. "Please come in."

"Father, the house looks wonderful. The fresh paint the congregation put on the walls is just as I imagined it!" Ada said.

"I'm glad you like it, and it's time for us to settle in."

"I tried to delay it, Reverend," Kate said. "Ada is such a blessing to me, I hate the thought of her leaving. And Billy? Goodness knows how he will react. Ada is his new best friend, you know."

"I'm so pleased my daughter formed a friendship with a God-fearing woman such as yourself, Kate. I fear we overstayed our welcome, and can only express again how grateful we are for both your hospitality and your friendship."

"Not at all, Reverend, but I assure you the gratitude extends both ways. Frankly, and with respect, I was hoping your out-of-town business would keep you a bit longer, I so enjoy having her."

"I hated leaving at such a time, but the business was pressing, and time sensitive."

"Did everything work out, Father?" Ada asked.

"I think so, but I'll know for sure in a few days' time." The Reverend reached down to retrieve Ada's two bags. Brushing against his daughter, she recoiled back.

"Ouch," she said, and drew her arms over her breasts.

"Are you all right?" her father asked.

"I'm fine, Father. It's...just a woman's thing."

"Ah, well…" the Reverend responded, snatched up the bags and hastened up the stairs with his daughter's luggage.

"Make yourself at home, Kate. I'll be right back."

He turned at the top of the stairs and glanced back at the two women. Kate stood in the doorway still, staring at his daughter with lifted eyebrows and downturned lips.

Yes, I should know in a few days.

* * * *

"I'm sorry, I didn't catch that?" the man asked.

"John…my name's John Dyer."

The man's gaze roamed over the cabin. He took in the papers scattered everywhere with hastily scribbled notes, and the dozen crosses tacked to the walls. His fingers traced the engraved letters carved into the wood of the table. The letters spelled 'Ladonna.' *What a coincidence.*

"Your name sounds familiar to me, son. You say you've been here a few months? Six months, maybe? You ever been to the town north of here, on the other side of the river? Place called Cumberland, Maryland?"

The man's jacket fell open, and he pulled it closed over the pistol he wore at his side. The man stared at John's shotgun resting against the bedpost.

"I don't believe I caught your name either, mister?" John asked.

"Campbell's my name, Sheriff Campbell of Alleghany County, Maryland. Setter's Run, Virginia, is a might out of my jurisdiction, but I figure on taking you back with me just the same."

John turned his head toward his bed, and before he moved, the sheriff's pistol cleared its holster.

"No need to do nothing stupid, son," Campbell said.

The pistol made a metallic click as its hammer locked back into place.

"Now you just take your eyes off that shotgun, boy. I'd rather not shoot you dead where you stand, but I surely will if I have to."

John turned to face the man and put his hands in the air.

"You don't understand, Sheriff. There's something bad about to happen down in the valley. I need to help…"

"It will have to wait until you get back. Don't reckon the judge will give you too much time for assaulting old Karl, even though he is the judge's cousin. Stealing that slave girl though…"

"Sheriff, Karl is the one who was after that little girl."

"Never mind that, you can take it up with the judge, but you were the one what run off. Dang shame there's no law protecting that young gal, but the law takes a dim view on thieving. Get on the floor, Dyer. Put your hands behind your back now."

John dropped to his knees, as the sound of another horse approached. When it was close, the sheriff yelled, "Got him, Karl. Get in here."

Campbell nodded at the sound of the man's boots thumping up the stairs and across the porch. Karl kicked open the door, grinning a mostly toothless smile.

"Now, ain't it good to see you again, half-breed. Remember me?" The big man kicked John in the center of his back, driving him to the floor.

The sheriff secured half of his manacles on John's left wrist, and John swung up and around, catching the man with his elbow, knocking him back. Karl swung his ham of a fist hitting the younger man in his temple, and John thumped face first into the floor.

* * * *

"Reverend Hartman, I respect your position in this matter, but being so close to it, are you sure this is the right thing to do?"

"I swear I don't know, William. It's indeed a terrible situation, and he's the last man on Earth I'd choose for a son-in-law, but I know Ada cares for him, and in fact is pining away for him," Reverend Hartman said.

"Then it's good we will confront him. Do you think John will do the honorable thing? Kate is convinced he will."

"I fear your lovely wife may be one of many swayed by the likes of John Dyer."

"What are you implying, Reverend?"

"Ah, William, I fear my brain and mouth are ill connected these past few days. I did not mean to imply any misconduct on your wife's part. She's as fine and pious a woman as I've known, save my own departed wife."

"No need to apologize, Earnest. I believe I understand what you are saying. I've known young women to be too trusting when it comes to the treacheries of disreputable men."

"That's my fear, William. I need to know Dyer's intentions with my daughter. He will either agree to leave her in peace, or he will court her properly, and not cause her distress."

"Has Ada expressed her feelings about John to you then?"

Reverend Hartman laughed. "It's good that your wife bore you a son, William, for you know little of fathers and daughters. No, she would not tell me how she feels, but a father sees his children's pain, and knows it as his own. Her appetite is off, and her days are spent at the window, just gazing out as if waiting for something…or someone."

"Are you hoping he courts her then?"

"If he does, what life will it be for her, wed to such an ungodly Lothario?"

"I confess my impression of the man matches yours. It hardly seems just, a man leads a woman on, then continues on with his life as if nothing happened. He is even lauded by our society for his prowess in deceit, but he is as guilty of impropriety as the woman—more so, as he's devoted his life to the practice of debauchery."

"What impropriety are you speaking of, William? Is there something you're trying to tell me?" The Reverend stared at his younger friend, but William focused straight ahead, not meeting his eyes.

"No, Reverend, I just mean if there was such, in these cases…I mean…there is no fair answer for it in this uncharitable world."

"I know what you allude to, William. You needn't act namby-pamby in an effort to spare my feelings. I am a Christian man, but have no doubt if Ada was forced to single parenthood, the man would *not* go unpunished. I am a Christian, but I am also a father, *and* a sinner."

William nodded his head in agreement and pulled back on the reins as the cabin came into view. "Well, we will soon see what the man has to say."

The men's eyes swept over the homestead. John's goats ran free, and a dangling piece of chewed rope hung from one's neck as it nibbled away at the elderberry bushes at the edge of the garden. Its udder appeared full and extended. The chickens were nearby, loose in the garden, picking away at John's fresh produce.

They tied off the horse and approached the cabin.

"Not much of a farmer, is he?" William asked.

Reverend Hartman shook his head and knocked on the partially ajar cabin door.

"John Dyer? Are you home?"

* * * *

"I heard you, Kate, but I don't believe it. John didn't run off on me! Something has happened to him, or he was called away on some emergency…"

"Ada, I love you like a sister, but you need to face the facts, and get on with your life. William and your father hauled all of his animals back here. They were uncared for, and his place is deserted. William said it looked like nobody had been there for a week of Sundays."

"He's exaggerating, Kate. It's been only three weeks since we saw him there."

"You know what he meant. John's gone. He left his home…he left…you. I'm sorry, Ada, but I can't call myself your friend and let you continue with false hopes."

"I have to go out there, Kate. I want to see for myself. Maybe he left a note or something…he wouldn't just leave me without any word…I know he wouldn't."

"It's not safe, Ada. You know that. That wild animal is still on the loose."

"It was safe enough for William and my father, and my father went out of town for days! I'm going, Kate, but I would enjoy your company."

"Have you had your woman's time, Ada?"

"What? No, but…"

"I've seen how you turn up your nose at foods you love, and some of the combinations you do eat would turn a vulture's stomach."

"Yes, I know. I'm scared, Kate, but with God as my witness, I don't know how. I had the darkest of dreams, but it was just a dream…it had to be."

Ada's eyes filled to the brim, and a lone tear spilled over, and she slapped it away. Kate saw the mixture of pain and determination in her friend's face.

"If I don't go with you, will you go anyway? By yourself?"

"Yes, I'm going."

"We will have to be sneaky, so the men don't find out. I hate keeping secrets from William, but he would stop us, and I will tell him…but not until after."

Ada jumped up and wrapped her arms around Kate's waist. "Oh, I love you. I love you! Thank you, Kate."

"There is one condition." Kate wiggled free from the embrace.

"Yes?"

"Promise me that no matter what, if there's no sign of him, no note or any indication of where he's gone, or of any plans to return, promise you will get that man out of your head! I'll have your hand on it!"

Ada grabbed her outstretched hand and squeezed her friend in another hug.

"We will find something, Kate. You'll see!"

* * * *

"I think it's time, Sally Ann, are you ready?" the dark one asked.

"Yes, Laris! The foolish guards have grown bored with their duty, as if they could stop us anyway!"

"We needn't draw attention to ourselves…not until we both get what we want from this hayseed town."

"What is it that you want, Laris?"

"Why, to make you happy, of course, my sweet princess. That's all you need know for now."

"I love when you call me that. My father did, before I started becoming a woman. He loved me back then."

Sally dropped her head into her hands and sobbed. "Nobody loves me now."

"Oh, but *I* do, princess, I do indeed! When we are done in this town, we will play together for an eternity. You'll never be forgotten. Let me show you, then we will find your cat!"

As always, Laris' ministrations were half pleasure and half pain. Torture blended with passion, her satisfaction limited only by her tolerance for pain.

When he allowed her relief, her spirit cat waited for her. Its tail switched with impatience, but with Laris at her side, she easily morphed into her feline form.

Frankie Johnson was next on her list, and she wondered if the blood of a rich man held any special bouquet? She hoped to spend more time with Mr. High and Mighty than she had with Lewis. Laris had cut her enjoyment short, fearing the nosy brat might sound the alarm. What was the little imp doing up in the middle of the night anyway? What kind of parents were Kate and William? At least they moved the crib. Billy wouldn't be able to see them now!

Swiftly yet silently they moved through the night. Again, Laris accompanied her embedded in his own black cat. Sally Ann felt more confident with him at her side, and it got crowded in her puma's head when they shared it.

The mansion belonging to Frankie Johnson (he preferred Frank now) stood at the highest point of the town. Sally Ann called it Frankie's Folly, knowing what the upkeep must be on such a palatial building, and for a confirmed bachelor no less. She suspected Frankie's parents footed most of his expenses. He never minded throwing their money around.

* * * *

Frankie spent a lot of money on her—at first. She came home with new brooches, rings, and necklaces, so much so that her father suspected her of prostitution! Sally Ann thought he was less concerned with her virtue than he was in getting his 'cut' of her action. His liquid lover was demanding, after all.

In fact, it was at her father's insistence that she began a relationship with Frankie. The Johnson family were coopers and distillers, so her father's approval was guaranteed.

"He is from a good family, and will inherit a ton of money when old man Johnson finally meets his maker. Frankie will be able to look after you when I'm gone, Sally Ann."

Sally Ann heard the stories about the man though, gossip that proclaimed he impregnated two different women. One, Dorothea Claire, disappeared overnight. Her parents said she moved back east to spend the year with her elderly grandparents until they were safely through the winter.

The other girl's parents, domestics in the Johnson's employ, were less affluent, but Harriet Trotter likewise disappeared from everyday life. Frankie was never seen spending time with Harriet, but they did share the same household, allowing lots of opportunities, according to the local chattering chinwags.

Sally Ann did not call either woman friend, but empathized with their plight, and that of their children, if indeed the stories were true. She knew too well the sting of flapping tongues attached to idle judgmental minds.

Between the gossip mongers, and her belief that she was beneath the attentions of this high-born man, she avoided Frankie altogether. Her freckled face, kinky hair, and voluptuous body stuffed into natty clothes—like Mr. Franklin's link sausages—were no match for the svelte socialites Frankie courted.

Despite, or perhaps because of, Sally Ann's coolness towards him, Frankie 'discovered' her like a child might with a toy and seemed determined to win her heart. He milled around in the street outside their home, finding excuses to speak with her, and stealing glances at her in church. At the time, she found his dogged pursuit endearing. With hindsight, she knew he wanted her because she unintentionally made herself into an unattainable conquest.

The gifts began then, some left at her doorstep, others delivered by the shop they were purchased from, and even one left at the grocer's for her, wrapped and tied with a bow.

At an early spring barn dance, they were officially introduced—by her father—and Frankie hung on her every word. His attentions doubled over the following weeks.

"I'm not ready," she told him. "My last break-up is too fresh, just give me more time."

"I'd like to put a thrashing on that Lewis. He has no idea about how to treat a woman," Frankie replied, winning her over with his willingness to stand up for her, to be her protector.

Most evenings, he beat a path to her door with presents, and promises of undying love. Sally found herself looking forward to his visits, and wondered if it was love she felt for him, or if she was in love with how desirable he made her feel?

On his birthday, she knew his parents were visiting relatives in Keyser, while Frankie stayed home to mind the business. She wrapped his gift, a draft horse carved by Jeremy Redmond, and smiled at the thought of the parallels as she dressed in her newest outfit. She slipped past her father dozing on the couch, and out of her house.

Frankie's parents' home was just uphill from her own, and moving in the shadows, and watching for prying eyes, she soon found herself at his door. She knocked to find the door already ajar, and spoke his name, entering when there was no response.

The implication of the sounds emanating from the top of the stairs left little doubt, but still it drew Sally Ann on, step by labored step…she must know for sure!

The sounds stopped just before she reached his open bedroom door, and she poked her head around the door jamb. The skinny, bone white, and very nude Lily Ferguson reclined on Frankie's bed filing her fingernails.

Sally Ann's mouth flew open, and a sound she didn't recognize screeched out. She stepped backwards as a side door opened and Frankie hurried into the room.

"Sally Ann, wait!" But already her feet were propelling her down the stairs, taking over from her stunned mind. At the front door Frankie caught up and snatched her arm back.

* * * *

The clanks and creaks of the farm wagon caused John to stir, but the veil of unconsciousness still held him. He tried to answer the questions swarming his brain—where was he, how did he come to be here, who was driving the wagon, and why?

His hand went to his head, felt the dried blood, and the realities of his situation slowly returned. He sat up, and saw he was manacled at the wrists with a long chain passing through an eye bolt on the cart's wall. His legs were tied with a stout rope around a wagon board.

"Sheriff Campbell, is it? Wonder if you'd return the favor? Sure could use a drink of water."

"Well, now, we thought you might be out all day, sleepyhead," the Sheriff said.

"He's just a lazy half-breed is all," Karl said.

"Oh hell, Karl, I once saw a man sleep for days after you slugged him. I reckon we can stop here for a piece. That ford we just went across put us back in my jurisdiction, so welcome back to Alleghany County, John Dyer. You are now officially under arrest."

"Sheriff. I told you, it was Karl attacking that gal…"

"You are a damn lying, lily-livered half-breed, and you struck me when I wasn't looking!" Karl said.

"I never did, you big ox…"

"Yeah, yeah, and you never done nothin' to that girl either, right, Dyer? Save it for the judge. Now do you want this here swaller of water, or not?"

John reached for the tin cup and drank greedily. His swollen throat had trouble swallowing.

"Easy there, boy. Don't want you puking up all over my wagon." The sheriff snatched back the cup.

"I have animals that need to be taken care of, Sheriff. Think we could swing by Setter's Run?"

"We turned your critters loose, Dyer. Goats and chickens—they do just fine foraging for themselves. They'll be fine. I reckon you'll be back before winter sets in hard."

"Even still, people will miss me, be worried…"

"I doubt it. I figure we saved your bacon, Dyer. No sooner did we get past the fork in the trail from your place, then two fellers come barreling up the other side. They looked fired up too. I figure they had a bone to pick with you!"

John squinted and rubbed his chin. "What did they look like? Did you know them?"

"Well now, they were both dressed up right smart. Used to be city folk, unless I miss my guess. One of them was all of 30 years old, I reckon…what do you think, Karl?"

"Yup, thirty sounds about right."

"Dark haired feller, appeared to be on his way to a bald head like Karl's there. Now the other fellow, he was older, sixty maybe, and he sure enough did look familiar."

"How so?"

"He looks just like the man what showed up at my office with the clue on how to find you. Reverend somebody or other…"

"Reverend Hartman?" John asked.

"Yes sir, I believe you're right on that one. Not sure where he got the note though. He said it was pushed up underneath the front door of his house."

"Note?"

Sheriff Campbell reached into his vest pocket, and pulled out a slip of stained crumpled paper, and unfolded it. John held out his hand for it, but the Sheriff snatched it away.

"This here's evidence." Campbell pulled out a pair of spectacles. "It says, 'It has come to my attention that one of our neighbors, John Dyer, may be a criminal on the run from the law in your county. He has been courting me, and now I fear for my safety. If this is not the case, please send your assurances back with Reverend Hartman.'"

"That's it? That's all it says?"

"Well, she was smart enough to draw up a tiny map with your homestead on it."

"Nothing else?" John yanked at his chains.

"Calm down now, boy, or so help me God, I'll have Karl slug you again. No, nothing else, just the poor woman's signature—Sincerely, Ladonna Nephi...Nephilim, I reckon it is. I bet she's a purty Italian gal, huh?"

* * * *

Ada slipped around the back of the Jordans' home and made her way to the stables. William was already at work, and the Reverend slept in after a late night composing his sermon for the Sunday service. She saw the soft glowing of a lantern inside, and knew Kate waited for her, just as she'd promised.

The women hitched the horse to the carriage, and led it outside, only climbing on when they were out of earshot of the street.

"We have to be fast and quiet about this, Ada. In and out, and no dawdling around at John's place. Are we agreed?"

"Yes, I pray we find something...anything that will tell us what happened to him," Ada said.

"I pray that big cat is gone too. The town sentries are cancelled, so the thing could be watching and waiting for us right now."

"I know, waiting...hungry...ready to pounce." Ada clawed at Kate's shoulder. "Rowl!"

"Damn it, Ada! Now you've gone and made me curse! That wasn't funny!" She bit her lip, but still her laugh bubbled over. "I hope we didn't wake the whole town."

"We will be fine; besides, George Farris killed a mountain lion out by Lonely Gap. He thinks it's the one that killed that man."

"I hope you're right, Ada, but William said the cat that Farris killed was a young one, no more than a yearling."

"Still, it's been weeks now, and weeks since John..."

"I know you are worried, and you probably think me unfeeling, but I'd like nothing better than to find John...assuming he has a very good explanation for his absence! Otherwise, I'm gonna have a very serious conversation with that young man."

"I hope you get to have that conversation, Kate. I can only see two possible answers—either John is hurt and needs me, or John never wanted me and left before things got too serious."

Kate raised her eyebrows and touched Ada's stomach. "*Before* they got serious?"

The comment knocked the wind out of their conversation, and they rode on in silence until they pulled into John's yard.

"Please, please, please open the door, and wave to us, John! Tell us everything is fine," Ada said, but the door remained closed. They knocked on it anyway and went inside when there was no answer.

"John? Are you here?" Kate yelled.

Ada walked over to the table, while Kate gathered up the loose sheets of paper.

"What's with all the crosses on the walls?" Kate asked.

"I guess my father finally got through to him. Come and look at this," Ada said. She pointed to the letters carved in the table. "What do you think it means?"

"Ladonna? Strange name, but maybe an old girlfriend? Wife even? Maybe that's where he went, Ada?" She put her arm over her friend's shoulders, but Ada brushed her off.

"No, I don't believe that. Something's happened to him. He wouldn't go, not without telling me."

"Ada, you have to…"

"Please don't, Kate. Finish gathering these papers for me? Maybe there's a clue in there. I'm taking this book," she said picking up the leather-bound volume. "It looks like it was important to him."

Kate turned back to the task at hand, trying to ignore the bizarre scribbled notes John had written.

"If we hurry, we can be back before William comes home for his lunch."

* * * *

Sally Ann's cat slipped inside an open window, and Laris' black cat followed. On the way to the stairs, she passed the locked front door, and thought back to the fateful night, years ago, when Frankie caught her on her flight from his bedroom, just there, but on the threshold of a different house. After he grabbed her, she swung an open-handed roundhouse blow, and hit him hard on the left cheek.

"Stop it, Sally Ann! What did you expect? You've been playing hard to get, and Lily is my betrothed!"

Sally Ann's mouth dropped open. "You're engaged to marry? And all the while you've been courting me!"

"Is that what you thought?" he asked with a smirk, and Sally Ann pulled her arm away.

"Please, let me explain! Lily doesn't care for the physical aspects of marriage, but we make a perfect couple otherwise. It's just a financial merging of two great families, but a man still has needs. That's where you fit in. You know I love you, and I will keep you in style as my paramour, my treasured mistress…you'll see, but my wife? Surely you can see that's ridiculous?"

"I'd never sell myself so short, you arrogant ass. I'm a good woman, no matter what you've heard! I think I'll march up those stairs and tell Lily everything, if she hasn't already guessed!"

"Guessed? Sally Ann, it was Lily…she suggested this arrangement! She's a very progressive…"

Sally Ann's closed fist punched him squarely in the nose.

"Oh my God, you've broken it!" he whined, covering his face to stem the flow of blood. Her next swing knocked him to the floor.

Many years had passed, but the fire for revenge Frankie ignited that night still burned, hotter than ever. The two cats leapt up the stairs, taking several at a time until they reached the top. Sally Ann's cat paused at the bedroom door, savoring the moment.

Frankie didn't just destroy her reputation as Lewis had, even though he did his best to do so. No, Frankie destroyed her self-esteem. After Frankie, she became what they'd made her out to be all along.

At the foot of the bed, she scented Lily, and stood on her hind legs to get a better view. The couple emitted the sonorous breathing of deep sleep, Frankie's sounding like a gasping snort.

Sally Ann drew closer until her whiskers tickled the woman's neck. Lily stirred, and her eyes flew open in shock. Sally Ann sank her teeth deep into the soft throat and ripped at the muscles covering her windpipe, severing the carotid artery. The pulsing spray of hot sticky blood covered Frankie's face and he woke screaming.

"Oh my God, no!" he shouted, and jumped from the bed. He ran toward the door, but another cat, as black as perdition, blocked his escape. Laris herded the man back to the bed where Lily flailed in an uncontrolled death spasm, and the last weak streams of blood spurted from her neck.

Sally Ann's cat smiled, dropped down beside the bed, and returned to her human form. She stood before him, in the outfit she was born with, splattered in blood.

"Isn't this what you always wanted, Frankie? Me, all to yourself? Well here I am—no strings attached!"

"Sally Ann! What in the name of God…?"

"God again? Say your piece to Him, then. Pretty sure He doesn't know you though."

The black cat's talons hooked into Frankie's shoulder, and pushed him back down on the bed. As Frankie tried to pull away, the claws sank deeper.

"Aarrgh! Sally Ann, please…!"

"Tell me you love me, Frankie."

"Yes, yes, I do love you, Sally Ann. I've always loved you! Oh God, have mercy!"

"Oh Frankie, it's too late for mercy, but I'm willing to settle for a little revenge instead." She smiled and ran her tongue slowly over her bloodstained lips. "Ready or not, here I come!"

"No, please, we can work something out! I have money, I'll pay…"

"Wrong answer!"

Neighbors, four houses down, woke to the sound of his screams.

* * * *

John tried to get comfortable in the windowless cell in Cumberland. After spending a week there, he still hadn't grown accustomed to the accommodations.

The hard, wooden cot provided by his jailers gouged him with splinters in his backside but was nothing compared to the confinement of the soulless cage. There was no light, no way to tell night from day, and no opportunity to breathe free air.

The sheriff dropped food off to him before noon, or so he guessed the time to be. More food arrived as the shadows grew longer on the walls, and just before the flicker of a lantern at the end of the dark hall was blown out. Then came the sound of a key twisting in a lock. After that, the jail was still for the night, except for the whisper and scratch of small rodents creeping out of the walls.

John had asked for a pencil and paper that he might send a letter to Ada but was refused.

"You scoundrel!" the sheriff said. "That poor girl, Ladonna something or other, is waiting for you, and here you are in jail, and still trying to bait this here Ada woman. I'll not be a party to it!"

John picked up a crumb of bread missed during his previous meal and flicked it toward a particularly fearless rat in the corner of the cell. The rat grabbed it and ate it while standing on his hind legs like a squirrel with a nut. Then it scurried into a hole in the corner of the cell and disappeared.

Wish I was a rat. As a skin walker, he could 'climb aboard' the rat, project his consciousness, if he tried really hard, but interaction with such a primitive mammal always had its price, usually a pounding headache lasting several days! But if he made the jump, he'd still be stuck inside a cramped jail cell on Main Street in Cumberland when he came back to himself!

He could effect change when shifting. Any wound he suffered, while with his spirit animal, carried over when his consciousness returned to his body. Perhaps as a rat, he could unlock the jail cell door?

Better to be a shapeshifter, he thought, but even in his current predicament, there was no desire to call forth the powerful and malevolent entities required! He was *not* his father! Besides, the law would hunt him down again, and he wanted this phase of his life over. John had found a home, even if he couldn't go there, and a love, even if he couldn't see her.

Dejected, he waited for the sound of the key turning in the lock to signal the new day, perhaps some good would come from it. The sheriff assured him the county magistrate would be in town today to settle his case.

Assault was not much of a crime in the backwoods, and when the judge took one look at the massive Karl Bauer, cousin or not, he was likely to release John on the spot! Worse case would be another week or two in this hellhole of a cage!

Soon, he could go home again! He reclined on his bunk, hoping to dream again of the life they would carve out for themselves.

* * * *

Reverend Hartman stepped down the stairs reciting his sermon for the day's services from memory.

"What are you mumbling about, Father?" Ada asked.

"It's my sermon. You know I don't like to convey my thoughts—nor the Lord's—from a slip of paper. If I have it committed to memory, it seems more from the spirit, don't you think?"

Ada rubbed her eyes and pulled them away from the worn leather-bound book on the kitchen table.

"Still reading that profane diary, child? Did you sleep at all? It's time for you to forget about that irresponsible sot and move on."

"I already know how you feel about him, Father," Ada said, and absently touched her belly.

"I fear you've laid out a rough road ahead for yourself, Ada." Her father's face fell, turning the lines in his face into deep gouges, as if from a woodcarver's tool.

"Do you want me to have a listen, then? To your sermon?"

He nodded. "Yes, I'd love that, Ada. The men patrolling the streets kept me up half the night yelling back and forth to one another, so my mind isn't very sharp this morning."

"I heard them too, but I guess that means they were awake and on the job. I'm surprised they are still so active. When was the Johnson man killed? A month past?"

"Over six weeks I think, and I'm not complaining about our protectors. I suppose we must give up some sleep in the pursuit of safety."

"Father…what if the killer wasn't an animal?" Ada asked.

"What would make you ask such a thing, Ada? There were huge muddy cat tracks leading into the house. Claw and bite marks were on the man's…corpse. Certain body parts were ripped off, and…eaten."

"I know you think to spare my delicate sensibilities, Father, but the man's condition was spread far and wide by the women in town, with all the gory details. I believe the consensus was even if he'd lived, he'd never father another child."

"Ada!" Reverend Hartman said, and shook his head. "No, I suppose that's true, and perhaps it helps everyone to understand the seriousness of the—"

"But what if a person did it?" Ada asked, and continued before he could answer. "I heard a woman was spotted leaving the house."

"Idle gossip, and the poor misguided drunkard O'Shea was the only such witness. Some foolishness about a black devil cat and a naked woman was the gist of it. No such animal has ever been seen in this part of the world. Doubtless he was in his cups at the time. Lord knows what he saw, if anything, and it doesn't change any of the facts, regardless. A big cat did the killing."

"But is it possible? Do you think someone could train a mountain lion to kill a man?"

* * * *

Sean O'Shea stumbled up the crumbling stone steps in front of his small house on Main Street. He absently noticed the rotted door trim, and the flower beds once so painstakingly cared for by his sluttish wife. That flower bed was her only joy in life apparently, well that and throwing away his hard-earned money. The rampant growth of grasses and weeds allowed no blooms to flourish there now, and Sean found great pleasure in that knowledge.

His life began its descent into his mortal hell soon after he'd met her, and the bottle that replaced her prevented him from crawling out of his quagmire! Sean knew this, but every attempt to improve his station shortly brought him back to his knees, and soon after, to another bottle.

His job at the distillery didn't pay what he needed to assure Sally Ann's future, so he'd taken a second job at the farriers. Things looked better for a bit, until Frankie Johnson up and fired him, without providing any reasons, just some fool suggestion that he and his daughter needed to know their place.

Sean grew angry enough to smash his fist into his employer's jaw, and it took three able-bodied men to drag him off him! After that, his reputation as an angry, violent drunkard further diminished his worth among the town's business owners.

He barely eked out enough working with the farrier to keep food on the table, and then that fell through too when the spoiled brat Lewis Boyle was hired at half his pay. Sean and Sally Ann had managed to live off his meager and dwindling savings for the past year.

Oh, Sally Ann!

Surely his eyes deceived him that night. He knew it was the booze distorting his senses! That's why he gave the vaguest description of the woman to the men. In hindsight, he wondered why he'd opened his sauce box at all! Was he seeking validation from the community that had turned its collective back on him? Was he that pathetic—to turn on his daughter—even as inebriated as he was?

Luckily, none of them believed him, at last his reputation stood him in good stead. Sean knew Sally Ann was the only good to come out of his marriage. *Oh, Sally Ann! What did you do?* It didn't matter, she was all he had, and he'd protect her until the end!

Sean heard the scrape of a shoe heel on his front steps and waited. The skeleton key turned in the lock, and then jiggled to release the rusted mechanism.

"Damn lock!" he heard his daughter say, then the lock twisted home and Sally Ann flung open the door.

"Welcome home, Sally Ann. What have you been up to?"

"Father, why are you still up? How are you still up? Did the barkeep close the tavern early?"

"Sally, we need to talk about the other night."

"What are you talking about, Father?"

"I saw you. When you came out on the street in front of that bastard Frankie Johnson's house? You were…you didn't have any clothes on, and the blood…"

"Oh, Father, you and your alcoholic fantasies! Just listen to yourself!" Sally Ann stepped behind his chair and reached down to rub her father's neck. "Think about what you are saying for a moment. You're suggesting that I killed a grown man, and his wife? Little old me?"

"I know you did it, Sally Ann. I just don't know how. I saw you! When I got home, you were on the couch, still undressed. You and the furniture were covered with short black hairs, and blood. If I was a betting man, I'd bet the hairs were from a black cat."

Sally Ann smoothed her father's hair back behind his ears, reached under her bodice and clenched the hilt of the knife hidden there.

"Don't worry, my sweet princess, it doesn't matter. Your secret is safe with me."

"Oh, I know it is, Father," she said smiling, and slid the blade across his throat.

* * * *

The steel bars of his cage were pitted with rust, looking like hardened pieces of honeycomb. John tested their strength again, pulling, twisting, and throwing his weight against them. All to no avail, as was the case so many times before.

He'd picked out shapes in the bars, one looked like the horns of a goat, another collection of rusted pits resembled the outline of a bear, and yet another formed a heart reminding him of Ada. He shook the bars again.

"If ya got all that energy, I reckon we didn't work you hard enough today, John," Sheriff Campbell said.

"No sir, Sheriff. I'll admit digging all those post holes for the new jail foundation tuckered me out. Ground being frozen doesn't help, but I guess I'm just getting stir crazy in here. No disrespect to your fine establishment."

"None taken. It's been a hard winter, but the thaw's coming." The sheriff walked back to John's cell, and wrapped his leathery hands around the bars, and gave them a shake.

"Solid steel, John, brought in all the way from Pennsylvania. A boar bear couldn't break out of my jail."

"I've been here too long to try an escape, Sheriff, no worries there."

"Well, you put in an honest day's work, especially for a man who's serving time. I'll see to it that Miss Laura piles you on an extra helping of taters tonight."

"Thanks, Sheriff…um, Sheriff, have there been any letters for me?"

"No, John. That girl you keep writing to ain't wrote you back. You know I'd tell ya if she did. I'm sorry, son."

"Yes, sir."

"I'm starting to think I got the wrong impression of you at the beginning, even though you didn't help yourself one bit. You were one ornery cuss. I'm thinking that gal has your heart on a string, boy!"

"I thought she was the one, Sheriff. I thought I'd finally found a place to call home, and someone to share it with."

"Sorry for how it all worked out. I never figured the judge would be so harsh on you, not with knowing the kind of man Karl Bauer is. I reckon you leaving him beat up so bad, and the condition of that slave gal, didn't help your case none either."

"For all I know, maybe the judge did me a favor, Sheriff. It seems like I was living a dream, and it took this to wake me up."

"Your six months are nearly done, John. You go home then, see what there is to be seen, and if it doesn't work out, well, just come on back here. We could use a fellow who's not afraid of a little hard work."

"I'm sure this town looks a lot more appealing to a free man, but I think I'll pass for now. Appreciate it, though."

"Don't burn any bridges, John. That's what my daddy used to say."

John nodded his head, and glanced back at the bars in his window, an upgrade from his former cell, and a testament to his improved standing with Sheriff Campbell.

"No sir, but I have some unfinished business there, Sheriff, something I broke, and I'm the only one to fix it—if it's not already too late."

When the sheriff locked up for the night, John squatted on the cold hard floor, and sought out his bear, and home, his only escape, the link to sanity that kept him from embracing the dark recesses of his troubled soul.

Perhaps at long last, he'd catch more than a fleeting lantern lit glimpse of his love through the shuttered windows of her home.

* * * *

The cackling crow of their rooster, Bob, woke the Reverend Hartman just before the first streams of sunlight assaulted his bedroom window. He scraped the crusty sleep from his eyes, wishing for another hour's rest, but the cold plank floor greeted his feet, as he resolved to start his day.

The smell of crisp bacon lured him downstairs, where he found Ada bent over the coal stove, adding more meat to the pan.

"You are industrious, and so early in the morning too," he said.

"I have a lot of errands to run this morning, Father, and I wanted to get off to a quick start, but I couldn't leave you here starving now, could I?" Ada smiled, and adjusted her stance at the stove to accommodate her growing midsection.

The Reverend sat at the small table and loaded his plate. His table manners did not reflect his life's station as he wolfed down the bread and bacon, crumbs of each dropping from the corners of his mouth.

"Are you sure that's a good idea, daughter? Going out, in your condition, for everyone to see?"

"I'm sure the whole town knows by now, Father. I am sorry for the scandal I've brought you. I swear I don't know how…"

"Don't be daft, child. Ada, the ever virgin, is it? Have I raised a bloody papist under my roof?"

"I'm not obtuse, but I don't recall…"

"I understand, Ada." Hartman sighed. "The pervert drugged you, as I've told all who would listen. Woe unto that man if he shows his face in this town again!"

"He's hurt me, Father, but I wish him no ill will, and I still fear for his safety."

"A fine Christian thought, but do not be a fool, Ada. The man is evil incarnate. He used you and left for greener pastures when he got what he wanted."

"I cannot believe that. What manner of man would leave no word? Surely even the basest coward would leave a note, and John is no coward."

The Reverend crumbled the last bit of bacon in his fist and dribbled the greasy crumbs on his plate.

"I've lost my appetite. Enjoy your day," he said.

The legs of the table screeched across the floor as he pushed away and stalked off to his study.

Shortly after Ada closed the front door en route to her shopping, Hartman heard a knock at his door, and peered out of the study window. Kate Jordan stood before his threshold. Her head moved left and right, then back the way she'd come, her lips in a pout. She held a woven twig basket in her arms.

When he opened the door for her, she scurried past him, not waiting to be officially invited in, and scanned the outside before shutting the door behind her.

"Hello, Kate. I'm sorry, but Ada isn't in just now. Doing her shop—"

"I saw her leave, Reverend, and I'm not here to talk to Ada today, but to talk to you *about* her."

"Oh?"

"May we sit?"

"Yes, of course, where are my manners?" He led the way to his study and remained standing until Kate took her seat.

"Now, to what do I owe the honor, Kate?"

"I wanted to talk with you about Ada's situation. First, I must say I'm impressed with the way you've handled it…as a man of the cloth and all."

"Thank you, Kate. I try to convey to my congregation the rules our Lord gave us to live by, but we are all human, all sinners, just as He made us. Don't forget, 'He who hath no sin should cast the first stone…'"

"Noble thought, but many discount their own shortcomings by pointing out another's, and I don't want my friend to suffer as some theological scapegoat."

"I also fear for her, and the child, but what is to be done?"

"I look at Billy, and I wonder how anyone could desert their own blood? It isn't human, Reverend, but I have a recently widowed cousin in Philadelphia. He is a good man and was a good husband. He'd make a good father to your grandson too."

"This cousin of yours, you think he'd take on another man's child?"

"He's a good Christian man, Reverend, and has made a fine life for himself. I haven't spoken to him about Ada, but we have corresponded often about his situation, and his desire to have a mother for his children. I'm confident he would be interested in a fine woman like Ada."

"Ada would never go for it. Not as long as there is any question in her mind about this Dyer man, his whereabouts and intentions. I fear only the sight of his remains or word of his marriage to another will cure her obstinacy."

"She loves him, Reverend. Have you forgotten love's undeniable allure? She gave him her heart, and I would have sworn, he did the same. But I was wrong, and he's long gone, forgotten all about her by now, just another feather in his cap. What else could have kept him away for so long?"

The Reverend dropped his face into his hands, and froze in place, statue-like.

"Reverend? Are you all right?"

"I thought it was the right thing to do. I only thought of her and the baby, but I am a blind, self-righteous fool."

"What have you done, Reverend?"

The Reverend sucked in a huge draught of air and blew it out. He lifted his head and rubbed his eyes.

"Never mind, and forgive me, Kate," he said, clearing his throat. "I'm a foolish old man, but I fear I haven't been a very supportive father. I didn't think ahead. I didn't help her plan for the future in my self-righteousness. Thank God Ada has you for a friend."

* * * *

James Henry Haas III knew both of the men killed in recent weeks. Some might call them his contemporaries, but Jimmy knew better. Yes, they were men of the same age, and played together as youths, but he would have laughed if anyone suggested they were his equals.

Jimmy had bested them in every competition growing up. Lewis Boyle got no more than he deserved in life, and perhaps death as well. As for Frankie Johnson? Well, being born with a silver spoon up his arse is what propelled him to small town greatness. Any buffoon could do as well with the Johnson family's money.

James knew the townspeople recognized their inferiority to him, and that alone kept him from reaching the heights he was capable of!

Managing Frankie's distillery was never enough for a man of Jimmy's abilities. His talents were wasted there. He considered moving away, finding a town where he was unknown, where his excellence would be self-evident, and not clouded by the petty jealousies of this town, but the Johnsons' silver spoon never visited the Haas family's buttocks. Money to begin a new life didn't come easy when everyone was against him.

Haas had skipped the funeral for Lewis Boyle but thought it appropriate to attend Frankie Johnson's. Besides, he hoped to make some contacts there, rubbing elbows with the affluent families, but it didn't work out as planned.

As he stalked away from the gravesite, he heard a scurrying of feet on the gravel behind him, and Sally Ann O'Shea caught his elbow.

"It's been a long time, Jimmy, how have you been?"

"I'm doing well, thank you. Shame about Frankie. I've turned his distillery into a huge success over the years. Now I imagine all my hard work will be for nothing. His father is taking over again, but I'll be fine. Can't keep a good man down, you know?"

"Yes, how terrible that is for you…and how have *you* been, Sally Ann? Oh, fine thank you!" She rolled her eyes.

"What? Hey, weren't you involved with both Frankie and Lewis? Funny, huh?"

"Hilarious, and with *you* too if I recall correctly?"

"I'm quite sure you do. Tell me the truth, after all the men you've been with, wasn't I the best you ever had?"

"Oh, you were special, Jimmy. I haven't forgotten *you*. Now you do take care and do keep an eye out for cats in the night."

A self-satisfied smile lit up his face as he said his goodbyes and walked home.

Haas thought about the funeral throughout the evening. Not so much about the pain he saw on the grieving parents' faces, or about how old friends only gathered for weddings and funerals. He wondered what it would all mean for him.

The skinflint, Old Man Johnson, always had an ax to grind when it came to him. James received no promotions or raises in the five years he'd worked for the ingrate. Frankie, at least, recognized what a failure the distillery would be without him, but Frankie was cat food now. His uppity mortal remains were no more than worm fodder, just like any other corpse.

Sally Ann looked surprisingly good considering she'd needed his advice for everything from what to wear to when to speak. The months they'd spent together were probably the best of her life! Her social standing surely rose after being seen with him. Perhaps that was the reason for her glow? She hoped for a little more Jimmy Haas action? He considered the pros and cons of taking up with her again, just for fun.

The sound of shattering glass came from downstairs! The front parlor windows!

He raced downstairs, nearly tripping on a loose section of board half way down. Entering the unlit parlor, he saw…nothing. Darkness and silence greeted him, and he wished for a lantern as his eyes adjusted to the blackness.

Green shining eyes stared at him from the gloom. He backed away from the unseen danger, but behind him another creature growled.

He saw a movement in the vague outline in front of him, but couldn't get out of the animal's path as it leapt upon him, pinning him to the floor.

He opened his mouth to scream, as the toothsome jaws opened wide…impossibly wide, and snapping, sinking into his face. He felt the fangs penetrate his cheek and scrape against the bone beneath, as the lower teeth slid in under his jaw, clamping his mouth shut. His scream was left unheard.

His eyes bulged in their sockets as he noticed the heart-shaped emerald necklace. The cat loosened its grip to seize another purchase, and he screamed, "Sally Ann!"

Then the suffering began...

Part V
The Way Home

"I reckon you figured this day weren't ever coming, John," Sheriff Campbell asked as he turned the key in John's jail cell for the last time.

"It sure didn't come fast enough, Sheriff, not that I don't appreciate the hospitality of yourself and your fine town."

The sheriff paused, and held the door, as if considering relocking it. "I'm not sure if we have any regulations about being a smart-ass, but I can check with the judge if you want to hang around for a bit?"

Then Campbell smiled, opened the cell door, and held out his hand. It reminded John of a rough piece of sandstone when he grabbed it in his own.

"Are you sure you won't take me up on that offer? We can use a hard worker."

"No sir, I know you were just doing your job, and I hold no ill will to you, but like your good book says, I need to shake the dust of this town off my sandals and get home. If it still is home, that is."

"I suspect it will all turn out for the best—one way or t'other. Is there anything I can do for you, John?"

"I would like my knife back, Sheriff. It has sentimental value to me. It belonged to my great-grandfather."

"Almost forgot that! I wondered about that knife, it's about the purtiest blade I've seen. I kept it nice and safe for you John, squirreled away here in my desk. Injuns done it up for him, didn't they?"

"Yes, sir, and I appreciate it."

"Stay out of trouble, son, and watch that temper of yours! If we meet again, I'm hoping it's under better circumstances."

John waved goodbye and began his trek back home along the same route he'd followed nearly a year ago.

The river continued to flow, and the sky still shone in as brilliant a blue as he remembered in the beautiful mountain country. The last shreds of winter melted away with the warmth of the spring morning, and it was as if all that happened didn't matter. He hoped that was the truth of it. He wanted only to get home, back to the life he'd begun, and back to the woman he loved!

What if Ada found another? There were no letters in response to the many he'd written. Had she forgotten him? Was the love he felt unrequited? Did his past turn her away from him?

There was only one route to the answers, so he quickened his pace, wishing for a horse.

He thought about his Great-Pa and the journey he took as a lad to be with his one true love. He braved the wilderness alone, walking from the small colony in Southern Maryland northwest to the range of mountains that his tribe still called home.

John dropped his head in silent supplication. "I hope you are with me, Grandfather. I seek your council. You said you'd always hear me, wherever I roamed. Am I too late? Does my true love's heart belong to another? If it is so, I wish her happiness, though the knowledge would break my heart!"

He crawled under a small rock outcropping and tried to find a comfortable position as night fell. Tossing, turning, he wished his mind would shut up, and grant him peace.

He lifted his head at the scuffling sound in the leaves near his leg. He remained still, frozen in time, waiting. A small albino field mouse poked its nose out of the leaves, and stood on its hind legs observing him, the strange intruder in its small kingdom. When satisfied that John wasn't a threat, the mouse crawled up and over his booted foot, and disappeared into the leaves as easily as it appeared.

"Thank you for that, Great-Pa, all is well." He fell asleep dreaming of Ada, cats, and his bear.

* * * *

"Foolish human bitch! You got your childish revenge, but there are greater schemes in the offing! Now we must leave before the child is born!"

"I'm sorry, Laris. I didn't see…"

"You allowed him to scream! Scream your name for all to hear! Fool! You had the weakling at your mercy! Why didn't you claw his heart out? Chew out his tongue?"

"Why didn't you finish him, Laris?"

"You question me? I care little for taking human life, foolish girl, I prefer souls. I am the inspiration to others to do what needs to be done." His nostrils flared, and he raised his hand to strike.

"I am not yet as adept with my tools as you are, my dark prince."

Laris smiled at her description of him, but his lips peeled back exposing his teeth. He slapped her across the face, and Sally Ann flipped across her bedroom. She used the edge of her bed to climb back to her feet and rubbed her cheek, as Laris paced back and forth across the room.

"Who was the man who saw you slinking away from the house?"

"He's William Jordan, Kate's husband."

"Did he recognize you?"

"I…I think he did, Laris, but it was so dark, he couldn't be sure."

This was followed by another slap, and Sally Ann remained where she fell, curled up, balling up her lacy bed cover in her hand.

"Then he must die."

"If he recognized me, then he's told others by now, and others may have seen me."

Laris kicked her in the ribs.

"Grab what you need, spend the night at the old abandoned cabin near John Dyer's homestead, where we began. They won't think to look there, not right away at least."

"And you?"

"I will be with you tonight, and until you are safe, and I have your mess cleaned up. After that, you won't see me until it's time to proceed. You must fulfill your end of the contract. Don't look so worried, Sally Ann, I *will* find you."

Laris faded from her sight. She blew out the air held in her lungs and winced at the pain in her ribs. She glanced out of her window at the stars, and tried to remember better days, but no such memories were forthcoming.

She grabbed a few meager items of clothing and went downstairs to the cabinet that held the family Bible. She opened the book and drew out the dwindling stack of bills. Her father said an honest man wouldn't steal it, and a thief would never think to look there.

As she passed the couch where her father's body rested, she pulled a tattered old woolen blanket over him.

I love you, sweet princess. Her father's voice echoed in her mind. A lone tear drifted down her cheek and plopped on the floor as she quietly slipped out of the back door, and into the night.

* * * *

The wind whistled through the trees outside Ada's open window. One lone oak branch tapped and scraped against the plank siding, like her father's fingers on the wooden table top, waiting for her answer.

"I don't know what to do," she said, but the branch, again like her father, continued its impatient assault, not hearing or caring about her inner turmoil.

The stars were few on this moonless night, and her lantern remained unlit, matching the darkness of her spirit.

Ada listened to everything her father said, and knew it was time for a decision to be made, but what to do?

John had deserted her, body and spirit, it had to be so. He left her with a broken heart, and a child to raise on her own. She reached down at the feel of her little one's kick. He was getting stronger! Kate assured her the baby was a boy due to it being carried so low on her belly. The thought gave her a momentary reprieve from her angst, and the faint hint of a smile touched her lips.

Kate visited that morning, and told her about her cousin in Pennsylvania, a Robert Turner, and his interest in her. He'd expressed his desire to wed again and provide his children with a mother! Fire flew to her face, and she nearly threw her friend out of her house! *What right had she? Who did she think she was? What kind of friend was she, to make these plans behind her back? Damn her!*

She calmed down after she had some time to think. Kate was her friend, and was always there for her, never asking anything in return. She was only thinking of her, and her baby, nothing more. Still, she should have asked before she threw Ada's name out as a possible contender for his hand. Perhaps she did not as she anticipated Ada's answer.

At lunch time, she walked over to the Jordans' house and apologized. It was a weepy, yet wonderful visit, a renewal of a tested friendship.

Kate told her all about her cousin, and how excited he was to meet her. She promised there was no pressure, and she invited him to come for a visit anyway, and he accepted. Robert was arriving in Cumberland on the stagecoach the first of the week. A carriage borrowed from a friend would complete his travel there.

He must be a desperate man to consider taking a stranger to wife! She must be too, to even contemplate a relationship with this unknown man, or worse yet, a marriage without love! Her father said this was the type of thing parents do for their children. *But he never did so!*

She sat on the edge of her bed, and dropped her head in her hands, only to find herself pulling her hair.

John, oh John, why did you leave?

* * * *

John moved through the brush, no longer following the river, but cutting through the forest where the river looped back towards itself. He hoped reducing his hike by five miles made the greenbrier cuts and potential poison ivy worthwhile.

He pushed on, determined to reach his homestead before nightfall. He'd been away for too long, but the woods still whispered his name. He was no stranger here, but a child of all creation. The woods made him feel at home, as no other place could.

The leaf buds were beginning to open, and the dismal grays of the woodlands reluctantly exploded with creation's life force, changing to the lush green of the leaves, and the yellows and reds of the earliest blooms of spring.

The temptation to join with his spirit bear was strong, made stronger by the natural surroundings. Still he resisted, pushed on, toward Ada, towards home.

As the daylight faded, and the night birds began their songs, he sat and built his fire. Home was still a half day's walk away, but the rocky terrain here promised a broken arm or worse for a hurried and reckless wanderer. There was no recourse but to wait until dawn.

As he finished his simple meal of dried fruit and venison jerky, he prepared himself to find his bear. If not bodily, at least he could see his home through his spirit animal's eyes.

He sought his place of calm and released the frustrations of the day. His craving for home, and his quest to get there, faded into the background of his mind.

As he moved within the bear's consciousness, he wondered again if his bear was a real animal, or a mere spiritual projection of himself? The bear always appeared where he most desired to be. In this case, his bear lurked just shy of the ancient oak marking the edge of his homestead.

John recognized the dilapidated cabin where he'd saved Ada from Sally Ann's vicious attack. The memory was strong, and John smelled cat in the night air, just as strong as he did those many months ago.

His steps were slow and deliberate, as his nose tried to separate the memory of past scents from the present spoors. He detected two distinct smells, Sally Ann's cat he remembered well, but another cat traveled with her, its scent pervasive, and...dark. Mixed with its feline's essence, it evoked images of graveyards and fire, torture and insanity...malevolence. The demon stalked his woods!

John backtracked, ears perked, and nostrils aquiver. He should shed his bear, and return to himself, not yet prepared to risk a confrontation with the malicious entity.

Finding cover under the thick low hanging branches of a spruce, the bear sat on its haunches. The first tendrils of consciousness pulled away from the animal...when the mountain lion pounced!

John felt the cat's fangs embed in his hindquarters, and he swung his huge paw, slapping the animal away. He leapt out of his hiding place, and stood on his hind legs, then fell forward onto the cat, his jaws catching the cat's skull, but before he could clamp down on his attacker, another set of claws sliced across his flank.

John shook his head, the cat in his jaws moving with him, its hind feet slashing open his chest, as the other bit into his thigh. For a brief moment, he was the rope in a tug of war between the two cats! He released the mountain cat and turned to face the other.

The black cat screamed its defiance and sprang. The giant black bear tumbled backwards at impact, slipping from the edge of a cliff, and bouncing off the rocks to the bottom of the ravine.

John heard the two cats screech in anger, as he gave way to the darkness. *Sally Ann, what have you become? What did I bring you to?*

* * * *

William Jordan held the envelope in his left hand as he knocked on the Reverend's door with the other. He hung his head at the sound of the approaching footsteps inside the house.

"Good morning, Ada…um, is your father at home?" he asked, tucking the envelope under his arm.

"He is, William, and I know he'd love a visit with you. Are you all right? You look concerned? Did you get more of Father's mail?'

"No, ah…yes, but I have a business matter that I'd like his advice on." William tapped the envelope under his arm.

Ada ushered William inside, and he followed her to the door of the Reverend's study.

"Father, William is here to see you," she said, as she tapped on the door.

The door flew open, and a smiling Reverend Hartman greeted them.

"Come in, William, please. Thank you, Ada." The Reverend closed the door behind them.

"Earnest, I have another…"

Reverend Hartman held up one finger, and William watched as he listened at the door for Ada's receding footsteps.

"Please have a seat, William."

"No, not today, but I have another one for you, well for Ada." William shook his head. "I'm feeling very duplicitous about this, Reverend. Are you quite sure it's the right thing to do?"

Hartman reached for the envelope and ripped it open. "How else can I protect my daughter, William? What would you do to guard your son from the wickedness of the world?"

The Reverend quickly scanned the crumpled page.

"The letter details the scoundrel's desire for my daughter, things he'd like to do to her! This note is dated two weeks ago and describes his release from jail the following day. If he was a decent man, with honorable intentions, he would have been here days ago. Look here, William."

William glanced at the page where Hartman's finger pointed out the date, and quickly wandered over the note, most of the writing covered by the Reverend's hand, but the last line and signature was visible. "Ada, please say you'll be my wife! My eternal love and devotion, John."

"Indeed, Earnest, still, should we hide this from Ada? Doesn't she have a right to know his intent? It might even help her get over him."

"Someday when the time is right, William. I know what's best for her, trust me on that." He placed the paper back in its envelope, folded it and placed it in his bottom desk drawer with the others. "Thank our merciful Lord that the filthy heathen only knew to send his illicit missives to your home. You have spared my daughter untold grief, William, and again, I find myself in your debt."

William said his goodbyes to Reverend Hartman and avoided Ada's eyes as she escorted him out.

I must tell Kate.

* * * *

What had she done? Sally Ann tried to recall the events of the night before through the heavy cloud hanging over her, but she remembered enough, too much in fact! She could see John's pain and she knew his anguish.

No! She'd acted in self-defense! Why was John there? Was he following her? Trying to get her to pay for her crimes? The bear was moments away from crushing her skull! He might have killed her! Why didn't he? He certainly had the advantage. Why did he hold back?

He attacked her, but no…didn't she pounce on him first? Laris tickled her with the glimmer of thought, and she followed his lead like a well-trained hound dog.

John befriended her, and she'd repaid his friendship by killing him! He couldn't have survived the mauling, and the plummet over the cliff surely sealed his fate. John was done, his bear smashed at the base of the ravine, just food for the carrion eaters now.

She thought back over the past few months. Her father dead at her hand. He was not a great father, but he didn't deserve such an end, unlike the three ne'er-do-wells she had also sent to meet their maker. They could rot in hell, as she surely would as well.

What was she to do? She could no longer control her cat! Anger burned in her heart, leaving ash in its wake, tainting all that was once good in her. She must stop, and not call on her cat again.

She looked around the old barn where she'd spent the night. Took in the weathered grey boards and smelled the sweet scent of decaying hay. She couldn't stop. Her cat was freedom and power, and when she wore that hide was the only time she'd known either. For now, she planned to lay low, and wait out the encroaching tribulations.

She dressed in the clothes Laris left for her. He always took care of her. He was her friend, her only friend now, with John gone. He often lost his temper with her, but she knew it was only what she deserved. She didn't know why she had so much trouble pleasing him, but she'd try harder. She'd do better.

* * * *

Rolling over, a burst of pain woke him as his hand landed in the coals of his nearly spent campfire. He jerked it away, only to feel the ache in his thigh and buttocks as he pulled back. His ribs felt as burnt as his hand, but he wasn't able to sit up to examine them.

His fingers crept over his body, seeking out the major areas of pain, discovering a chunk of flayed meat sliced from his thigh to his butt. His hand lingered at his ribs, feeling the bone laid bare there.

An ooze seeped from his stomach, but he couldn't bring himself to touch there, knowing too well the end result of a stomach wound in the wilderness. He recalled every strike from Sally Ann's cat, and from the demon cat, all too vividly.

The sun burned into his eyes, and he clamped his eyelids shut. He existed on no other plain except his agony, and so he prayed. Prayed to his father's gods, and his mother's god, to take the pain away, to end the anguish that defined him, but none of the deities heard his plea, or they chose to ignore it.

Then he remembered Ada. Sweet Ada waited for him. He knew it in his heart, for no truer soul ever drew breath in a world defined by deceit!

He tried to sit up, and his hair felt glued to the rock upon which it rested. He touched the drying blood at the back of his skull, remembering the crash down the rocks, and pulled loose his hair. Bright lights flashed as the world swam around him, and the welcome blackness took him again.

* * * *

Robert Turner never did anything impulsive in his entire life. He was a man of reason, not action. He weighed the most insignificant decision by its pros and cons. A man didn't become a bank president in one of the more affluent banks in Philadelphia by being reckless!

Yet, here he was, on the edge of the wilderness en route to meeting with a cousin he'd not seen since childhood, in the hope of finding a prospective wife for himself, and mother for his orphaned children. Kate surely inherited her gift for persuasion from her father!

When the stagecoach driver announced their arrival in Cumberland, he thought the man mad. How could the mud streets and rough-hewn buildings he saw around him be the vaulted gateway to the west? The last bastion of civilization? The children playing in the street were clothed in rags! His cousin described it as the 'big city,' but it reminded him more of the poorest ghettoes in Philly!

He marched down to the general store to ask directions to his friend's home. The sooner he could borrow a carriage and be on his way, the better!

The proprietor of the establishment was engaged in a heated discussion with a woman over the cost of her selected dry goods, and how did the proprietor expect that she might fund her daughter's wedding outfit with such onerous charges.

While he waited, a broadsheet tacked to the wall caught his attention. 'WILD ANIMAL ATTACKS CLAIM LIVES!' the headline proclaimed, and Robert read each word, using his finger under each line to guide his eyes over the poorly inked parchment.

"Excuse me, sir. These attacks?" Robert thumped his index finger against the flyer. "Where did they occur?"

The shopkeeper lifted his eyes from the arguing woman and thrust out his thumb. "Twenty miles that-away, give or take."

Robert strode toward the back of the store, and pulled down a rifle hanging from the wall, twisted it around in his hands, and returned to the shop owner at the front of the store.

"What do I need to make this work?" he asked, placing the rifle on the counter as the bickering woman slammed the door behind her.

"Ever shoot a gun before, mister? I don't mean no harm, but you gots the look of a city-bred feller about ya."

"No offense taken, but I'm confident I can figure it out if you will outfit me with what I need and point me in the direction of Charles Ramsey's place."

Armed with a new .58 caliber flintlock rifle, powder, ball, and directions, Robert left the establishment and navigated the edges of the sloppy streets attempting to keep his polished shoes out of the mire.

Ramsey's farm was situated beyond the town proper, and Robert prayed to reach it before nightfall. A misplaced step landed his right foot in a puddle overflowing his shoe and soaking his sock with a gray colored slime. He pulled a handkerchief from his pocket, wet it with his tongue and dabbed at the splatter on his pants leg, but only succeeded in smearing it further. *Damn!*

He hoped his cousin's celebrated cooking made his journey worthwhile, because no woman merited all of this trouble!

* * * *

"Well, if you don't think he left of his own accord, what in God's creation do you think happened to him, Ada? You say you've searched your heart, perhaps this is a question better decided by your mind? Honestly, I'm close to giving up on you!"

"Kate, if you'd just hear me out."

"Ada, your blind trust is so naive! Surely you can see that? Look at you! My God, you are almost a mother. I think it's time you act like one!"

Ada wiped the seeds of a tear from her eye. A more determined look crossed her face. Tight lipped, and stern of visage, she stared at her friend.

"Enough! Tell me this then, who do you love, Kate?"

"What? What do you mean?"

"It is a simple basic question—who do you love?"

"Very well, if answering your silly question will assuage your heart, or bring you to your senses, I will play along. I love my husband, William, and my son, Billy. I love my parents, and I love you, dear friend. I think I know how you'd answer the question."

"I lost my mother before I had a chance to know her. I've traveled up and down this country, never seeking a home, or family, because other than my father, a loving, if cold man, I didn't know what either represented. A home held little fascination or yearning in me because I didn't know it. I didn't care where I was, because no place gave me what I desired—a sense of belonging and love."

"I know, Ada, and I am so sorry about your mother. I—"

"Please let me finish, Kate. John lost his mother at a young age. His father deserted him in a manner even I don't know, as the pain on his face wasn't worth my pursuit of the knowledge. The only person he's ever loved, and who stuck by him, is his great-grandfather, a man he revers like no other. John told me he loved me, and that he'd never spoken those words before."

"Men speak those words so easily, Ada." Kate shook her head.

"He swore on his great-grandfather's life that he'd always find his way to me, through thick and thin, and no matter what anyone threw at us! He saved my life, Kate! How can I turn my back on him now? I cannot help but believe in him. He is my love."

"Ada, I know the depth of your feelings, and of your stubbornness. I do not plead with you to hurt you."

"You've called me naïve, Kate, and I do not feign experience in love, but I do know what I want! I had a teacher once who said a person needed knowledge of a thing to ask an intelligent question about it. I discovered the answer to a question I never asked. I was too oblivious to ask it, but I won't ignore the answer I've found."

Kate shook her head, searching for the one thing to say that might sway Ada's thinking, but came up empty.

"My cousin will be here soon, Ada. Will you at least give him a chance?"

"Kate! And you call me hard-headed! I have one more question for you before I'll answer that."

"Please, Ada, stop with these questions, I don't…" Kate saw her friend's eyes contract, as her lips formed a tight pout.

"Very well, what is your question?"

"What is your idea of hell?"

"I don't know. I guess it is as your father preaches, hellfire and brimstone, eternal damnation? Why? What do you believe?"

"I believe it is a beautifully appointed room, with a soft bed and linen sheets. It's never too cold, nor too hot. The room has everything you could possibly need—food, drink, books to read…."

"That's your hell?" Kate asked, her eyebrows raised high. Ada licked her upper lip, drew it under her teeth, and glared at Kate.

"All right…sorry. Go on, then."

"The room is locked, and just outside the door, you can hear the voices of everyone you've ever loved. You feel their happiness, you hear their laughter, but you cannot see them, or touch them, and they cannot see or hear or touch you.

"The Creator is also on the other side of that door, the embodiment of perfect love, a love no living human ever knew…but He is also beyond your reach. You can feel His warmth. You can hear the whisper of His loving words but can't quite understand them. You know the love and joy that is on the other side of that door, and you ache for it with every fiber of your being, but knowing you will never, ever have it. Now what do you think of my version of hell?"

"An eternity of loneliness, never to see His face, or bask in His glory? If we turn our face from Him while in this world, He wouldn't force us to do so in the next. Is that it?"

"Yes, forever alone—a desolate soul. It's lonely too when you are the sole person who believes something you know to be true. I need your support as my friend, Kate. I've had a glimpse of true love, and having found it, I'll not callously toss it aside and face a lifetime of regret."

* * * *

When John next woke, the moon replaced the sun in the sky. Despite his tortured uneasy sleep, he had no idea of the amount of time passed, one day, two?

Sweat dripped from his brow, yet he shivered from the chill of the evening. *Not a good sign. Must get out of here.*

He moved slowly, with much deliberation, avoiding pulling against torn muscles. His torso was loosely wrapped with material ripped from his shirt, although he had no recollection of doing so. *At least my guts won't fall out!*

An old logging road passed through the valley below the abandoned homestead. The road was little more than a deer path now, and seldom used. An occasional traveler, referencing outdated maps, followed it on their way to town. If he could only reach it, perhaps…

John tried to sit up, but pain shot up and down his core, and an uncontrollable trembling shook his body. He rolled over slowly, and dug his left elbow into the rocky soil, his right side useless. Inch by labored inch, he began his descent.

His burned hand touched wetness, and thinking his wounds opened, he examined each in turn. His thigh oozed clear fluid, and his chest and stomach wrappings were soaked through, but not yet dripping.

He fought his way down and found the source of the dampness to be a small spring seeping from the mountainside. Unable to lift his arm enough to cup his hand under the tiny flow of water, he lowered his head, and lapped at it with his tongue.

Refreshed and energized by the fresh water, he renewed his downward assault on the mountain. The rocks dug into his elbows, drawing new blood, but still he pulled himself on.

John felt a difference in the terrain under his arms and raised his head enough to look ahead. The moonlight offered little clarity of vision, but the obstacle was clear enough.

A drop of ten feet lay before him, not a cliff, but enough of an incline to disallow a controlled descent. To avoid it would require a twenty-yard detour to a gentler slope. A detour John was unwilling to take.

He shook his head gently and twisted his body to present his side to the slope. He gritted his teeth and gave a final push to the edge.

He rolled, or more precisely, bounced down the incline, feeling every rock as it dug into his skin and bruised him to his bones. With the last bounce, his ribcage landed on top of a rounded stone projection, knocking out his wind. He gasped trying to catch his breath.

I'm coming, Ada!

* * * *

Kate walked home unable to shake the feeling of impending doom and not knowing the reason for her anxiety. The darkness of the night reflected her gloom and doom mood.

The tree branches overhead reached out like skeletal fingers scratching at the darkness, grasping for her, as the sullen breeze whispered her name. She shook her head to dispel her dark thoughts and hurried toward home.

Kate made it a habit to avoid the streets after dusk, in light of the recent killings, but it seemed Ada needed her as a sounding board, if nothing else. She certainly didn't heed her advice!

It bothered her that Ada so casually tossed aside the prospect afforded by her cousin, but it was her decision to make, and Kate made sure Robert entertained no expectations beyond a visit. As Ada's friend, she worried about her future, and that of her unborn child. The world was harsh enough, without raising a child alone.

Kate entered her home with William's name on her lips, wanting to share Ada's conversation with him. Perhaps he could see a means to help their friend, something she'd missed, or an approach to get through to her. William was good with words.

Instead, William confessed his falseness to her. He spoke of the dozen letters addressed to Ada and delivered to their door, in care of his name.

"I've done her wrong, Kate. I see that now, but Earnest was so sure of himself, and he is Ada's father after all! I know his vision was clouded, but I was clear-headed. I'm complicit in his deception. God have mercy on my soul!"

"There's nothing to be done, William, but consider this. If the letter is dated as you say, he'll not be coming back. He would have been here a week ago. So perhaps the Reverend was right? I think it best if we keep this to ourselves a bit longer."

"Keep living this lie? I may burst from the evil I've done to her if I don't come clean. I want to wash my hands of the whole affair."

"Now you are thinking only of yourself, Will. You'd only be easing your own conscience, not helping Ada, though we must do something...if we tell her the truth, all at one fell swoop? She loses her love, her father, and her two closest friends, not that we've earned that title."

* * * *

Robert regretted getting such a late start from his friend's house the day before. His original intent was to spend the night, and get reacquainted with his childhood friend, but it soon became apparent that despite Charles' earlier assurances, he was not welcome there.

He'd never met the man's wife before, and she made it quite plain that she wasn't partial to visitors. Rebecca Ramsey was a shrewish woman with a face like a hawk.

After a hurried supper of stale bread, and heavily salted ham, Charles escorted him to his barn to hitch up his carriage.

"I suppose you'll be wanting to get on your way, Robert. I sure did enjoy your visit."

The carriage was, in actuality, a farm wagon with slats for sides and an oilcloth tarp hastily stretched across the wooden uprights to serve as its roof.

To add insult to injury, Charles, with hat in hand, asked his old friend for a fifty-dollar deposit on the rig! Robert doubted the wagon, and the old nag provided to pull it, were together worth that much! His friend assured him he'd get the money back when he returned, but it would make his wife more comfortable. What with her not knowing Robert and all…

Robert left soon after, and made his way into the wilderness, mere hours before dusk. He camped at the edge of the road, without a fire. His lantern and the rifle across his knees were his only comforts.

Strange noises beset him every time his eyes closed. Hoots and screams from all manner of creatures that haunted the night. He'd sit up, listen, and if the sound drew no closer, he'd again recline to attempt a much-needed rest, only to be assailed by the howls of some other woodland beast!

Between the splinters in his backside from the rough planks of the wagon floor, and the boisterous night creatures, he doubted he slept a full hour.

He stirred from the wagon and stretched as blessed dawn finally broke, or the half-light of early dawn, the sun not yet cresting the mountains. The horse started at a snail's pace, trudging along the rutted path, in no hurry to bend its will to Robert's bidding.

By midday, the chill of the night air was a distant memory, as the sun now scorched his skin. His pale complexion born from years of indoor office work did nothing to thwart its sizzle. A small creek crossed the trail ahead, and he reined the horse toward its waters, pulling the animal to a stop under the shade of an ancient maple. He unhitched her and tied her up with a long rope to a limb.

He splashed cool water on his face and rested in the shade as the horse drank its fill. Lack of sleep took its toll, the weight of his eyelids too heavy to bear, and he slipped away.

* * * *

John's fevered brain transported him to another, simpler, and less painful time. He woke as the child he once was, wrapped in deerskin blankets and bear furs, with the sound of his parents' argument ringing in his ears.

"You promised you'd take me home when we wed, Sebastian. John is of an age where he needs to begin his schooling, and he deserves to know his other people. All that the world can offer is waiting for him."

"But this is my home, Iris. It's our home. The tribe accepted you as one of their own."

"Sebastian, please! They kidnapped me as a child and made me a slave for two years! They gave me the filthiest jobs they could devise. I was a hated outsider! Yes, they accepted me, but only when you married me. Still, this isn't about me. It's about your promise and our son's future."

"Iris, I know no other life. I am their shaman. Do you know how rare an honor that is for a half-breed like myself? We've built a good life here."

John's mother squatted on the dirt floor and dropped her head into her hands.

"Please don't, Iris. You know I love you and my son...if this is what it takes to make you both happy, I will speak with my grandfather tomorrow."

John's dream memories faded in and out, blurring the times and places. Images flashed in his mind of Zachary presenting him with the stone knife, their family's tearful departure, and the journey to the white man's world.

He recalled frozen snippets of time—mental pictures of wooden plank buildings, strange clothes, and a teacher with a paddle! Their pale-skinned children were equally colorless in spirit, spending their days sitting in hard back chairs, and scribbling squiggly lines on flat pieces of slate.

He twisted in his sleep, felt the burning across his thighs and buttocks, remembering the teacher's many lessons in proper behavior! Those meant nothing to John as the only lesson worth learning at the white man's school was the gift of reading. He engulfed books like a rat snake with a mouse.

His eyes opened a slit, the sun blinding him, and he wiggled to find a more comfortable position, then returned to his restless dreams.

What he remembered most of all was the happiness on his mother's face, something he didn't remember seeing there before. That alone made the effort to acclimate in this peculiar new world worthwhile. As his mother's joy grew, his father's demeanor turned darker than the depths of the narrow cave near his people's camp.

John saw the city eating away at his father's soul, enslaving his spirit. He recalled the last night they lived as a family. His father paced the floor of their small home.

"This was a mistake, Iris. This is no way for human beings to live. There are no woods, the trees are gone and the animals with them. The river smells foul, and the people have forgotten what it means to be alive!"

"You've not given it a chance, Sebastian."

"It's been eighteen months of hell!"

"Sebastian, look around this city, open your eyes to what's here! There's a library, restaurants, a theater, and schools for John! It will grow on you!"

"There's scraping your fingers raw trying to earn enough to barely feed your family, and to keep a roof over their heads. There's a life of drudgery and enslavement to procure what is given freely among our people."

"Your people, Sebastian."

"I hate it, Iris!"

After that night, the hole his father punched in the wall remained as a reminder, but his father did not. Oddly enough, many months later, and on the night of the very day it was repaired, his father returned.

John recalled being snatched from his bed in a room lit only by moonlight.

"It's time to go home now, son."

John, still half asleep, was carried from the room. He smiled at first, then frowned. "Wait! Where's mother? She has to come too!"

"I pray that she will follow later," his father answered, but John never saw his mother again.

* * * *

The receding shade woke Robert, as it now only offered relief to his once shiny shoes. He glanced at the sky, and then at his pocket watch, confirming the time to be noon.

His borrowed horse stared at him. *Judging me for my slothfulness.*

"You are right," he admitted to the horse. "We've wasted enough time here. At this rate, we'll be a week getting to Kate's house. Are you ready to go?"

The horse offered no comment, only looked at Robert, and then gazed longingly off to the side of the trail.

"Some tasty treat down there, old girl? Well, you've left little graze here, let's have a look. Can't have you getting all peckish on me."

Robert untied the horse from the tree limb and took two steps off the path.

"Ahh, umpf," he heard from behind a rock, and he retreated to the wagon, returning with his rifle pointing the way forward. He held his hand up to the horse, palm out, "Steady," but she ignored him. Her head dropped back to feed, indifferent to any danger.

Robert stepped forward lightly, difficult with the fresh blisters on his feet, and edged his weapon around the boulder.

"Who are you, and why are you hiding there?" he demanded of the prone figure of a man.

Receiving no answer, he prodded the man's side with the rifle's barrel.

This brought forth a grunt, and the man twitched his leg. Robert walked around him, noting the torn clothes, and gaping open wounds. Blood seeped out in puddles in the clay soil around him.

Robert leaned his weapon against the rock, realizing a man in such condition was no threat to anyone!

"What in the hell happened to you, mister? You get in a wrestling match with a bear?"

The man didn't respond, didn't even blink, his gaze fixed on some distant horizon.

Robert pulled saddle pads from the boxes of supplies Charles provided, and sleeping blankets from his own luggage, and used them to line the floor of the wagon. The man was face down in the dirt when he returned.

"Mister, I'll do the best I can, but this is going to hurt. There's nothing else for it."

Robert squatted, and slid an arm under the man's shoulders, and the other under his knees. A bloody flap of meat from the man's thigh slapped against his hand.

"Ugg…Ugh, ahh…" Robert lost the little breakfast he'd enjoyed that morning. He wiped his mouth on the lapel of his waistcoat, grunted, and then stood with the man in his arms.

"Father, where…you…taking…" the man stuttered.

"Mister, you're hurt really bad, and I'm trying to get you to some help. I'm taking you out of here."

The man tossed his head from side to side.

"No, no…where's mother?"

"Mister, you're hot as the hinges of hell, and not seeing things right just now."

Robert drove the wagon as fast as the rutted road and the man's condition allowed, although he appeared to be unconscious since Robert first plopped him onto the wagon's bed.

A shack sat just off the road about a mile from where Robert found the man, and he managed to convince the elderly couple inside to look after him as best they could. Robert offered a wad of cash to defray any expenses, but they'd not take a penny.

"Mr. O'Connor, please. Take it to pay the doctor then," Robert said.

"There ain't no doctor in these parts, Mister. One comes by Frankfort ever so often, but between us, I doubt this here feller makes it 'til morning. Maw knows near as much about healing as they do anyways. But you done your Christian duty, and we'll do the best we can by him too."

Robert assured the couple he'd be back in a few weeks' time, on his return trip to Philadelphia. He asked them to tally up any expenses, and he'd straighten up with them then.

He expressed his appreciation, and said his goodbyes, then climbed back on the wagon, and flicked the reins. Before Robert's backside properly settled into the oak plank seat, the cabin had disappeared in the dust kicked up by his wagon's wheels.

At the sound of the departing hoof beats, the man inside the shack suddenly sat bolt upright, grimacing in pain.

"I'm coming, Ada," he said and fell back to the bed.

* * * *

William Jordan had ridden hard since daybreak on the small Arabian he'd chosen for the trip. Time and again, the horse proved himself to be sure footed, with a strong back, and a stout heart. Hoping to get to Fort Cumberland and back as quickly as possible meant bypassing the established roads. The chosen route cut through tight ravines and mountain passes, but was the fastest way. The old Arabian was the best horse for the job.

His effort this day didn't amount to much, but it was the best idea he and Kate could come up with. Maybe John lingered in Cumberland for some reason, or maybe he wasn't released as soon as anticipated? Those were the maybes, William thought, but the probably? He figured John Dyer got word of the baby and ran in the opposite direction as fast as his legs would carry him!

William hoped that whether he managed to bring John home, or discovered his betrayal, that his own conscience would at least be soothed!

He had no delusions about his undertaking and recognized his journey for what it was. A feeble attempt to make up for the wrong they'd done to Ada. It was like Pope wrote, 'Hope springs eternal in the human breast.' Truer words were never spoken, William thought. He hoped and prayed his mission bore fruit.

Twilight enveloped the town as William tied old Abraham to the hitching rail in the center of town. A young lad raced down the street rolling his hoop with a polished stick. He stopped the boy long enough to obtain directions to the jail, and crossed the street to the unpainted grey boarded structure.

A new post foundation with completed floor joists and stick framed walls stood adjacent to the jail, and William correctly assumed that this building would house the next generation of inmates.

William knocked, and entered the jailhouse. An elderly, but wiry man with a weather-beaten face stood up from behind the desk.

"What can I do for you, young man? New in town, are ya?" He held out his hand, and when William shook it, he recalled grabbing a marble statue's hand as a child.

"No, sir, just passing through. I rode up today looking for a friend of mine, John Dyer. You wouldn't know what became of him would you?"

"What did you say your name was?"

"My name is William Jordan. I rode here from the next valley over, and—"

"You live that close by, William Jordan, and only now come by for a visit with your friend? After six months?"

"Well, yes sir. It's been a busy time at work..."

"My wife's hands seen more work than those puddin' paws of yours. How busy did you say you were?"

"Not that kind of work, Sheriff. Now see here, are you going to tell me what happened to John or not?"

"It's like this, son, I count John Dyer as a friend of mine, and I ain't got all that many. I know that's hard to believe given my sweet disposition, but then here you come, pretending to be friendly with a friend of mine? I'm not sure I'll buy that dog, and it just don't sit well with me."

William's shoulders sagged, and he looked the sheriff in the eyes.

"Very well, in truth, I don't suppose I'm exactly John's friend, an acquaintance then, but I am a friend of the woman who loves him."

"I reckon it's that Ladonna something or other?" The sheriff squinted his eyes.

"Who? No, Ada Hartman is her name."

"Miss Ada? Is she all right?"

"Yes, Ada's fine, but John?"

"Thank Jesus," Campbell said, and wiped the sweat from his brow. "John talked about that woman so dang much, I swear I went and fell in love with her myself. Don't you tell the misses, hear? Sit down, and take a load off, son. Now, what's the problem?"

"John is. Which way did he go when he left town?"

"He ain't got back yet? He lit outta here like a man afire, but that was weeks ago. I knew dang well I shoulda lent John a horse."

"Do you think he headed toward home? Or run off somewhere? Ada is heavy with child, you know. Did he tell you his plans?"

"Ho! Slow down, son! Miss Ada is in the family way?"

"Yes, but…"

"Well, you are right about one thing, William, you ain't no friend of John Dyer. In fact, you don't know the man at all, not if you figure he'd run off on the woman he loves, and on his own blood too."

"Look, Sheriff, there's another man interested in courting Ada, and she needs to know the truth about John."

"She needs to know? Or you do? Because it don't sound like the sweet, faithful Miss Ada I've heard tell of all these months. Maybe this other feller is someone of your choosing, and not Miss Ada's at all?"

"Guess Ada thinks it's time to move on, Sheriff, one way or the other."

"Uh-huh, could be. Women can be fickle creatures."

"That's a fact, sir!" William laughed and lightly tapped Campbell on the shoulder. The sheriff stared at the younger man's hand.

"You know, there's something else what don't quite sit right with me, William."

"Oh?"

"How come Ada never answered any of John's letters? Did she ever receive 'em you reckon? She never came to visit, but now has you come all the way out here to check on him, her being so fickle and all?"

William pursed his lips, scratched his cheek, and stared over the sheriff's shoulder. "I've been a married man for six years, Sheriff, but I can't understand what goes through their heads sometimes."

"Yup, so how about you run along on home now, William. You can tell Miss Ada I wish her well, but she needn't worry none about John Dyer. Ain't nothing shy of God's own wrath, or Satan's fury, that's gonna keep him away from her."

William stalked out of the jailhouse, and down the street to the boarding house. One thing was for certain, Dyer sure pulled the wool over that sheriff's eyes! He now narrowed it down to two probabilities: John Dyer was the snake in the grass he always thought he was, and ran off with the Ladonna woman the sheriff let slip, or John was killed on his way home by the same cat that terrorized his town!

Either way, Ada was better off not knowing the truth of the past few months. Either way, John Dyer was dead to her, and their betrayal could remain a secret!

* * * *

The pain swallowed him whole and was all he knew. People moved around him, but he could not see their faces, nor hear their words. They were a distraction, noises from far away masquerading as words. It was hard enough focusing on the man's voice!

He felt the hard-unyielding surface, like rock, beneath him and then recognized the voice—it belonged to his father.

"The gods are capricious beings, John, but they're never above coercion and always hungry for sacrifice."

John tried to speak, but his voice deserted him. He tried to sit up, but something unseen held him securely to the rock.

His father turned away from him, chanting strange mumbled incantations to his gods. He stood just above him, yet his face was blurred, as were the figures stretched out on the rock around him. His world appeared as if viewed through lenses of hand blown glass.

His father raised his arms towards the heavens. "Great and fearful Okeus, ruler of the underworld, punisher of those who bring harm unto your people, hear me! I am Sebastian Dyer, elder kwiocosuk of the Conoy! I walked away from my people and my gods, but I've humbly returned to offer you this blood sacrifice, the blood of my people's present, the blood of our future, and the blood of my blood."

John concentrated with his mind's eye, and saw the young woman tied beside him. He saw his stone blade, given to him by his great-grandfather, now in his father's hand! He watched the blade's arc, heard the squishing, gurgling sound as the blade met flesh. Blood pulsed from the woman's neck.

"Blood of my people, cleanse me now." The woman thrashed about on the rock altar, soundless but for the whispering scuff of her moccasins flailing against stone. On the other side of her, the young child wailed, and Sebastian placed his hand over the toddler's mouth.

"Grant me the power of my forbear, Moll Dyer, the master of demons, now bound in the darkness. Blood of our future, imbue me with her strength."

The intense and strangely familiar woman's voice echoed in his mind...*do not invoke my name in supplication to the darkness, grandson. My family has suffered enough!*

John saw the flash of the blade as it began its descent to the child. "No!" He jumped upright from the rock and caught his father's shirt in his hand as a red flower bloomed in the center of his chest.

A different woman's voice yelled, "Here now, turn me loose, young man! It's all right, your fever's broken."

John's eyes jerked open. An old woman, and certainly not his father, stood over him. "You were having a nightmare. Now please turn me loose."

John's released the fist that was knotted up in the woman's shirt. "I...I am sorry, ma'am, who are you? Where am I?"

"I am Henrietta O'Connor, and you're in our cabin. You been hurt bad. Do you recollect?"

John's head swam, but he remembered Sally Ann's attack, and…the demon cat!

The woman swabbed the sweat from his forehead and pulled back the blanket that covered him. John felt the air wash over him and snatched at the blanket.

"Too late for modesty now, young man, I've been washing you down every day for quite a spell now."

He tried to swing his legs over the edge of the bed, but his head wouldn't cooperate, and he fell back against the stuffed mattress.

"Now you behave, you're on the mend but a far cry from being well. You ain't even strong enough to pee on your own."

"How long have I been here?"

"I reckon you're in a hurry to get back to that Ada gal? Or was she just part of your nightmare too?"

"No, not a nightmare, but maybe a dream I've been living…how long was I out?"

"Couple weeks now, I suppose. Henry and I figured we'd be burying you, but here you are. Proved us wrong."

"Henry and Henrietta?"

"Yes, my husband is named Henry, and isn't that the sweetest thing—Henry and Henrietta? I told my ol' maw ages ago, it was like we was meant to be. Like we discovered the half of ourselves we was missing all along. Don't pay me no mind, son. I'm just a crazy old woman flapping her jaws."

"No ma'am, I know exactly what you mean."

"You need some sleep now. Get your strength back." Henrietta pulled the covers back over him, much as his mother did so many years ago, and he smiled.

"Thank you, Henrietta."

She nodded, and moved toward the door, then paused and turned to face him again.

"If you don't mind my asking…that nightmare you keep having? Great-Pa? Did he save that baby boy in your dream?"

"Yes, ma'am. He sent an arrow through the beast's chest and saved us all."

* * * *

Sheriff Isaac Campbell saddled up his own horse, and another borrowed from his part time deputy, and rode out of town. He didn't know what it was about that William Jordan, but something didn't add up about him. The man was hiding some secret!

If he was telling the truth about the rest of his story, John must have run into something he couldn't handle on his own. Heaven only knew what that could be, but Campbell's gut told him it was so. John was in trouble and needed help! If his friends were all the likes of William Jordan, then he needed Campbell's help!

William Jordan had left a week back, and the sheriff couldn't get the whole situation out of his head. He left his sheriff's badge on the top of his desk, in case he needed to act in a manner contrary to his oath of office.

His part-time deputy, and full-time hounds man, Samuel Nelson, would keep the peace in town. The jail was empty, and Jeremiah Coombs was nursing a hangover. He wouldn't be stirring up hate and discontent in the saloon for a couple more days.

The morning was brisk, a great day for a ride, but dark clouds haunted the horizon, dotting the blue of the sky. He followed the same trail John used, hoping for any sign of his friend and former prisoner. *Odd how things work out.*

His horse made good time, and Campbell prayed John did not deviate from the road. The sheriff was a good tracker in the woods, as his job required, but he'd never catch up with John if forced to travel on foot.

* * * *

"So, tell us all about yourself, Robert?" Reverend Hartman asked.

"There's not a lot to tell, sir. I have two children, Rachel is six, and Ben is four. I'm in banking back in Philadelphia, and doing fairly well for myself, as you know."

"Robert is being very modest, Reverend. He's the president of the biggest bank on the East Coast!" Kate said.

"Perhaps not the largest, cousin," Robert answered. "Would you pass the green beans, please, William?"

"I suppose your business suffers by your absence, Robert? Are you planning on an extended visit?" Ada asked.

Robert smiled, and took Ada's hand in his own, touching it lightly with his lips.

"Please pardon my boldness, Ada, but my plans are in your hands, as I await your answer! None of the fine ladies in Philadelphia can hold a candle to you..."

Blood flushed Ada's face, and her eyes dropped to her dinner plate. She withdrew her hand.

"I am so sorry to hear about your wife, Robert," the Reverend said. "I'm sure she's in a better place now and knows no pain."

"Thank you, Reverend Hartman. She fought a valiant fight." Robert dabbed at his eyes.

The dinner continued in silence for some time, allowing Robert to gather himself. He cleared his throat and turned his attention back to Ada.

"What are you hoping for? A boy or a girl?"

"A boy, I think. I'd name him John after a man I thought I once knew." Ada took a turn swabbing at her eyes.

The chicken was reduced to bones, and the mashed potato bowl scraped clean when Ada and Kate gathered up the dishes and excused themselves from the table.

When the dishes were cleaned and stacked, Ada put her hand to her head.

"Kate, my head is pounding, would you offer my apologies? I need to lie down."

"Of course, and I hope you feel better! Get some rest, and I'll see you in the morning."

Ada dragged herself upstairs thinking of nothing but John, and the news her father had of him. Reverend Hartman said he'd received word of John. An old parishioner reported seeing a man fitting his description in Cumberland. As he wished to spare her feelings, her father kept the story to himself. Instead, he convinced William to travel there to verify or disprove the gossip.

William reported back to Earnest the week before. Her love was long gone from Cumberland, and he'd found another to share his life! A woman named Ladonna *(why did that name sound familiar?)* claimed his heart! The people who'd known him there said the couple seemed happy together, but none of them knew anything of John's former life.

Ada suspected Robert heard about John's betrayal, as his courtship efforts doubled since William returned from Cumberland!

As for his unexpected proposal, what did he anticipate her response to be? She was a woman consumed by sorrows! Surely, he understood, being so recently acquainted with his own grief? Her soul was mangled, torn in two, no other love could ever make her heart whole again!

Did he want no more than a stand-in mother for his children? A woman to warm his bed? She could offer no more than that! She was an empty vessel, and the basin of her heart was a sieve!

It was time to think of the child, her father advised. He said her choice was not John's love or Robert's money. Her choice now was friendship and security, or loneliness and despair. But she knew a loveless marriage equaled an unhappy home. Was that the best she could do for her baby?

Even with such grim prospects, Ada remained undecided. She promised Robert, and her father, an answer by week's end, but she had something to do first. Tomorrow,

she'd again visit the last place of happiness she'd known—
John's cabin.

Part VI
Paradise Found

"Now you listen here, young man. You are in no condition for traveling, especially on foot! Get yourself back in that bed!" Henrietta punctuated her words with a shaking index finger pointed at John's chest.

"I'm appreciative of everything you've done for me, Henrietta, but it's time for me to get home. I've been away for too long."

"Now, John Dyer, you're no help to nobody the way you are! You'll end up dead on the side of the road, and the critters will be gnawing on you before the sun goes down!"

"I promise, I'll go slow. I won't undo the fine work you've done."

"Why not stay another day or so, John? Ain't no woman worth dying for," Henry O'Connor chimed in from the doorway.

"Ada is," John answered, as Henrietta glared at her husband.

"Well, course you are, Maw. I didn't mean you," Henry amended, his head hung low.

"I wish I could talk you out of it, but I know you to be one mule-headed so and so. I got a sack of vittles put together for ya, then, if you're so dang determined to get yourself dead."

"Thank you, Henrietta. I'm not sure how I'll ever repay you both for all of your kindness, and your friendship. I owe you my life!"

He pulled the woman into his arms and winced from the stitches in his chest.

"See there, that's what I'm talking about, John!" Henrietta said.

He limped toward the only outside door and turned back to his benefactors. "I won't forget...if there's ever anything I can do..."

The steady beat of horse hooves sounded outside, and John snatched open the door, and squinted from the intense brightness. Two riders approached, but the road, muddy at his arrival, now sent up clouds of dust to obscure his vision. It swirled around the horses in a whirlwind, then slowly cleared. John realized it was one rider with two animals.

"Well, hello, son." The rider pulled back on the horse's reins. "If you're done stirring up trouble, I thought you might be up for a ride?"

* * * *

Kate placed the picnic lunch in the wagon and waited for Ada's arrival. She hoped a nice lunch and understanding companionship would make this farewell pilgrimage less painful for her.

William and Earnest both asked to join them, but Ada got her hackles up, wanting no parts of their company on this trip. It took some persuading on Kate's part to be allowed along, but perhaps her friend realized a sympathetic confidante might be welcome before the day was done.

Ada met her outside the stable, placed a canvas bag under her seat, and climbed aboard with yet another basket of food.

"We certainly won't go hungry!" Kate pointed at the basket and laughed. William waved his goodbyes from across the street, as did Earnest, loitering and watching from his doorway as the wagon rumbled past his home.

Their route up the mountain was familiar, but the worn pattern of buggy wheels was no longer imprinted on the trail's surface, erased by the past few months of rain with little or no traffic. Ada said it was sadly fitting that the road was as forsaken and derelict as her soul.

"Not at all, Ada. Look around," Kate said. "See the pale green blades of fresh grass sprouting? The wild flowers blooming on the abandoned path? I only hope the allegory holds true, and it's a sign. A prophecy that your heart will also nurture the growth of love again!"

Despite her attempted cheer, Kate felt the ride was anything but cathartic for Ada. She noted the swelling around her friend's eyes. Eyes that leaked more of Ada's emotional essence with each turn in the road, and every new vista.

The cabin loomed ahead like a vaguely recalled scene, one that started as the sweetest dream and ended in nightmare. Kate knew some details would be remembered as in a fog, while others promised to haunt Ada for the rest of her days.

"We're here, Ada. Are you sure you don't want to just turn around? We don't have to…"

"No, I have to see it once more. Do you think…maybe John's been back?"

"Ada, don't…"

Ada shook her head and bit her lip. "It's all right, Kate. I'm all right. I ache to know what happened, but it's not to be. I'm here to say goodbye."

"Come on then, let's go and get it over with. I'll be with you every step."

Other than the layer of dust, and the cobwebs everywhere, the place looked the same as before. Ada went to the bedroom, and scanned every corner of the dwelling, then sat at the table with Kate.

"I can wipe the table down, and we can eat here if you'd like?"

Ada looked at her, or rather through her to some faraway place, or to some distant memory.

"Or we can go down by the meadow if you'd rather?" Kate added.

"No, not at all—this will be fine. A long ride always makes me hungry too!" Kate cleaned the table as Ada retrieved the food baskets.

The conversation over their food was light, the name of John Dyer never once passing their lips. Kate saw color returning to Ada's cheeks, and one or two of her jokes even elicited a smile.

"This was good for me, Kate, I needed it, thank you."

"Anything for you, Ada."

"I have one more thing to do before we go home," Ada said, and went outside to the wagon. She pulled down the canvas bag, and half dragged, half carried it back to the cabin.

"What on earth do you have in there?" Kate helped her hoist it up on the table.

Ada opened the bag and pulled out several small bound journals.

"These are my recent diary entries, containing every word I've written since I met John. I'll leave them here where they belong, part of my past."

"Are you sure..."

Ada reached in the bag and pulled out a huge leather-bound book. "This is John's, a memoir of sorts from several generations of the Dyers. Maybe he'll come back for it someday."

As she reached out to set the book on the table, Kate heard a wet, splashing sound, and Ada's eyes grew as wide as saucers.

"Kate! Oh no, it's the baby!"

"Oh dear God, Ada! Your waters have broken!"

* * * *

"What did you get yourself into anyway, John? You look like you went a dozen rounds with a grizzly bear."

"Big cats, Sheriff. Two mountain lions. I'm lucky they didn't eat me for dinner too, I guess."

"Yup, lucky, that's what I'd call it, all right, and I reckon you can call me Isaac now, being as how ours ain't a professional relationship no more."

"Isaac it is then."

"Two cats, you say? Mated pair, you reckon?"

"That wouldn't surprise me a bit, Sheriff...um, Isaac. How did you happen to be out this far from your home county?"

"You know me and that whole jurisdictional thing, it never did set right with me."

"That I do know." John laughed, grimaced and pressed his hand against his chest.

"I meant to tell you. A friend of yours dropped by asking after you, a William Jordan. Didn't seem to have a real high opinion of you though. You know him?"

"Not well, but he's a good friend of Ada's, and his wife Kate, more so."

"But you? Not so much?"

"I don't know, but I never did any wrong by the man."

"I didn't trust him a bit, tried to sell me a dog about how Miss Ada had some new man. I thought he might mean you harm, but for sure, he's hiding something."

"He said Ada was with someone else?"

"He did, but come on, John. Don't put no stock in anything that feller said. Put me in mind of the man in that story what traded beans to that boy for his cow? Said they was enchanted beans? You know the story?"

John shook his head and turned his face away from the sheriff. "I do, but the beans in that story really were magic, Isaac."

"I think you might be right at that, but..."

"It makes no difference. We're almost home now, and then down the other side of the mountain to town...to Ada. We'll know the truth of it all soon enough," John said, his face turned to stone.

"John? There's one other thing he said too. I didn't want to say anything to you about it. Not until we were close to your place, knowing him to be a liar and all…"

"Go ahead then, Isaac, what else was said?"

"He says Miss Ada is heavy with child, John, and that you're gonna be a father."

John paused a moment, his eyes dark, then slapped the horse's reins, and raced down the trail.

"John! Whoa, wait up!" Campbell yelled, but John only responded by whipping the reins, and kicking in his heels, pushing the horse even faster—intending to head straight on to town, and to Ada.

Spotting the Jordans' wagon tied to his hitching rail, he slowed his horse, and slid from the saddle, but the strength of his wounded leg did not support his anxious rush. John fell heavily to the ground. The first several yards towards the cabin were on his hands and knees as he propelled himself on.

Isaac caught up with his friend's horse just as John climbed the steps to the porch. Thump. Thump. Thump. The only sound John heard was the pounding in his own chest. Silence inside. John paused at the door for but a moment, then reached for the door handle.

The shriek of agony filled the air! A sound of horrible torturous pain, Ada's scream!

"Ada!"

Campbell ran to the steps as John threw his shoulder into the door. The momentum carried him across the room, and he slammed into the table. For a moment, the room swirled around him, and his eyes blurred. He shook his head, and squeezed his eyes shut to regain his equilibrium.

"Ada!" he yelled again, and stumbled toward his bedroom door.

"Who's there?" asked a voice from behind the door. Kate's voice?

"Kate? It's John."

The bedroom door flung open, cracking into John's knee. A red faced and angry Kate materialized in the doorway. Her fist flew out, smashing John in the nose with a liquid, plopping sound.

"Congratulations, you son of a bitch. You're a father," she said.

* * * *

"I thought he was long gone? What do you mean he's back?" Reverend Hartman demanded. He tossed his pencil and his fledgling sermon down on his desk and stared out of his study window.

"Yes, he's back, but didn't you hear the rest? You have a grandson, a healthy baby boy!" William said.

"Who brought this news, and where is my daughter now?"

"Ada and the baby are both doing fine. They are at John's cabin. He made a friend in Cumberland it would seem, an Isaac Campbell. Kate sent him on ahead, so we wouldn't worry about them."

"I need to get to her and see what there is to be done. Ada may need help, especially if that Dyer is up there too."

"What do you mean, Earnest? John came back for her. I'll be the first to admit it, but I was wrong about the man. Sheriff Campbell said John went through hell to get here and was nearly killed by those damn rogue cats!"

"No, William, I've been wrong a time or two, but I'm not wrong about that heathen, and he hasn't seen hell...not yet! Why didn't your wife bring Ada home?"

"For the love of God, Earnest, she just gave birth! Campbell says they will be home as soon as Ada is up to it. Kate is staying up there with her until then."

"The man who told you this? Campbell? Where is he, and why didn't he tell me himself?"

"He's gathering some supplies to take back with him. I told you I met him in Cumberland, remember...and Kate sent him down here, so..."

"So he's probably running his sauce box all over town about it. We can't let Robert Turner know about Dyer's return." The Reverend rubbed the stubble on his chin.

"Are you joking? You're not continuing this charade, it's—"

"Don't forget, you were complicit in keeping him away from her too!"

"I remember all too well! I followed your lead because you are her father, and I did dishonorable things. I justified my actions and yours, by saying we were protecting Ada."

"And we will *continue* to do so!"

"I will not. My soul is likely damned, and Ada deserves better than this."

"Do not fear for your soul in this undertaking, William. God has revealed his plan to me."

William raised one eyebrow. "God? God told you this, Reverend?"

The Reverend paused and glanced over his shoulder. "Of course not, but I am well versed in His Word."

"The father of her child is back, Earnest, despite everything he's been through, and Ada loves him."

"Love?" Hartman laughed. "She's no more than a child. I've protected her all of her life, shielded her from the world, perhaps too much."

William opened the pine cabinet next to the desk, took two glasses down, and poured them both a drink.

"Here, Earnest, drink this. It will help clear your head. You aren't thinking straight."

"I'm the only one who is! We must find a way to protect Ada from that godless man, William!"

"What you are describing isn't being protective, it's being spiteful, although I don't know what the man ever did to make you hate him so."

Reverend Hartman lifted his glass and took a hearty pull on the amber fluid inside, only setting down the glass when it was drained. He smiled, and a twinkle returned to his eye.

"I know what to do, William! Go and see Robert. Get him out of town for a few days. Tell him you want to take him fishing, or…"

William held up his hand.

"Stop it, Earnest." He snapped his empty glass down besides the Reverend's. "I'm done!" William turned and left the room.

* * * *

Campbell gathered boxes of food: leather britches beans, salted meats, links of winter sausages, dried fruit, eggs, and two loaves of fresh baked bread. He added a bottle of Rattle-Skull to his purchases, both to celebrate and to restore Miss Ada's strength.

He didn't know much about birthing babies, never having children, but suspected Miss Ada was plum wore out, and he was sure all that effort worked up a hearty appetite!

He had left John sitting on the floor beside Ada's bed, his son wrapped in his arms. Small rolls of cotton cloth stuffed up John's nostrils stemmed the flow of blood compliments of the Jordan woman.

Miss Ada welcomed John with open arms, and a flood of tears, as he hobbled to her side. He related his misadventures and explained about his months in jail. He told her about the Good Samaritan who found him beside the road and carried him to the O'Connors to heal. He owed the man his life, and he didn't even know his name! Sheriff Campbell was there as a witness to his tribulations, but Ada hushed him after the shortest of explanations.

Kate seemed to be the only unhappy person in the cabin. Seeing Ada and John's reconciliation, she stomped out of the bedroom, acting mad as hops, and sat alone at the kitchen table. Campbell could respect her wanting to protect her friend, but he suspected she was hiding something, just like her husband.

With the wagon loaded, the sheriff headed out of town. He passed the Jordans' house and remembered William's happiness at hearing of John's return. Guess some people were just plain hard to figure.

On the edge of town, Campbell noticed a gathering of mangy looking cats on the threshold of a small house. He pulled up the wagon, and a sickly-sweet smell struck him immediately. A smell Campbell knew well—the stench of death.

He knocked on the door, and yelled, "Hello in the house," but there was no response. The door was unlocked, and he pushed it open. The smell of rot rocked him back on his heels. He pulled his handkerchief from his pocket, covered his mouth and nose, and entered the home.

 The thick cloud of noxious vapors emanated from the central room. Campbell stepped through the doorway and spotted a blanket-covered lump on the couch. A grey hand hung out from the blanket's edge.

Campbell backed out of the house and went in search of any local law enforcement. He spotted a young lad who directed him to a home housing a county deputy. He'd been stationed there since the second cat killing and knew most of the locals. The deputy said the dead man's name was Sean O'Shea.

* * * *

Sally Ann woke from her troubled dream with the demon's name on her lips. She climbed out from her nest of coal that she'd covered with a discarded horse blanket and looked forward to the day's prospects for the first time in weeks.

The disused warehouse, on Water Street in Cumberland, proved a haven for her, but as fall approached, and coal's demand increased, so would the daily traffic to the warehouse. Burly men would begin loading the coal on flat boats at the dock for transport downriver, but she would be gone before then.

Things were looking up for Sally Ann. There were no more visits from Laris, and she hoped he'd forgotten her, or lost track of her in the squalor she'd been reduced to. She'd not been with her spirit animal since and lost her desire to do so after the fight with John.

The day before, one of Sally Ann's gentlemen, Peter Sullivan, offered her a position in his household as a chambermaid. It was a job no different than what she'd done for her father for years, but now it would pay!

When Sullivan heard Sally Ann's sad story, he had to do something to help her. She explained how she came to Cumberland on a business trip with her husband to be, but soon after their arrival, he met up with an old girlfriend, a childhood sweetheart, who'd broken his heart many years before.

Sally punctuated her tale with an onslaught of tears, especially when describing how her ex-fiancé left her destitute in a strange town, without so much as a note saying goodbye!

As an orphan, she had nowhere else to turn except the streets. Sally Ann wailed when she spoke of her dear departed mother and father, both falling victim to consumption when she was but a sprout of a girl. Such kind, God-fearing people they were, her Ma and Da.

Mr. Sullivan frowned sadly and nodded his head throughout. For a moment, Sally Ann thought he might break into tears matching her own display.

He promised that her duties would not include any indecent activities—it was, after all, the home he shared with his wife and children.

She was to dress in her best clothes—meaning the one decent though threadbare dress in the bottom of her traveling bag—and interview with his wife at his Centre Street home. Sally Ann suspected what an 'interview' with her really meant—an inspection and interrogation by her one-time gentleman's wife!

* * * *

"Isn't he the most beautiful baby you've ever seen?" Ada asked.

"He is, but isn't handsome the word to use for a boy? He got his good looks honest, straight from his mother. That part's plain." John leaned over the nursing boy and kissed the back of his head.

"I've got some walnut planks under the cabin. I can make him a fine cradle out of that."

Ada smiled, yet a tear flowed down her cheek.

"No, please don't cry, Ada! It doesn't have to be walnut, I have some cherry wood also!"

"Oh John, it's not that, you silly man. These past months, I thought I'd lost you. All sorts of terrible things went through my head. You were hurt, or worse…or maybe you'd forsaken me, and never loved me! My heart ached with the not knowing."

"I'm here now, my love. I wrote you often, but I never heard back. I also lived in fear. Then the rumor that you'd found another…"

"I never got your letters, John, and I suffered because of it. But you are here now, so I guess it shouldn't matter. We'll have the rest of our lives together."

John nodded his head, his eyes gazing off into the distance. "It may be better that I don't know, Ada. From what Isaac told me, our friends plotted to keep us from one another."

"But they are our friends, John. Whatever they did, they did out of love for me, misguided as they were."

"Yet Kate still remains angry at my return."

"She will be fine—she's thought only of me for so long and shared my agony over loosing you. She hasn't had time to process the new reality—our new reality."

"You make me want to be a better man than I am, Ada, but it worries me too. People take advantage of anyone so generous in nature."

"I'm not so good, John. Robert asked for my hand, and I considered it, even though I knew I'd never give him my heart. I'm also in need of forgiveness."

John lifted her hand from the baby's back and kissed it.

"Enough unhappy thoughts, John. Today is a day more glorious than any I've known!"

"Indeed, it is a day of miracles."

"So on a happier note, I believe you said it is my job to name the baby?" Ada said.

"You did it all without me, so it is only fair."

"Well, I've decided. How does John Zachary Dyer sound? We'll call him Zachary."

In answer, John wrapped his small family up in his arms.

"John?" she whispered in his ear.

"Yes, my love?" John whispered back

"I don't want to go back there…back to my father's house I mean. This is my home now, with you."

"The good Reverend would kill us both, like as not."

"He will do no such thing, John Dyer. He's my father and must learn to accept us together."

Again John swooped up her hand, and looked deeply into her eyes, so deep that Ada felt him caress her soul. "I know I've not asked, but I love you, Ada. Nothing would give me more pleasure in this life than to have you as my wife."

"Was there a question in there somewhere, good sir?"

John sat on the bed and held her hand in his. "Please be my wife, Miss Ada Hartman, or you will damn my soul to eternal torment and yearning! Will you marry me?"

"I've been married to you in my heart for a very long time, Mr. John Dyer, and yes. I will marry you!"

The bedroom door popped open, and Kate ran in.

"I'm so sorry, but I couldn't help but hear. Congratulations to both of you!"

John's eyes became slits as he turned to face her.

"I really am happy for you, both of you, John, and I'm…so sorry! I heard your story and hope someday you can forgive me."

"I'm just relieved you're not hitting me anymore," John said, forcing a laugh, and touching his nose.

* * * *

Kate woke at the thunk of the cabin door closing. With a crick in her neck, she turned her head left and right, back and forth, trying to relieve the pressure.

She stood and folded her blankets—her functional, though negligible—bedding. She felt another presence behind her and turned to see Ada sitting at the table nursing Zachary.

"I hope I didn't wake you?"

"No, my aching neck did that."

"I'm sorry about the sleeping arrangement, Kate, that hard floor. John will be adding a room for Zachary when he gets older, but that doesn't help now."

"It's fine, Ada. I think I'm getting too old for sleeping on the floor, but it is time for me to get back home anyway. It's been nearly a week, and I miss my little Billy. William's sister has helped, but he's had his hands full with him."

"I know you must miss him, and William too! I don't know how I'll ever thank you and Sheriff Campbell for all you've done to help us."

"Campbell isn't the ass I thought he was, a good man in fact—despite his rough manners. He's probably back in Cumberland by now, but I won't be far away if you need me."

The cabin door opened and John walked in. He looked back and forth between the two women.

"This is scary, what are you two fine ladies plotting?"

"Kate said she's going home today. I'm going to miss her."

"You're always welcome here, Kate, but I'd be proud to escort you down the mountain when you go," John said. "I need to gather our animals and bring them home too."

"Perhaps you'll come, Ada? I'd bet your father is dying to meet his grandchild."

* * * *

The soft, rapid knocking at his door shook Earnest Hartman from his reverie. He inserted the red ribbon bookmark in his dog-eared Bible, stood and stretched. The morning was early for callers, but as God's local representative, business hours were whenever the faithful needed him.

On his way to the door, he snuck a glance out of his study window, and saw Ada waiting on his doorstep. He paused with his hand on the doorknob, then pulled the door open.

"So, the prodigal daughter has returned. It's been weeks, Ada, where have you been?"

"With John, as you know, Father. I made sure that Sheriff Campbell and Kate spoke with you, and kept you apprised so you'd not worry."

"So, it's true. The savage heathen is back. Is that why you feel the need to knock on the door of your own home? Shame?"

Ada's face flushed, but she took a deep breath, and bit back her retort. "No, Father, but rather because Kate told me how you feel, about John, about us…but speaking of us, I've brought someone for you to meet." Ada picked up the covered basket at her feet and pulled back the cloth. The tiny baby inside yawned, placing his entire hand in his mouth.

"Father, meet your grandson, Zachary. Zachary, this is your grandfather…or how would you have him call you, Father?"

Reverend Hartman pulled the cloth back further, exposing the baby's upper arm, then traced his finger over three pronounced parallel birthmarks.

"Ada, this child is from an unholy union and is an abomination! I've prayed and prayed to our Lord for direction, knowing John Dyer to be evil, and the Lord answered my prayers. Your betrothed is a demon, Ada. Turn your back on him now, and not on our God!"

Ada stood open-mouthed, at a loss for intelligent thought! "You…what? My baby's an innocent, and John's treated you with nothing but respect! How could you? I came here to ask you to preside at our wedding, and you…"

"Robert is a decent, God-fearing man. If you decide to choose that godless demon over him…well, there's another preacher in Romney with less discriminating standards."

"Father! How dare—"

The Reverend's nostrils flared as he slowly closed the door and turned away from his child. A sob burst from his throat, and a single tear formed in his eye. He sat at the base of the stairs with his head held in his hands.

The sound of rustling sheets, and the woman again appeared before him, just as her kind once did to the mother of the Lord!

"Fret not, Earnest. You did well in His service."

Her coppery hair flowed in waves over her shoulders, and her alabaster skin held little color, except the slight blush at her cheeks. Her glowing green dress matched her eyes, and unhidden by the gown's plunging neckline, hung an emerald necklace.

Even before she had identified herself to Earnest, he suspected who and what she was. Her heavenly beauty was unnatural, far beyond the imagination of mortals. She was malakhim, Ladonna—an angel of the Lord! Earnest bowed his head in supplication.

"I've done as you asked...to save my daughter, and the child. Please protect them from evil!"

"Did you see the demon's marks, as I told you? Have you shed your disbelief?

"Forgive my doubt, Ladonna, but the disciple John warned us to not believe every spirit, but to test the spirits to see whether they are from God."

"And after testing me is your faith restored?"

"Yes!" Hartman wailed, openly weeping, and fell to his knees before her.

"Then do not challenge my orders or my patience again." Ladonna bent forward and kissed the tears from his face.

"Fret not, loyal servant of God," she said. "Every disciple is tested. All will be made clear to you in time."

* * * *

John and Kate drove their wagons on after dropping Ada off to visit with her father and give him time to get acquainted with his new grandson. William appeared at the front door of the Jordan home, his face lighting up when he saw Kate.

"Kate! You've been missed, my love," he said, and helped her down from their wagon.

"It's wonderful to be home, William. Where's Billy?"

"Inside with my sister and Robert. He's saying his goodbyes. He's headed home today. How are Ada and Zachary?"

"John dropped them off at the Reverend's house. She thought it best if she spoke with him alone at first."

"Understandable. John, won't you come in?"

"I think not, William, but thank you...and thank you, Kate, for all of your help. It won't be forgotten."

"Of course, and please don't be a stranger, John. Let us know if you or Ada need anything. I must get reacquainted with my own son and see my cousin off." Kate hurried inside, leaving the two men alone.

"It would seem I owe you a substantial apology, John."

"I never did any harm to you, William. Never treated you as anything other than a friend. I don't know what to say to you just now. Just lead me to my animals, so I can avoid saying anything I might regret."

William nodded. "I can't say as I'd feel any differently, John. Let's go get your animals."

He led the way to the stable, and the two men gathered the chickens and goats, and loaded them into the wagon. When they were done, John climbed aboard, and William reached up and held out his hand. John stared at it for a moment, and then took it into his own.

"Matthew tells us, 'If you forgive men for their transgressions, your heavenly Father will also forgive you.'"

John stared at him and raised one eyebrow. "I believe your Jeremiah says, 'But look, you are trusting in deceptive words that are worthless.'"

"You are well versed in the Good Book."

"In many good books," John replied.

"In my defense, John, I misjudged you. I acted in what I thought to be Ada's best interests. We love her too, so perhaps you will understand."

"I will…with time."

"As a friend, I will tell you this—beware of your future father-in-law. His resentment toward you knows no bounds, and in fact, I fear for his mental state."

John nodded and slapped the horse's reins. In front of Reverend Hartman's house, Ada sat with Zachary, dabbing at her eyes as he approached.

John sat in silence, holding Ada's hand, as she shared the conversation she had with her father. His own heart felt tortured with the shared pain.

"My father turned his face from me, Isaac is gone, and many of our friends prove to be so in name only. Now, your father considers our happiness unholy, an offense to

God? It seems the whole world moves against us, Ada, and we only have each other."

"Each other, and our family," she answered, and drew Zachary closer.

* * * *

The party was large, well-attended, and formal, as was appropriate for the upper crust of Cumberland society. The men were attired in fitted single-breasted tailcoats, with neck choking cravats up to their chins. Their breeches clung so tight they walked like pigeons. The women were not to be outdone in their high-waist dresses, and short matching single-breasted jackets. Necklines left little to the imagination, but likely gave some degree of relief from the hot, confining outfits. They wore their hair in the latest fashion—sharply parted in the center with tight ringlets over the ear. Slaves to fashion, Campbell thought.

There wasn't a single oilcloth jacket, or pair of work boots to be seen. If there was any buckskin in the place, he suspected it was in old Mrs. Perkins' corset. It was not the sort of affair Isaac Campbell was comfortable attending, but one he recognized as necessary to his position as sheriff.

Mrs. Evelyn Campbell found a comfortable spot on the couch and chatted gaily with the chatterbox church-bells from town. *She's in her element.* Her folks always said she'd married beneath her station, but Isaac did the best by her that he could. As near as he could tell, they'd both done well by each other.

Here in his brother-in-law's home, with its opulent furnishings, he realized how much she'd given up to marry him. Peter Sullivan was no slouch with all the local financial doings and provided well for his family. Isaac said as much to Evie earlier that evening.

"Isaac, don't you go comparing yourself to that man. He's a snake, a thief, and a whoremonger. I married you for love, not money, and besides, we do just fine." She punctuated her remark with a kiss.

The sheriff winked at his wife and wandered toward the quietest corner of the room. Finding no decorous manner to sit with his tight breeches, he plopped down in a leather chair.

One of Peter's house girls approached with a tray full of tiny food tidbits. The pretty red-haired woman bent down to offer the plate to him, and her plunging bodice gaped open, as if to offer even more. He closed his eyes, but not before noticing her firm youthful beauty.

She tugged at her blouse, and the tray jiggled in her grasp. Campbell reached out to steady it, but two pickled oysters fell into his lap.

"I'm so sorry, sir. I'm so clumsy!" A cloth napkin appeared in her hand, and she reached out to mop the juices from his pants. Isaac caught her hand.

"I think you better let me see to that, Miss. I'm not sure my wife would understand."

"Truly, sir, I am so sorry."

"At least it wasn't the hot soup! But I haven't seen you here before, are you new?" Campbell asked.

"Yes sir, only a month or so."

"What's your name?"

"Sally O'Shea, sir. But please don't say anything to Mrs. Sullivan."

"No real harm done, Miss O'Shea. Are you by chance related to the O'Shea family down in Setter's Run, Virginia?"

The girl's eyes flicked to the left and right, and a quick flush colored her cheeks.

"Distant cousins, maybe, but I don't know of any kin down that way. I must get back to work…"

"Feller down in Setter's Run, name of Sean O'Shea, got himself killed a while back. You ever heard of him?"

Her mouth fell open, and Isaac noticed her eyes well up. She rubbed her face against the shoulder of her dress.

"It's the garlic, sir. Please excuse me." Sally turned away and scurried back toward the kitchen.

* * * *

Reverend Hartman rubbed the crusty sleep from his eyes and glanced cautiously around the room. He sat up and listened for any movement in the house. She was nowhere to be seen or heard.

He stretched and yawned. The past few weeks were too much for an old man, he thought. His knees creaked as he swung his legs off the bed, and he padded barefoot to the bedroom window.

It was a grey misty day, the kind favored only by lazy men and ducks, a day like Ada's wedding day. He'd hated hiding in the back of the small church, lurking like a threatening predator instead of a loving father. She never knew he was there. Ladonna demanded so much of him!

Knowing that tainted blood flowed in John Dyer's veins, Hartman could never accept his daughter's marriage. He assured Ladonna of that! Still, he'd never forget the glow of happiness on Ada's face that day. Smiling, laughing, and even dancing through the street with her small family. Her beauty shined from within, a glorious sight to behold! He wouldn't allow Dyer to destroy her happiness!

Hartman climbed down the stairs to the kitchen. On the way down the hallway, he peeked into every room. The house was empty.

Who knew angels could be so domineering, yet invigorating? Six months ago, he doubted his ability to be with a woman, but now? The angel Ladonna made all things possible, some very surprising things!

When he was first with her, he worried over his immortal soul. Ephesians warned, 'among you there must not be even a hint of sexual immorality…because these are improper for God's holy people.'

His lust argued that it couldn't be wrong if directed by an angel of the Lord! But didn't the Lord punish the world, and his fallen angels, when they mated with the daughters of men?

For days, weeks, and months the arguments raged in his mind, at least whenever Ladonna was absent. When she was with him, he was powerless to deny her anything. He was her slave.

* * * *

Robert Turner released a sigh of relief as he pulled the battered wagon into the farm lane of his friend. The entire trip west was a mistake that he wished to be done with.

He never realized how special his children were to him until he took a business trip, and that is how he would remember this latest adventure—as a business trip gone wrong.

He enjoyed Kate's company—for the little bit of time he got to spend with his cousin. Ada was a bricky girl, full of life and with no qualms about speaking her mind. Robert liked that, not being a fan of timid, fawning women.

He thought she'd fit in nicely with his life and his children, but when Ada's intended returned out of the blue, both she and Kate disappeared from Setter's Run.

The how and why of it Robert never heard, but he couldn't understand how a woman like Ada, even a pregnant Ada, would allow such a man back into her life.

William was pleasant enough, and hospitable, but for all his pretentions, he was just a small-town boy. Robert found no common interests with the man, and his Bible thumping, holier than thou attitude quickly wore on his nerves.

Robert's trip back to Cumberland took longer than expected. He stopped for a short visit at the O'Connors, to settle any debts he might owe for their care of his charge. He thought to maybe say a prayer over the man's grave, but Henrietta O'Connor had other news.

"That John Dyer healed up faster than a body has a right to. He's got somebody looking out after him." She pointed up to the clouds.

"John Dyer, you say?" Robert asked.

"Yes, that was the feller's name. Hey, are you all right there, Mister? You look like you done seen a ghost."

Robert spent that night with the O'Connors, and they shared all they knew about John Dyer's miraculous recovery. He found it difficult to depart their company and got off to a late start the following day.

His horse threw a shoe at dusk, just outside of Frankfort, Virginia. Luckily for Robert, it was one of the largest trading posts in the area. They had a farrier that set him right and got him on his way the next day.

Now, with the Ramseys' house in sight, this leg of his journey was finally done! Robert tied the horse to the rail outside the stable, and his step quickened as he strode toward their front door. The noisy, cluttered streets of Philadelphia were but a stagecoach ride away!

Charles stepped down the steps just as Robert reached them.

"Well, hello, Robert! Glad to see you made it safe and sound."

"It is good to be back."

"Did you have a good visit with your cousin?"

"Pleasant enough, but I'll be glad to see the city lights again!"

The front door opened again, and a tall rugged-looking older man stepped out.

"Robert, this is Isaac Campbell. He's the sheriff of our fair little town. Sheriff, this is an old friend of mine, Robert Turner. The sheriff came out because some low life scoundrels stole a mess of my chickens last night," Charles explained.

"Robert Turner? We never met, but aren't you Kate Jordan's cousin?" Campbell asked.

"I am one and the same, and pleased to make your acquaintance, Sheriff, but how is it you know of me?"

"Kate mentioned you when we met recently."

"You must have a good memory for names, Sheriff."

"Occupational hazard, I suppose. You ever meet any of the O'Shea family when you were in Setter's Run?"

"Not that I recall, but…wait a minute. I do remember some talk about an O'Shea family. The daughter was a friend of my cousin. Kate said she'd just up and left without a word some time back. She left a note on the door. I don't remember much else…"

"Do you remember her name, son?"

"Sharon or Sandra, something like that?"

"Sally, maybe?"

"Yes, that's it! Sally Ann O'Shea was her name. Kate said she and her father Sean just up and left."

* * * *

"John, come see!" Ada yelled.

"What's wrong?" he asked, running into the bedroom. Ada was poised over Zachary's crib, grinning from ear to ear, and pointing at their son. John looked down and smiled. "He's a handsome boy, Ada, truly he has your features."

"Well, you certainly can't deny him either, John. Not with the triple squiggly lined birthmark you both share, but that's not what I meant. Just look, he's rolled over, all by himself!"

"That's good, right?"

"Of course it is! He's so strong for his age!" She wrapped her arms around John's shoulders.

He dropped his hands to her waist and lifted her, touching his lips to hers.

"John, you are my heart, and I love you, but I swear you don't know anything about babies! I guess I need to talk to Kate about such things."

"I'm learning as we go, but of course you can, and should, visit with Kate. I will hitch up the wagon today if you like?"

"It's going to rain all day, John, and I don't want to take Zachary out in this. Besides, I love rainy days."

"Do you really, Ada? I expected it today after hearing that rain crow squawking the day away yesterday."

"Rain is mother's milk to the soil."

"The cabbage and kale will love it, but I won't get much done today I'm afraid."

"Exactly! Today I get to spend the whole day on the porch with my loving husband and sweet son watching the rain nourish the earth. Come on, John."

Ada ran to the front door and flung it open.

"See?" She stepped out to the edge of the porch, opened her mouth and caught several droplets of rain.

"There are no chores to interfere, and I plan to take advantage of it."

"I may take advantage too, but not on the porch." John smiled.

Ada wet her lips with the captured rain and stared deeply into his eyes.

"You may take any advantages that you'd like, my love."

Falling into each other's arms, they stumbled back inside to their bed. Ada nibbled at John's bottom lip.

"God, I love you!" he said.

"Show me, John."

He traced the outline of her body through the light cloth of the night dress and felt her response.

Zachary screamed.

John laughed. "Oh, little man, I know I must share, but please not now."

"He's hungry, he's a growing boy. Don't worry, his hungers are satisfied much faster than yours." Ada winked at her husband, and lifted Zachary from his cradle. She slipped off her top and moved her son to her breast. She pulled the blanket up to her shoulders.

"Please don't," John said, and gently tugged on the blanket. "It's the most beautiful image I've ever beheld…so pure, a mother nurturing the new life she created."

She pulled the blanket away.

"The new life *we* created."

* * * *

Sally Ann tossed and turned in her bed. Was it an unfamiliar sound, or an odd scent that jarred her fully awake? She sat up and pulled her covers up to her chin.

"Hello? Is someone there?" No answer. She sniffed at the air, and noted the ashen smell, the odor of a freshly doused fire. Perhaps it was from the lantern she blew out? No, that was many hours ago. A quick glance out of the window showed a new dawn breaking.

Laris was out of her life for many months now. Surely he'd forgotten her? Lost sight of her whereabouts? She prayed it was so.

A deep purring sound came from under her bed, then scratching, like a huge house cat on a hitching post.

"Laris? No, not again! Please leave me be," she moaned.

"Get out! You're in danger—go, now!" the rasping, inhuman voice commanded.

Sally Ann threw clothes in a traveling bag and slipped on her shoes. She reached the door just as someone knocked on it!

"Sally? Sorry to disturb you, but the sheriff is here to see you. He has some questions for you," Peter Sullivan said.

Sally raced to the window and pulled at the sash. It wouldn't budge!

"Sally? Did you hear me?"

"Just a moment, Mr. Sullivan. Let me get decent."

Sally heaved against the window, and it creaked open, but one of the glass panes popped from its frame and shattered on the hard wood floor. The quiet of the pre-dawn house did nothing to dispel the sound, and the pounding on the door started immediately.

"Open this damn door right now!" another man's voice shouted.

Sally Ann stepped up on a foot stool and lifted her left leg through the window opening.

The door crashed open with a splintering of wood, just as her upper body ducked through the window. Sheriff Campbell snatched at her dress, and she kicked him in the jaw. Sullivan watched with his arms folded over his chest.

"You'll pay for that window, and the door too, young woman!" Sullivan warned.

Sally Ann aimed another kick, and Campbell snagged her foot, and grabbed one arm. With two of her squirming, thrusting weapons under his control, he dragged her back inside.

"I just wanted to ask you a few questions, Sally, but I think we'll do that from your jail cell now."

"What do you think I have done? Whatever it is, I'm innocent!" Sally wailed.

"Let's see—there's assaulting an officer of the peace and resisting arrest in our fine county. Also, you're a missing person from Setter's Run, Virginia, and a person of interest in a murder there. That's plenty enough to hold you on, Miss."

"Who told you those crazy things about me?"

"The local charges I just saw with my own eyes, now didn't I? The rest, I put two and two together from what a visitor fresh out of Setter's Run told me."

"Where is he now? You made all this up so you could get me alone in that jail cell, didn't you? Peter, do something! He's a pervert, a rapist!"

Peter waved his hands in front of himself and stuttered. "Well...I just d-d-don't...now...Isaac, I..."

"Wait outside, Peter," Campbell commanded, and waited for his brother-in-law to leave.

"Ma'am, the gentleman has returned home to Philadelphia, but…"

"I demand my right to confront my accusers!"

"He didn't accuse you of anything. He only revealed your lies. Besides, that's only the case come trial time, ma'am…if it even comes to that. We'll see to the charges here first, then I'll carry you on down to Setter's Run, and be shed of you."

"So, nobody in Setter's Run knows I'm here? Just some fancy gent passing through…and you? If you put me in some dark cell, I'll scream rape so loud the whole town will hear."

The Sheriff shuddered as a chill ran down his back.

"Somebody is walking over your grave," his mother would say.

"Um, yeah. Peter, run on down to the jail and get the deputy. He hasn't gone home yet, and I want help with this one."

Lord help me, I'm supposed to be the professional, but this wisp of a girl might outfox me. I'm gonna have to watch my back with her.

* * * *

Kate loved her visits with the Dyer family. Today's social call was no different, and the most fun Kate had in ages! Billy and Zachary played so well together. Although Billy was an accomplished walker, and Zachary was just getting the hang of crawling, that didn't stop the two boys from enjoying each other.

They laughed, and threw grass at each other, rolled in the dirt, and raced around the yard. On his hands and knees, Zachary was almost as fast as Billy!

Zachary put everything he found in his mouth, as if he didn't trust his hands and eyes to tell him the truth about a thing. Each time, Ada swept her baby up, and swung him around, then they'd both end up on the ground. John joined in, and the three of them rolled around in obvious delight with their world, and each other. They tried to draw Billy into their play, but he sat and stared at them and his mother.

"Billy isn't too sure about us." Ada laughed. "I think he questions our sanity. Come on, Kate, don't be so prim and proper, Billy wants his mommy to play too."

"Billy's mommy doesn't want to get grass stains all over her good dress. Next time I'll wear work clothes or play clothes!" Kate stifled a giggle observing their antics.

"Ma ma ma ma ma," Zachary murmured.

"John, did you hear that!" Ada asked.

"I told you. He's been saying that all week—every time you leave his sight in fact," John said.

"Say it again, Zachary. Mama. Mama."

"No, say da da da this time, Zachary. I haven't heard that one yet. Come on, say it—da da da…"

"Oh, you are so jealous!" Ada slapped his arm, and they rolled around on the ground again, laughing like feral children.

"I swear, the two of you are like an adolescent Romeo and Juliet. I can't imagine any two people who were more meant to be," Kate said, and noticed Ada's face drop.

"Maybe you are right," Ada said. "Their love story also caused family division, but they didn't survive the discontent." She got up off the ground and sat on the bench by her friend.

"I was hopeful William would come with you, but it's a blessing to have you here, Kate," Ada said.

"He's sorry, Ada, really. It is only his guilt and shame that keeps him away."

"I never doubted your friendship, Kate, but William's deceit hurt us. Still, we must reconcile our differences. I trust he did what he did from a place of love, not hate."

"And does John share your feeling?"

"John too."

"William will be glad to hear that, but we've been arguing a lot, Ada. He's spending too much time with Earnest again. He says he's trying to help him—that your father's mind has slipped. But William's become so self-righteous, he talks like he's some Old Testament prophet. I'm afraid the Reverend's rubbing off on him. I'm concerned about William just being around the man."

Ada's arms wrapped around her friend and pulled her head onto her shoulder.

"I'm sorry, Kate, but you'll work through it. You're both good people."

"Ada, that's not all. There's something I need to tell you…"

"John, Zachary just put something in his mouth! I'm sorry, please go on, Kate."

"Earnest came to see William yesterday, and they spent half the morning sequestered in the study. I prepared lunch, and well, I'm ashamed to say it, but I listened at the door."

"My goodness, Kate. What a sneak you are!"

"Ada, they were discussing your family. Earnest wanted my husband to annul your marriage and asked about taking possession of John's land."

"He can't do that, can he, Kate? But maybe you misunderstood?"

"When the Reverend left, I confronted William about it. Ada, I was so mad I could feel the heat of anger in my face, and my vision blurred with red at the edges of my sight."

"What did William say?"

"Just what I told you. He thinks your father wants to take everything from you, or from John anyway. William said there's no legal way he can do that, and suggested he leave, but your father…well, he's not himself these days. Be careful, Ada!"

211 • His Father's Blood

Part VII
The Sacrificial Lambs

"Would you please take these manacles off me, Sheriff? You're not scared of a little girl like me, are you?"

"It's protocol when transporting a prisoner, Miss O'Shea."

"I heard you did this to John Dyer. Was that protocol too, Sheriff? No, it couldn't be, could it? A sheriff from Maryland arresting a man in Virginia?"

"I believe in the law, ma'am. Without law, there's no society, and sometimes the law needs a little helping hand. But don't worry yourself, miss. I will get you there safe and sound."

"Was it the law when you made an illegal arrest on the basis of a note from some woman you never met? Ladonna, I believe? Acting without due cause is kind of what you do, huh, Sheriff?"

"How is it that you know any of that?"

"I guess I have a trusting face, Sheriff. People tell me things, sometimes even in my sleep."

"We're setting up camp here, Miss O'Shea, before it's full dark. Springfield is just over that rise, and that puts us better'n half-way there."

"I heard there's big predators in this part of the country—vicious cats and hungry bears. Are you afraid of the dark, Sheriff?"

"No more than the daytime, ma'am. Don't worry, like I said, I'll get you there safe and sound."

Sally Ann lifted her head as if listening to a distant voice.

"Laris says this will do just fine," she said.

"Who said what? Never mind. I'll get a fire going and heat us up some beans."

Sally Ann sat fidgeting by the fire. Campbell kept his eyes on her as he heated dinner over the flames. Pulling at her restraints, she tried to stand.

"I need to go potty, Sheriff. Will you take these off, please?"

Campbell stood, and helped her to her feet, and led her into the woods beyond the reach of the campfire light.

"This just won't do, Sheriff. Is this how you treat a lady?"

He shot her a dark look.

"Here will do," he said. He released one of her hands from the shackles and reattached it to a wrist sized tree.

"Sheriff, really, I must protest!"

"Give me a holler when you're done with your business, ma'am."

Sally Ann waited until she heard the clinking sound of Campbell's spoon in the bean pot. She squatted, dropped her head, and sought her spirit animal.

"Finally," Laris said in a gravelly voice ending in a growl.

Sally felt her mind and limbs melding with her cat. Shrinking in some areas, expanding in others, her paw slipped from its restraint. Rolling on her back, she slithered from the confines of her clothes. Freedom!

She padded over to the edge of the firelight. Campbell sat unawares, still stirring the pot.

She crouched. Step by step, she drew nearer. Closer, then closer still. When the firelight reflected in her eyes, her muscles constricted. Prepared to pounce. Claws dug into the dirt.

The man looked up, startled. *Too late!*

Muscles clenched and sprang. The cat pounced on her target. Claws slashing, jaws snapping.

Boom!

Searing hot pain! Her leg...

Warm fresh blood dripped from her teeth, and flowed down her throat, tasting of copper and invigorating her. The prey was fallen. Gnashing, bones crushing, she feasted. Laris shared.

"Savor him. There's much more work to be done," Laris said.

* * * *

As daylight failed, the deer paused in the clearing, ears focused forward like a radar dish. He tasted the air, and sensing no imminent threat, dropped his head to feed. The newly dropped acorns were sweet and rich in protein. The predator crouched in the shadows, watching, waiting. His mouth watered at the thought of fresh meat.

The buck took a step forward, providing the hunter with a clear view of his vitals. John drew the bow string back and anchored it against his cheek bone. The buck glanced at the odd shape in the brush. *Wait...not yet.*

As the buck turned his head away, the string slipped from John's fingers.

The stone-tipped arrow flew to its intended target, just behind the deer's shoulder. The animal tossed its head back toward the arrow's impact, acting as if stung by a bee. He walked off into the woods, twice dropping his head to browse.

John saw the arrow embedded in the dirt beyond where the deer stood. Good shot, through and through.

He backed off the killing field. He'd give the deer time to expire peacefully before he picked up its trail.

John felt pleased that his Conoy brothers' archery lessons stuck with him and bore fruit, or more precisely, meat for his family.

Leaving that morning for the hunt, his gun was nowhere to be found. Ada said she'd seen it in the corner just the day before when she swept their bedroom.

"It has to be here somewhere, John. There isn't many places for it to hide in this cabin, and it's not like anyone would steal that old thing, held together with twine and snips of wire." She laughed.

When John left the cabin, he'd instructed Ada to lock the door and windows in his absence. He swore he smelled the lingering scent of rose water.

He left his horse grazing in a small meadow, dropped his pack and settled in for the night. No sense trying to track the deer in the dark. The evening promised to be chilled enough to keep the meat from spoiling.

Ada would be pleased. He wouldn't have to kill one of their goats to provide the family with meat. A nursing Ada meant she was eating for two, and the goat milk would be important when she weaned their son from her breast.

* * * *

Reverend Hartman reclined on his bed. A shiver ran down his back, and to his groin, as Ladonna traced her nails between his shoulders.

"You will do as you are told, Earnest. We are at war with demonic forces. Do you not care what becomes of your grandson? Would you leave him in the hands of darkness?"

"Of course not, but…"

"Did you think this would be easy? That the heroes of the Bible didn't have doubts, and fears? No, they were heroes because they were afraid, and overcame it, not because they were fearless."

"Are you certain? I mean…are you sure this is what our God intends?"

Ladonna smiled. "I assure you, this is exactly what my lord wants."

"But the boy is my daughter's child!" Hartman exclaimed.

Ladonna did not answer, and he rolled over to face her. The other side of the bed was empty.

* * * *

The deer's trail was easy to read, and John knew he'd find the buck soon. Broken branches, heavy prints where it stumbled, and frequent blood sign led him on. Vultures floated in lazy circles above him and caused his pace to quicken. He'd not allow the woodland clean-up crew to take his kill!

The path of the tracks turned, and John spotted his quarry, nestled in a hollow formed by the roots of a fallen tree. He combed his hand through the hairs on the deer's head and neck, then placed a handful of greens between the animal's teeth. He dropped his head in silent supplication.

Thank you for your sacrifice, brother. Your flesh will feed my family. Your hide will warm us on the coldest nights. Your life will not be wasted, nor forgotten. I look forward to the time we will meet again when the creator calls me home.

He drew his great-grandfather's stone knife from its sheath and dressed the animal. Death begets life.

The wind changed, and his nose flared, assailed by the smell of death and decay. He dropped his head to his kill, but only smelled fresh meat. Black vultures still soared above him, but further down the valley.

Curious, he tied his deer to an overhanging branch and crept forward to investigate. He no longer needed to follow the trail by sight, but rather by scent. Its flavor was overpowering and sickly sweet, the obnoxious taste of death on the morning breeze.

The carrion birds croaked their indignity at his trespass, flapped their wings in agitation and stumbled around the woods, graceful in flight only.

The old worn work boots were his first clue of the man's identity, and John ran toward the body. Face down in the dirt, the man's face was protected from the birds' feasting.

The same did not hold for the bloated offspring of the green bottle flies. As he flipped the body over, the moist fat larvae fell from the man's mouth and eyes, forever squirming, and rooting in their quest for growth, consuming the corruption of flesh. Death sustains life.

The face was ravaged, but the hair, clothes, and tin star on the man's chest were enough.

"I'm sorry, Isaac. You were one of the few I called friend. I wish I'd been here in your hour of need."

As was the way of John's people, he wrapped Campbell in the hide of the deer, and placed him in a grave dug in the soft ground. Over the body, he placed a mat hastily fashioned from cattails, the sheriff's gun, and his own hatchet.

"Forgive my haste, my friend. You were a lone warrior, and left too long after your final battle. I'll not have you further dishonored."

He knew either Sally Ann's cat or her traveling companion were responsible for his friend's murder. The marks on the body were too clear, even after the defilements. If Sally Ann's cat killed Isaac, John was equally complicit in his death, and that knowledge tore at his conscience.

John camped by his friend's final resting place. He burned sage and prayed to the Creator to guide Isaac's final steps home. Thoughts of Isaac were enough to provide a restless night. He was not surprised that he woke often, and in a cold sweat. What was the voice he heard? A woman speaking a warning from far away? It was a familiar voice even if only known from his dreams. *Moll!* Nothing met his gaze, and his head fell back to his rolled-up jacket, only to repeat again and again throughout the night.

Dawn found John heavy of heart as he said his final goodbyes and turned his steps toward home.

* * * *

The sharp ache in Sally Ann's upper thigh snapped her from a fitful sleep. Campbell's bullet tore a gaping hole, luckily only passing through flesh.

She gathered dead-nettle leaves to use as a poultice, as John had taught her, and tore strips of cloth from the blouse left by Laris to bind the wound. It was an uncomfortable night of pain spent on the uneven floorboards. Exposed nail heads poked at her skin, and biting insects plagued her.

Sally Ann limped through the abandoned cabin and out the door to sit on the stoop. She shivered at a sudden chill in the air and turned to see Laris staring at her. A smile, containing way too many teeth, split his face.

"You did well, my sweet princess. All is proceeding as planned." He wet his lips with a snake-like tongue.

"Are you ready for your reward?" he asked.

"What is the plan, Laris? You helped me get my revenge, but what is it that you are after?"

His nostrils splayed open, and a growl crept up from the recesses of his chest. He took a deep, labored breath, and smiled again at her.

"You've been a good soldier, so I will grant you this one indulgence. It's quite simple. The child is a Cambion— half human, and half demon. I will make him ours."

"Zachary, you mean? John and Ada's child?"

"The same. He's far from the first of his kind—even in the Dyer family, but we made a mistake with the last one that had power such as his."

"What mistake?"

"A child this powerful can only be born of parents of power, and we will not allow them to interfere this time."

"Them? The poor child has no one but his mother now."

"Do keep up, Sally Ann. John Dyer still lives, though not much longer I think."

"He's alive?"

"Yes, although his nine lives are about spent. Who knew that a bear got them too?" Laris laughed.

"What will you do with Zachary? You cannot raise a human child!"

"No, but someone we control can, and the parents are too strong. They would not bend to our will."

"What are you going to do to them?"

"Don't act all squeamish, as if they were your friends! You were fighting Dyer when he fell from the cliff, and not so many months ago, I had to pull you from the woman's throat!"

"No, Laris. You can't! John is…"

Laris snarled and landed a sharp kick to her thigh. She drew up in pain, and he punched her in the mouth. She fell back on the rotted boards of the porch, bleeding from the mouth and her reopened leg wound. He glared down at her.

"Never tell me no, harlot! I'll roast you on a spit in the fires of hell myself. Get in my way, and your death will be the last kindness you will ever know."

* * * *

William was strolling to his office when John pulled his wagon to a stop in the road beside him.

"Good afternoon, John. I just finished lunch, but I'm sure Kate would love to rustle you up something?"

"No, but thank you, William," he said dismounting. "I ate some jerky on the trail."

"Sorry I haven't been out to your place to visit with Kate. The way we left things…"

John stuck out his hand, and William grabbed it and firmly shook it.

"Friends are few and far between, William. We all do things we regret, things we can't take back."

"Thanks, John. I appreciate that more than you know. So what brings you to town today? I'm curious about what it takes to get you off that mountain."

"I need to get word to Cumberland, to the wife of a friend. It would be better done in person, but the news might be easier if it comes from her sister."

"What can I do to help, John?"

"I need to send a letter, and I won't be here when the stagecoach picks it up. I want to be sure it goes on the next trip. You're good with words, and I was hoping…"

"Let's go to my office."

The men walked down the street discussing their families, the weather, and the harvesting of crops.

"Did you get Zachary to say daddy yet?" William asked.

John laughed and threw his hands in the air.

"I see Kate has been talking about me! No, our Zachary is a stubborn lad, and he's definitely his momma's boy."

"Don't worry, before you know it, you won't be able to shut him up!"

John nodded, and William stopped suddenly. He turned to face his friend.

"Has Ada visited with her father lately?"

"No, I'm not sure when, or even *if,* that bridge can be crossed. Why do you ask?"

"I'm not one to spread rumors, but you should know. Earnest is…he's a changed man, and not in a good way."

"How so?"

"There's a darkness about him. I fear he is planning something, and that it won't end well for you or Ada. He tells me…"

William paused when John nodded at a point beyond his right shoulder. He turned to see Reverend Hartman approaching. The preacher mumbled and waved his hands in the air as he spoke to himself.

"I know what to do…kill the demons. Yes, I love the Lord…his servant…his will be done…all over soon…" the Reverend muttered.

Hartman bowed his head repeatedly, then noticed the two men for the first time. His face contorted into a mad man's mask, eyes bulging, and nostrils flaring. His mouth formed into the snarl of an angered beast as he lumbered off.

"Who is he talking to?" John asked.

"Angels I believe. The elders are considering relieving him if he doesn't snap out of this state he's in."

"You and Kate are good people, William. I wonder if I might ask a favor…a big one."

"Doesn't hurt to ask." William laughed, and stopped abruptly after seeing John's face.

"If something happens to me…will you keep an eye out for Ada and Zachary?"

* * * *

Ada stared out of the cabin window, hoping to catch a glimpse of John returning. Again, she was disappointed. He should be back by now. It was their first separation since they were reunited, and it came hard.

Her dreams the night before did not improve her outlook. In fact, her hands still trembled from the memory. She glanced again out of the window as the siren call signaling Zachary's hunger sounded from the bedroom.

She reclined on the bed with her back against the headboard as she fed her son. Exhausted from lack of sleep, she closed her eyes, and the woman's face from her dream immediately jumped into her mind's eye.

"I know who you are, Moll Dyer. I've seen the picture drawn of you in John's book, but I don't understand what you want?" Ada said.

The specter pointed to the cabin door.

"You must go!" the spirit said, with no movement of her lips.

"Why do you haunt me? I know nothing of a ghost's needs. Tell John, he's your descendant! He knows about these things."

"I am weak here, child. My spirit is too far removed from my mortal remains, but I have tried. John's heart is in a dark place, in anguish. His spirit is cut off. He cannot hear me now."

"What is wrong with John? Is he hurt?"

"No, it is another—but you must go! Protect the child, they're coming!"

Ada's eyes popped open at the sound of horse hooves pounding up the road to the cabin. With Zachary at her breast, she slid out of bed and hurried to the door.

Seeing his wife at the window, John approached the house in a trot.

"What's wrong, Ada? You look terrified," John asked as he pulled Ada into his arms.

"Thank God, you are here. I'm fine...terrible dreams...that woman, your witch ancestor from the book? She's been visiting me in my dreams."

"She often visits my dreams. Sometimes to comfort or warn me, and often to chastise me as well."

"She told me to go, and that you were in anguish!"

"It's Isaac, Ada. I found him in the woods, dead. He was attacked by a big cat."

"Oh dear God, John. I'm so sorry. I know how close you were with him. He was a good man."

She took John's face in her hands, and gently kissed him, then wrapped her arms around him with tears in her eyes.

"He fought valiantly," John said.

"John, if the cats are back, maybe that's why Moll is telling me to leave?"

"Ada, there's something I need to tell you about those cats, and about me..."

* * * *

Thick clouds obscured the sky, bringing dusk early to the mountains. The two cats moved silently toward the cabin. Circling...closing in. Testing the air and licking their lips in anticipation.

The man guarded the porch. Weak, vulnerable, he was easy prey. They smelled his blood, heard the beat of his heart...and waited.

* * * *

He twisted and pushed through the thick brush, accustomed to paved roads, and gas-lit walkways. The shotgun rested heavily on his shoulder, the manifestation of God's wrath waiting to be unleashed.

His head swung to his left and right like a pendulum, investigating each sound of the night, but identifying none.

Sweat soaked his shirt on this cool night. Demons were afoot. Death was in the air.

"Lord, I am a willing martyr to your glory, but as our savior prayed, so do I. If it is possible, let this cup pass me by, but your will be done."

* * * *

John paced back and forth from one porch rail to the next, and hoped his assurances to Ada allowed her to get some rest. He shook his head at his own foolishness. Perhaps Isaac's death made his own mortality seem too real? Letting a twisted dream, and a vague warning about his senile father-in-law, drive him to waste a night's sleep guarding his home?

No, he'd learned long ago not to discount any messages from the spirit world. Listening to them saved him on more than one occasion, but Moll Dyer? He knew to ignore her was madness.

Great-Pa spoke her name with reverence, and even his Conoy brothers honored her memory. Her name wasn't just a wisp of ink on a wrinkled, discolored page. Her spirit held power and stood all these years as the family's last bastion against the darkness that haunted them. But why would she seek him out now, when his happiness exceeded any he'd ever known?

Ada took his story very well, better than he had a right to expect. He wasn't sure that she believed him, but if not, at least she pretended.

"Husband, there are many things I do not understand in this world, and much that I take on faith. If I chose not to believe you, I'd surely lose you again. Maybe to believe you is to give in to madness, but I still choose to believe."

She did elicit his promise not to skin-walk around Zachary. It would take time for her to trust his bear.

A faint scent reached his nose, and he drew in a great draught of air, wishing for his bear's senses. At the snapping of a branch, he stepped down from the porch to investigate.

* * * *

Ada sat on the edge of the bed, listening, waiting. She'd never seen John show any sign of fear. Her blood ran cold when he slid from their bed, crept from their bedroom, and walked into the night. Protecting his family, she knew, but from what? Did he know?

She got out of bed and checked on their son. Zachary slept peacefully, chewing his thumb and smiling at the angels whispering in his ear.

Ada walked to the window. John was nowhere to be seen. Indistinct shadows moved in the faint moonlight. She went to the door and stepped out onto the porch.

"John? Where are you? Come inside."

A rustling to the left of the porch. Turning, the cat so close! A pouncing blob of fur! The shrill scream of pain hurt her ears. Her scream?

"Ada! Ada, no!!" John's voice.

The black cat's teeth raked over her scalp, skidding over her skull. *I love you, John.* Then darkness.

* * * *

Too late, Earnest Hartman saw the black cat leap for his daughter from his hiding spot behind the big oak. As he lifted the gun and took aim, a second cat slammed into the first.

The cats rolled away from his Ada and fell to the ground in front of the cabin, biting, scratching, and clawing. Blood flew like rain around him.

He saw John run up on the porch to Ada, and heard his wail.

"Ada!"

The black cat had the other's throat in its jaws. *Boom!* As he squeezed the trigger, the blast from the load of buckshot knocked him from his feet, and both cats fell.

"Remember why you are here."

"But Ada!"

Hartman ran up on the porch and paused. The air deserted his lungs. So much blood! Surely, she was dead. Reverend Hartman's spirit also died then. Zachary screamed inside, and he ran to him.

* * * *

John sobbed, his anguished cry bouncing from the heavens.

"God! Oh God, no! Ada, my sweet Ada, please…"

He felt a vibration on his side and touched his stone blade.

He kissed Ada's forehead, and felt her eyelids flutter. *Sweet Jesus, she's alive!*

"Zachary?" her small voice asked. "See to Zachary."

"Oh, Ada, dear God, thank you."

A raspy voice behind them said, "What a shame, but I doubt she'll survive the night. So sad too, really it is."

John turned away from his wife and stared at the intruder. Black hair and eyes, he exuded evil, darkness.

"Who are you? Why have you done this?"

"I am the demon Laris, but surely you knew that? I'm so pleased you decided to face me, man to man, or man to demon." The creature laughed. "Ah well, just semantics after all, isn't it?"

"I know your name."

"I should hope. Your family and I have been close for centuries!"

"It was you! You attacked Ada!"

"Indeed, you are a bit slow, aren't you? Whatever does she see in you?"

John pulled his blade from its sheath. An unearthly glow lit its stone surface.

"I'll kill you!" John shouted.

"Foolish man, you can't kill me, I'm immortal!"

The ground shook beneath John's feet, and a white mist seeped from the leaves in front of the demon. Green glowing eyes appeared first, followed by a shock of wavy red hair. The mist congealed into an opaque figure of a woman. Two other towers of swirling fog grew beside her.

"Well, it's Moll Dyer and her merry band of losers. How's hell treating you and the girls, Moll?"

The figure ignored the taunt and turned toward John.

"Demons lie," she said. "It isn't easy to find you, grandson. Forgive me. Your father did not prepare you, but perhaps your Great-Pa? Still, you have all you need."

John felt the heat of the blade in his hand.

"You have no powers from your prison in hell, witch," the demon snapped.

The ghostly image turned toward to Laris.

"Hell no longer has a hold on me, demon, but you are right, my powers were not released."

"Then why are you here?"

"I've come to see my many times great-grandson send your scurvy ass back to hell, you demon scum."

"GrrRahh!" Laris screamed. Charging at John, he plowed into his chest, knocking him from his feet.

The demon thrust his hands into John's shoulders, pinning him to the ground, and head butted him. Stars flirted with John's consciousness. Laris' mouth opened wide. Sharp, needle-like teeth glistened. Too many teeth!

John threw up his knees and twisted. Laris slipped off as John's blade flashed. Slicing. Flesh. Bone.

"Ahh!" The demon jerked backwards, holding its shoulder. Black blood and acrid smoke seeped from the wound.

"So, you've got a toy, John? Good for you."

The demon's hands sprouted balls of flame.

"So do I!" He threw the fireballs playfully as one might with a child and giggled as John easily evaded them.

Laris rushed him then and leapt toward his chest. John dropped to his knees and swung his blade, its edge sliding over the demon's ribs. Laris rolled to the side, and smashed John's hand against a rock—the knife falling harmlessly to the ground.

The demon's arms encircled John's neck and squeezed. John slapped at its hands and arms, twisted his body and threw his elbows into Laris' side…but to no avail. John felt the tendrils of consciousness pulling away from him and blackness prevailed.

* * * *

Moll Dyer's glimmer floated near Ada and leaned over to place her mouth near Ada's ear. *Wake child. If the demon wins, your family dies.*

Ada's eyelids fluttered, then flew open. She saw the battle before her, gritted her death, and tried to stand.

Demons are prideful. Ada pulled herself up using the porch rails. Moll continued to whisper in her ear.

"But I can't, Moll. I'm not strong enough."

You can. You must!

Ada's eyes took on the visage of a terrified child, but she nodded and turned back to the sounds of the battle. The demon held her beloved in a stranglehold, and from John's color, Ada knew his grip on life was tenuous. She grabbed a rock and threw it at the beast striking him between his shoulders.

"Laris! Leave my husband and my family alone!"

The demon released John and he fell to the ground in a heap. He wiped his hands together, and turned to face her.

"You dare to order me around, trifling human? To so casually toss about my name!"

"Forgive me, dark prince, but don't we all know the name and fear the deeds of the demon Laris? First among the dark one's lieutenants—Laris, the most powerful, and the most beautiful to behold!"

Laris' face split into a wide toothsome smile. He nudged John's body with his foot. "He still lives...for now. What is it you would offer to keep him that way?"

"To be with my son, and to save my love? Anything. I would be yours. Although it would take considerable strength and skill...perhaps you can't..."

The smile melted from his face. "What? What is it that you think is beyond me?"

"Unless you are capable of possessing another? It is said only the strongest warriors of hell can do so?"

Moll's spirit raged as her image wavered. "No, Ada—do not do this thing! He is a demon knight of hell!"

"Be still, Moll Dyer, this is no affair of yours. John will live, and I'd be with my son forever. We can guide him together, Laris. Think of it. Ballads will be written to honor you, and songs will be sung by the hellish choir to the glory of your name."

"You and I together. That would be sublime." His swollen tongue rolled over pointed teeth. Drool dripped from his lips. He stepped over to her and bent down. He lifted her chin, and his lips touched hers. The reptilian tongue slithered in. When Ada choked, the demon giggled.

"It will be sublime indeed, but now you must say the words."

She knelt at John's side, took his hand and repeated the demon's words:

"I open myself to you, my great Dark Lord Laris. Enter me that we may be as one. I accept you and welcome you. My life, my body is yours." She opened her arms to him and Laris smiled.

Ada stared as the corporal figure of the demon dissolved, giving way to a smoky black mist encrusted with red pricks of light. It retained its human form for but a moment, then swirled around her in a tornadic fog. Unseen hands forced open her mouth and the demonic cloud streamed in. Her throat burned with the acidic flow, and she dry heaved against it.

"Oh, dear God, what have I done!" she choked out. The fires of the pit exploded in her belly and erupted through her bowels. The blackness of despair. Hopeless terror filled her soul! "No! No! No!"

She flinched at the myriad of images flicking through her mind's eye. She glimpsed the demon's plan for Zachary's tortured childhood, the corruption of her own soul, and John dead from her hand! *No, I meant to save John!*

He must die!

Little remained of the woman once called Ada, when she felt John stir beneath her.

"Kill him now," the demon inside of her commanded. Ada snatched the knife up from the ground beside John and lifted it over her head. *Now!*

John's eyes opened. "Ada?"

The knife descended in a slow arc toward him, then turned and plunged to the hilt in the center of Ada's chest.

"No!" the demon screamed.

"Ada!" John caught her as she fell forward into his arms. "Ada, my love, what have you done?"

"Remember me, John, and I'll never die. Remember I loved us so much."

John moved his hand over Ada's eyes, and a sob tore from his chest. As he cradled her, a demonic cloud—black as coal—lay upon the ground at his feet like morning fog on the swamp land. It moved as a living thing might, undulating but retaining its shape. The ground reluctantly absorbed the fetid mass, and a syrupy red fluid oozed from the earth's afflicted opening as its passage.

Moll Dyer's spirit was at his side. "It is done, John. Our family is again safe from hell's pestilence. You and Ada saved them this day, you've won."

John looked down at his wife, and tears flowed from his eyes.

"No, this isn't a win."

The mists that formed Moll's image spun and became less defined. Moll was slipping away. He squinted his eyes and stared at the face of his ancestor.

"Can ghosts cry, Moll?"

"I never knew until now."

John fought the urge to release maniacal laughter, his grip on sanity fragile.

"Grandmother?"

"Yes, my son?"

"What's a scurvy ass?" he giggled crazily, as a deluge of tortuous scenes replayed in his mind. Tears rained down his face. A sob began in his abdomen that threatened to splinter his ribs.

A sad smile distorted Moll's ghostly lips.

"Your price for victory is harsher than mine ever was, John. If it helps, the next world is far kinder, my son. I'm truly sorry."

"Is Great-Pa with you?"

"He is at peace, John."

"Why didn't he come?'

Moll looked at him as one might a stubborn child. "He's at peace, John. He committed himself with honor, and his battle is done. It is my curse to walk this land. It's not his to bear."

The mist that was Moll Dyer circled John, hung for a moment, and then drifted over the cabin mixing with the smoke from John's chimney. It faded away as her grief-stricken wail filled the night.

* * * *

Hartman was curled up on the bed beside his grandson's crib when John entered. Both men stayed awake through the night, listening. Praying it was over.

With the dawn, Hartman bundled Zachary up, and moved toward the door.

"Where are you taking my son, Earnest?"

"You need to leave this place, John. I know what you are. Rest assured I will raise Zachary in Ada's memory to be a righteous man."

"No, Earnest. He is all that I have left of her. All that is left of my family!"

"Think about it, John. You know they will hang you for murder."

"I can check with William, but I'm confident there's no law against killing demons and murderous cats."

"Who will believe that? And what demons, what cats? I see only two dead women. You have a record of assault in Cumberland, and the whole town remembers when you kidnapped Ada. You were having an affair with Sally Ann. I saw her naked in your yard."

"I never hurt Ada, and you killed Sally Ann, and I never…"

"Your gun did. Not many blunderbusses left in these parts. This is rifle country," Hartman said, and brandished the weapon.

"You stole my gun?"

"No, who would steal this old thing? It's a wonder it fires at all. It is a rather memorable weapon though. I found it in my study, no idea how it got there."

"I've done nothing…"

"Then there's that Sheriff Campbell. Isn't he the fellow who locked you up for six months? I heard he was killed, and you were the only witness? Convenient."

"We have graves to dig, Reverend," John snarled.

* * * *

The man was inhuman, John thought. How could he be so callous and unfeeling? It was as if all thoughts of his daughter were forgotten. Digging kept John's hands busy, and off the man's throat. Ada wouldn't want that.

Over the graves of their loved ones, both men said prayers related to their beliefs, and found many they shared.

"The natives are right, Dyer. Death and despair are all that grows on this mountain. I fear its soil is too thin to hold even the spirits of the dead. I pray my Ada finds peace."

When both had exhausted their tears, and grief left their bodies spent, John picked up his son.

"You will be hanged, John. They will never believe you. Get away now and maybe with time I can convince the people of your innocence."

"I can take him away with me. The woods will be our home."

"What life is that for a child? He's no more than a baby, John. Think of your son, what would Ada want for him?"

John sniffed at the air. "Right now she'd say our boy needs changing."

He sat the boy down on the ground to clean him but found him unsoiled and dry. John stared at his father-in-law. Saw the embarrassment written on his reddened face and felt a flicker of compassion for the man.

"It was a hard night," John said.

Hartman reached for Zachary, but John held fast to his son.

"John, the demons will never stop coming for you! I can raise him in safety, invisible from them in the Lord's house."

This stopped John in his tracks, and he held his son tightly against his chest. He knew what it meant to lose a parent.

"Consider your options, John. You can run off with him. Give him a miserable life where the law and demons will hunt you every day for the rest of your lives. Or I can take care of Zachary, and you can keep an eye on him from afar. They'll never stop coming for you if you take the child. I'll see to that. I'll not have my grandson raised that way. If you stay here, you'll be hanged."

"Why, Earnest? What have I ever done to you?"

"I know what you are, John. It's better this way."

"I loved them all, Earnest."

"You destroy everything you love, John. Have you learned nothing??"

* * * *

John turned his back on the cabin, and his son. Every step carving off another slice of his heart. Each step cutting deeper than the last. He paused for a moment—without turning to face what he was about to lose.

"I love you, Zachary. Take care of him, Earnest, I'll be watching!" John's vision blurred. He ducked his head and forced one foot to follow the other.

"DaDaDa," Zachary squealed, and John's knees buckled, his legs losing the strength to stand. He snatched at a locust sapling to keep his feet, its thorns digging into the palm of his hand. But the agony of his spirit nullified the pain of the flesh. He sucked in a deep breath… and took another step.

* * * *

The Reverend watched John until his figure was out of sight. Hearing the sound of many excited voices and the beating of hooves approaching, he turned back toward the cabin. A half-dozen men dismounted and tied their horses to the rail.

William took in the scene, observed the bloodied ground and the two graves mounded over with fresh dirt. Both were adorned with a rustic cross. The wood matched that of young Zachary's crib.

"What's happened here, Earnest? Did you…?"

"Dyer. John Dyer happened…my daughter…my dearest Ada! I saved the child, but Ada and the woman—I couldn't…"

One of the other men joined them. "Mr. Jordan, want us to get a posse together and chase down the killer?"

"Reverend? What do you think? How much head start does John have?"

"We'll never catch that man, not without a brace of good hounds. He's half demon and half beast and knows the wild lands as well as any furred critter. He's born to it, and there's no humanity left in him—if there ever was."

"We can't just let a murderer run free," William said.

"We'll get the word out far and wide. He'll never set foot among God-fearing people again. He'll be hunted until the end of his days, William. Until then, let him live with what he's done."

* * * *

Years passed slowly for the very young, and the past eight years represented a lifetime for Zachary. He understood why his grandfather was so harsh with him. It was to protect him and help him find his way to paradise. Zachary was a bad seed, from bad stock. The Reverend told him so often enough. Only through deprivation, prayer, and pain would he ever see the pearly gates.

Today was Zachary's eighth birthday, and it promised to be the most special day of his young life. His friend Samuel presented him with the gift of a prized laying hen. Even his grandfather wouldn't begrudge him the fowl. Samuel never mentioned that he snatched the bird from his father's flock—without his knowledge.

Old man Billings heard the cackling, squawking hen and followed the boy to the Reverend's house and demanded restitution.

Now Zachary walked the well-worn path to the spring house in the woods behind their home. It was out of sight and hearing of their nearest neighbors and for that, Zachary felt blessed. The Reverend wouldn't let his whole congregation know how wicked Zachary was.

The boy stripped the branches from a hickory sapling and handed it to his grandfather. He pulled off his shirt and fought back the tears welling up in his eyes. *Weakness.*

The hooded eyes watching from the cover of the woods observed the crisscrossing pattern of scars on the boy's back, and a growl issued from deep in the beast's throat.

Zachary leaned forward and grasped the stone wall of the springhouse waiting for the first sting of the switch. The roar that emanated from the brush caught him off guard, but he stood firm—to show fear now would demand additional penance. He stood his ground waiting for the latest punishment from the Reverend's all-knowing God.

The Reverend screamed, and Zachary turned to see him running away towards the house. A large black bear chased him, gaining ground even as Zachary watched. The Reverend stumbled over a rock and before he could regain his footing, the bear fell upon him.

Zachary could not count the number of times the great bear's claws slashed his grandfather, but he ran to help, slinging a large rock as he approached.

"Leave him be, demon bear!"

The bear looked up, and cowered away from the boy, sitting back on his haunches and groaning as if in mortal agony.

For years after, Zachary was to question his recollection of what happened next. As his grandfather beheld the beast towering over him, it was as if a light of recognition flashed in his eyes.

"Dear God, what are you?" his dying grandfather whispered. "Dyer...John Dyer? God have mercy on your soul."

* * * *

William and Kate were happy to bring Zachary into their home. They hoped in some way to repay the debt they felt they owed their friends, John and Ada.

They were devoted parents to him, and he soon felt a part of their young family. They never forgot John and Ada, and made sure Zachary knew of their love for him and each other.

Like his father, Zachary grew wise in the ways of the woods, feeling more at home there than in any town.

On his eighteenth birthday, he left their home and went in search of his Conoy brothers. Finding their village destroyed and deserted, he returned to Setter's Run and began homesteading at his father's cabin on Devil's Peak.

The books and diaries he found hidden under a loose floorboard opened his eyes to a new world—a world reflecting the generations before him.

For now, he was home—and for a while, he knew happiness.

The End

Afterword

Zachary grew in power and spirit in a manner that would make his paternal grandfather proud. His story is for another day, but he does make a mark in the final book of the series.

Kate and William did their best to keep their promise to John. They reminded Zachary often of his parents' love—for him and for each other.

Moll Dyer remains ever vigilant, her eternal love traversing the realms of flesh and spirit to aid her family and providing succor to a world responsible for her torment.

As for John, he never accepted Ada's death. He'd given her all of his heart and knew his desecrated heart had no room for any other. He wandered the mountains alone in present day West Virginia for many years. Memories were more painful to bear as a man, and he found some solace dwelling within his spirit animal.

If you ever travel these hills and spot an enormous black bear with white furred scars across his chest, think of John Dyer and pray he finds peace.

In Memoriam:

Sally Ann's transgressions paled by her final and ultimate sacrifice. She finally understood the meaning, and price, of friendship, and died protecting John's family.

During his life, Reverend Hartman was a man of strong faith and beliefs, a simple man, his path was always paved with good intentions.

Isaac Campbell lived and died a man. A rough-spoken, soft hearted soul, a lone warrior searching for justice in an unjust world.

Ada was too generous of heart to fare well in the world of men. In her short life, she found true love, and is an eternal beacon of hope for all. She was never forgotten, and what greater tribute can any life have?

www.ingramcontent.com/pod-product-compliance
Lightning Source LLC
Chambersburg PA
CBHW070837030726
47504CB00005B/1128